The
Witch Hunter's
Tale

Also by Sam Thomas

The Midwife's Tale
The Harlot's Tale
"The Maidservant and the Murderer" (e-book)

The
Witch Hunter's
Tale

SAM THOMAS

MINOTAUR BOOKS ✦ NEW YORK

THE WITCH HUNTER'S TALE. Copyright © 2014 by Samuel Thomas. All rights reserved. Printed in the United States of America. For information, address St. Martin's Press, 175 Fifth Avenue, New York, N.Y. 10010.

www.minotaurbooks.com

Design by Omar Chapa

Library of Congress Cataloging-in-Publication Data

Thomas, Samuel S.
    The witch hunter's tale : a midwife mystery / Sam Thomas.—
First edition.
        p. cm.
    ISBN 978-1-250-04575-1 (hardcover)
    ISBN 978-1-4668-4537-4 (e-book)
    1. Women detectives—Fiction   2. Midwives—Fiction.
3. Witchcraft—Fiction.   4. York (England)—History—Fiction.
I. Title.
    PS3620.H64225W58 2014
    813'.6—dc23
                                                            2014032393

Minotaur books may be purchased for educational, business, or promotional use. For information on bulk purchases, please contact the Macmillan Corporate and Premium Sales Department at 1-800-221-7945, extension 5442, or write to specialmarkets@macmillan.com.

First Edition: January 2015

10 9 8 7 6 5 4 3 2 1

For Laura Jofre, two books late

Acknowledgments

As always, I must acknowledge the support of a whole host of individuals whose patience and hard work made this book possible. First, of course, is my family, who put up with my absence in a number of guises, whether it is dashing off to book clubs, public presentations, or the office to sneak in a few hours of writing. I'm also grateful to my stepsister Laura Jofre for reading a draft of this book, and the two previous ones as well. Without her, I would be just another historian with an unfinished novel in my desk drawer.

I am also thankful for the work of my agent, Josh Getzler, and his intrepid assistant, Danielle Burby, not to mention my editor at Minotaur Books, Charlie Spicer, and his assistant, April Osborn. It is better to be lucky than good, and I count myself as incredibly lucky to have such great people to work with.

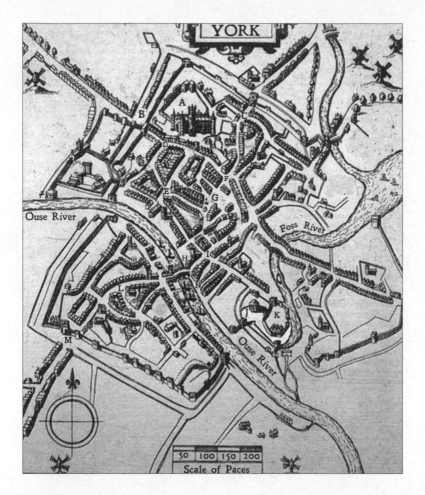

A. York Minster

B. Bootham Bar

C. St. John-del Pyke Parish

D. Corner of High Petergate and Stonegate

E. St. Helen's Stonegate Church

F. St. Martin-Coneystreet Church

G. Hungate Parish

H. All Saints-Pavement Church

I. Foss Bridge

J. Clifford's Tower

K. York Castle

L. St. Martin Micklegate Church

M. Micklegate Bar

The
Witch Hunter's
Tale

Chapter 1

The crowd cried out for the witch's blood, and the hangman obliged. Hester Jackson was so old and frail, the hangman pulled her up the ladder as if she weighed no more than a sack of grain. With a wave to the crowd, he put the noose around her neck and turned her off into oblivion. Many cheered as she clawed helplessly at the rope that slowly choked the life out of her, and they continued to applaud as her hands dropped and her body began to convulse. One spectator aped her suffering, turning her death into a jerky dance, the devil's own jig. Those around him cheered lustily, and I turned away. Despite the cold and wind, townsmen and -women leaned from the second- and third-story windows for a better view of Hester's death. Even from a distance they joined in the merriment.

I looked to Martha, my maidservant and deputy. She had seen—we both had seen—the aftermath of similar deaths not six months before, and it was not a sight easily forgotten. If a stranger had looked at Martha's face at that moment he would have found it impassive, and he might have been forgiven for thinking that the hanging held no particular interest for her. But I knew her well enough to recognize the horror in her eyes. Martha had been reluctant to come, but Hester had asked us and it was not the sort of request one refused. Hester's legs continued to jerk, and for a moment I feared that she might still be alive. If she'd had family in the city, someone might have bribed the hangman to ensure her death was a quick one, but she was old, poor, and alone. Finally Hester was still.

"Let us go," I murmured to Martha. She nodded, and we turned into the frigid winter wind that cut through our clothes like Satan's razor.

The summer before—already known by the jangling rhyme of "the summer-tide of forty-five"—had been brutally hot, and the farmers especially had given thanks when the rains finally came. But when the rains continued for weeks on end psalms of praise became petitions for mercy. It soon became clear that much of the harvest would rot in the fields, and by fall farmers found themselves up to their knees in mud so thick it defied description. The cold came soon after, and by November the Lord made it known that, in His wisdom, He intended to balance the viciously hot summer with a brutally cold winter.

As we passed the shops, I noticed how spare the shelves and bins were, and how much the prices had risen in the years since King and Parliament had gone to war. I could well remember the time when York's markets overflowed with the nation's bounty, and residents could find anything they desired: fruit from the city's orchards, grain from the countryside, fish and eels from the sea, cloth from France or Holland, even spices from India. Some said London could offer nothing more. But that was then.

Even though the contending armies had left Yorkshire, all

manner of goods, from rare silk to common corn, had become harder to find, and the poor had begun to suffer. Indeed, the faces in the crowd were gaunter than in the past, and their bodies were more skin and bones than flesh. Many had the look of rough country folk, come to the city to sell their meager wares. But I saw familiar faces as well, including women whom I had attended when they were with child, and their husbands. Perhaps they had come to the hanging in order to see someone less fortunate than they were. Even in times of shortage, the vendors found goods to sell, and many had taken full advantage of the execution. Grocers sold food and drink to those who had not brought their own, and chapmen hawked penny-pamphlets detailing Hester's crimes and shouting up the wonders, marvels, and omens that the Lord had visited upon England in recent months.

"A monster born to a woman in Surrey!" one chapman cried. "Come read about the sea-monster washed up near Whitby!" He stood on the corner of one of the streets that spilled into the market square, and from there he could hawk his wares as people entered and left. He must have arrived well before dawn to obtain such a prized spot, and I had no doubt the crowd would reward him for his trouble. He had pasted the coversheets from all his pamphlets to a board behind him, tailoring his offerings to the audience and occasion: Most of the titles included some combination of the words *Bloody, Strange, Terrible,* and *Horrid.*

I did my best to avoid him, but a boy thrust a sheet in to my hand. *A Strange and Wonderful Monster Born* shouted the title, and I felt my eyes drawn to the vile image on the front. It showed a headless child, with a gruesomely large face set in the middle of his chest and ears on his shoulders. His hands were on his hips, and he stared impudently from the page, as if daring the reader to doubt the reality of the story inside. A group of women surrounded the child: witches and papists, it seemed, for one woman suckled a rat at her breast and appeared to be casting a spell, while others held rosaries and crucifixes. It was not clear which group had called the monstrous child into being, but perhaps it did not matter. The world was out of order—what difference did it make whether witches or papists were to blame?

The chapman must have seen the look of disgust on my face, for he stepped in front of me and snatched the sheet from my hands, even as he doffed his cap. "Not what you are looking for, my lady?" he asked. "Not to worry, for I've got other news as well." For a man who must have lived much like a vagabond, travelling from town to town, he seemed almost respectable. He kept his clothes clean, knew a gentlewoman when he saw one, and had shaved that morning. He pulled a stack of pamphlets from his pack and with a flourish fanned them out before me. Now, rather than tales of witchcraft and monstrous births, I was confronted with the bloody acts of men, as the titles shouted of recent battles between King and Parliament, including one that had taken place at Marston Moor, not far from York. I started to push them aside when one title caught my eye: *God's Terrible Justice in York*.

Martha saw it as well.

"Oh, God!" she moaned.

The chapman misread her reaction as one of surprise rather than dismay.

"Oh, you never heard of the murders?" he asked. "You must be a stranger to the city, for all the North knows of the killings." His voice rose in excitement and the words poured out like water through a breached dam. It did not take long before a small crowd had gathered around him, ready to hear a tale they already knew.

"It was a horrid summer indeed!" the chapman cried. "Death himself stalked the city's whores; there were murders upon murders, hangings upon hangings." To my surprise he broke into song, telling the story of Betty MacDonald, a girl who had come to York in search of work, but fell into whoredom and met a dreadful end in the room where she plied her trade. It was close enough to the truth that I could not fault him overmuch.

"The shame of it is," he continued, "how many innocents lost their lives, and how many murderers went free. And the entire story—including the song I just sang—is here." He held up a pamphlet for all to see. "And it can be yours for just a penny." It was a masterful performance. A half dozen people stepped forward, eager to buy the pamphlet. Hester Jackson's hanging had not provided blood enough, it seemed.

Before Martha and I could escape the crowd, the chapman stepped in front of us and held the book before Martha.

"Surely you will buy a copy," he said with a smile.

"We know about the murders," Martha said. "We saw the bodies." Even over the hubbub of the crowd the chapman heard the steel in Martha's voice, and it brought him up short. He looked at us for a moment and then realized who we were.

"You're the midwife," he said to me as he bowed. "You're Lady Hodgson."

I nodded.

"And you must be her deputy," he said to Martha. "You found who killed these women. The two of you are famous, even in London!" I had not known that the news of the murders had spread so far, but it made sense that a man who carried books on his back would be the first to hear. He seemed thrilled to be in our presence, and I could not help wondering what mix of truth and fancy had found its way into his blood-soaked books.

"My lady," he said, nearly in a whisper. "I have a proposal."

Despite myself I leaned toward him, straining to hear his words.

"Have you ever tried your hand at writing?" he asked.

I started to respond, but he held up his hand—he'd not yet finished making the sale.

"I have friends in the Stationers Company, and they would pay handsomely for your account of the killings. It is better to tell your truth than let the vain scribblers tell their lies." He looked expectantly at Martha. "Surely so beautiful a woman as you could use a few shillings for your dowry. All you'd need to do is tell your story. We could go to an inn. I would even pay for the wine. My name is Peter Newcome, by the way." He offered us what he hoped would be a winning smile. I admired his audacity, but I had no desire to revisit the killings.

"It is a generous offer, Mr. Newcome," I said. "But we must decline."

Newcome took the news with good grace, bowing yet again. "In the event you change your mind, my lady, I hope you will search me out."

"I don't think we will," Martha replied for both of us. "We have dwelt long enough on that summer."

"Very well," he replied. "But if you won't tell your story, perhaps you'll buy another man's." He leaned forward again and spoke in a conspiratorial tone. "Have you heard of the witchings and hangings in Suffolk?"

Without meaning to, I shook my head.

"Ah, it's all here," he said. He held out yet another book, this one called *The Discovery of Witches*. The author was called Matthew Hopkins, and described himself by the unusual title *Witch Finder*.

"What in God's name is a 'Witch Finder'?" asked Martha.

I shook my head. While we'd heard of the trials and hangings—who in England hadn't?—I'd never heard of such an office.

"For that, you can buy the book," Newcome said with a wolfish grin. "But I'll tell you this—it is said that he strikes such fear in the hearts of witches that when he comes to a town, they search out a Justice and confess of their own free will. They say that hundreds have been executed. After today's hanging I shouldn't be surprised if the same thing happens here."

"Here in York?" Martha asked. "Are you sure?"

"Sure?" Newcome asked. He turned the word over on his tongue as if it were new and entirely unfamiliar. "Who can be sure of anything in such unsettled times? But it is what I have heard. And once the hanging starts . . ." His voice trailed off, and I looked toward the gibbet. Hester's body swayed slightly in the wind. I suddenly felt cold in a way that had nothing to do with the winter weather.

I glanced at Martha and saw the concern on her face mirrored my own. I thanked the chapman for his offer, and we resumed our journey home. As we walked away, I could hear Newcome crying out his pamphlets, selling blood to a bloody-minded people.

When we turned onto Stonegate, the street that would take us home, the north wind howled against us, seemingly intent on ripping our cloaks from our backs. I pulled mine more tightly around me, but it made no difference. I gave thanks when we turned out of the wind and onto my own little street. Though I'd lived in my house for nearly ten years I still found wonder in how much had changed in that time.

I'd made the long journey from Hereford to York as a young widow—could I have been just twenty-three years old?—promised in marriage to Phineas Hodgson, a man I'd never met. As it turned out, Phineas was among England's least competent merchants, and from our first day as husband and wife until he died in 1642, I spent most of my waking hours defending my estates from his foolish schemes. My two beautiful children, Birdy and Michael, were the only good that came of the union—God's way of balancing the scales, it seemed. But Michael died soon after he was born, and in the months that followed, death visited my home with terrifying frequency. After Michael, he took Phineas, and a few months later he returned for Birdy. In less than a year, my maidservant Hannah and I found ourselves the only survivors of this dreadful reaping.

It was midwifery that kept me afloat when I feared I might slip beneath the waves of melancholy that battered me so, as I threw myself into that work with what little strength I still had. When a mother was in travail, I could not think about my own lost children, and the friendships I made as a midwife kept my spirit alive. Soon after, Martha appeared at my door begging for a position as a maidservant. I took her in and began to train her in the mysteries of midwifery. A few weeks later, we met an orphaned boy named Tree, and he became a son of sorts. While he still lived at the Castle in the care of one of the jailors, he often came to my house for a meal or to spend the night in a feather bed. Though they did not know it, Martha and Tree, my newfound sister and son, had begun the work of healing my grief-ravaged soul.

When we opened the front door to my home, the newest member of my household raced out of the kitchen and, with masses of red hair streaming behind her, fell into my arms. "Ma," Elizabeth cried. "Hannah has made cakes, and they are almost done!"

Elizabeth's mother had been one of the doxies murdered the previous summer, and Elizabeth had come to live with me in the aftermath. When she first came to my house, she had been entirely unsure of what to call me. *Lady Bridget* seemed too formal for such a little one, better suited to friends than family. She'd called her own mother *Mum*, and wouldn't use that name. I had told her that she could call me whatever she liked, and eventually she settled on *Ma*. I could not have been happier. In her first months with me, Elizabeth kept a safe distance as she mourned her mother and the life she'd lost. But gradually her wounds healed, and while I still found her crying from time to time, such occasions had become far less frequent. Elizabeth took Martha and me by our hands and led us into the kitchen, where Hannah was indeed removing cakes from the oven.

"I thought you would need something sweet after such a day," she said. Hannah had been with me for over twenty years, and she knew me well. I gratefully accepted one of the cakes.

"Can I give one to Sugar?" Elizabeth asked. A small cat had entwined himself around Elizabeth's ankles and was meowing plaintively. Without waiting for an answer, she broke a corner off her cake and offered it to the cat. Sugar sniffed the crumb, concluded it was not to his liking, and stalked off with Elizabeth close behind trying to convince him to try it. Once Elizabeth had left the room, Hannah looked at me expectantly.

"They hanged her," I said. "Just as we knew they would."

Hannah nodded and looked away. It was not that I, or any of us for that matter, objected to the hanging of a witch. But having met her in prison, I could no longer convince myself that Hester *was* one. It is one thing to believe in the reality of witchcraft. It is another to see a neighbor hanged for the crime.

"We heard that a witch-hunt may soon come to the city," Martha said.

"A witch-hunt?" Hannah asked, her face suddenly pale and drawn. She had read the newsbooks about the trials and hangings. "In York?"

"You should know better than to give credence to such chatter," I said, a bit too sharply. "There is enough idle gossip as it is. There is no need to add to it."

Hannah nodded, but I knew that the rumor would soon spread throughout the city with or without her help. Once a chapman knew something, it might as well be shouted from the city's pulpits.

"Has Will come home?" I asked, eager to talk of something other than witchcraft and hangings.

"Not yet," Hannah said. "He's at Mr. Breary's and said he might sleep there tonight."

Will Hodgson was the final member of my household, having come to live with me in circumstances strangely akin to Elizabeth's. Will's father had died a bloody death just a few days after Elizabeth's mother, and this shared history brought them closer together.

The four of us sat down to supper, and by the light of many candles and warmth of the hearth we were able—for a few minutes at least—to forget the desperate winter cold and banish the memories of Hester's hanging. But when I looked at Elizabeth's hair glowing in the firelight, I could not help remembering the desperate straits from which I'd rescued her, and I said a prayer that I could keep her safe.

Once we'd eaten, I led Elizabeth upstairs to her room and put her to bed. We prayed for the city, the King, and the end of the wars. She added prayers for her mother, asking God to keep her safe from the cold. I lay with her until she slept, and then for a while longer. On some nights evil dreams still visited her. Usually they were of the man who'd killed her mother, and she'd awake screaming. I'd found that if I stayed with her after she fell asleep I could keep such nightmares at bay.

Later, I retired to my chamber, wrote one letter to my cousin in Hereford and another to the steward of one of my estates there, and then climbed into my own bed. I could hear the wind outside my window and gave God thanks for the warmth and safety that He had given me.

But a nightmare visited me not long after I drifted off to sleep, as my fevered brain transformed the howling wind into the dying screams of a bewitched child and mother. I woke with a cry, and I scrambled from my bed to splash water on my face in desperate hope of driving away the horrid dream. I knew that sleep would prove elusive and that the dreams would return if I did not exorcise them. While I had spent much of the day trying *not* to think about Hester's crimes, I now closed my eyes and recalled them as best I could. On that night it was the only way I would find a measure of peace.

Chapter 2

Hester Jackson's journey to the gibbet had begun the previous September with a child's fever. We were in the midst of those happy weeks after the heat had broken, but before winter's early arrival made clear that we had simply exchanged one curse for another. Looking back we should have known better.

Sarah Asquith appeared at my door early one morning, pale and drawn. I'd delivered her of a son a few months before, and as soon as I saw her face I knew that something had gone wrong. I ushered her into my parlor and sent Hannah for barley water.

"It is Peter," she said, even before Hannah returned. The words rushed as if she'd been holding them in for days. She probably had been. "He has a fever, and I've tried everything I can think of: oil of roses, a salve of poplar buds . . . nothing has helped." I could find no fault there. These were the same cures I would have suggested.

"Is he still taking the breast?" I asked.

She nodded. "And I've been taking cooling foods, but that hasn't helped, either. We even paid for a physician to come. He sent me to an apothecary for some wormwood and sea green, but—" She shook her head. Nothing had helped.

"Sarah, would you like me to examine him?" I asked.

"Would you?" she asked, taking my hands. "I would be so grateful, my lady."

"Of course," I replied, and the two of us set out for her home in St. Crux parish.

As we walked through the city, I noted with sorrow the many changes that the war had brought. With so many men taken off to fight—carried by their zeal for God or by Parliament's press-masters—it seemed as if York had become a city of women and old men. Wives became shopkeepers, daughters worked as craftsmen, and maidens searched in vain for husbands before resigning themselves to lives as spinsters. Every Sabbath the churches filled with prayers for the safe return of our men, but we knew that many would never come home, and few of us had any illusions that the time after the war would be the same as before. While I did not regret my own widowhood—marriage to Phineas would make any woman into a merry widow—I knew that few women had the wealth and family that made my own life so comfortable. Singlewomen, whether spinsters or widows, suffered a hard existence filled with poverty and want.

The Asquiths' parish of St. Crux lay in the heart of York, not far from Fossgate Bridge. After a decade in the city, I knew the twists and turns of York's cobbled streets as well as I knew the lines on my face, but when I'd first come to the city it had seemed to be a maze designed by a madman. London is said to be worse, but I can hardly imagine such a thing.

We passed through the Asquiths' shop and climbed the stairs to the rooms above. William Asquith, Sarah's husband, was one of the suppliers for Parliament's armies, and had done very well out of it ever since the war began. When the summer's drought made food even dearer, William profited yet again, and they had filled their home with rich furniture and covered the walls with sumptuous hangings. But I knew by my own hard experience that while wealth gives the illusion of safety, death is not so easily deterred. What had my estates done to protect Michael and Birdy?

Sarah led me straight to the chamber at the back of the house where her son lay. I caught my breath as soon as I saw the child, and Sarah cried out. The maidservant who sat on the side of the bed holding the child's hand looked up at us and burst in to tears. He seemed so pale, so still, that I knew we had come too late. I crossed to the bed and felt the boy's cheeks and chest, but I found neither warmth nor breath. I turned to Sarah, and she buried her face in my neck. I felt a wail rising up through her body before it burst into the room with a force powerful enough to shake the rafters themselves.

After a few moments, Sarah pulled herself away and lay on the bed next to her son. She cradled his head, kissed his hair, and told him that she loved him. Sorrow welled up inside me and I clenched my jaw to keep my own tears from bursting forth, but it was in vain. Like a flood intent on washing away all that lay before it, my tears poured out as I mourned the death of Sarah's son, the deaths of my own children, and the deaths of so many other young ones that God saw fit to reap like stalks of grain. I do not know how long I stayed with Sarah. She sent her maidservant to find William, who had gone in search of another physician. While we waited, Sarah and I held the boy and each other. Sarah cried. I prayed for her and wondered that God would take her only son.

We buried the child the next day, and I left William and Sarah to comfort each other. That night I prayed that Sarah soon would come to me, thrilled and frightened to find that she was with child once more. I would not encourage her with false promises that this time the child would live—my own example would give the lie to such words—but I would do my best to calm her fears. I would remind her which foods she should take and which she should avoid. I would visit her as her travail neared, and tell her that the second time would not be as difficult as the first. I'd say that she would be a wonderful mother and that together we would do our best for her child.

But I never got the chance to say any of this. Two weeks later Sarah was dead.

Looking back at the events that followed, I could not help wondering what evil might have been avoided if Sarah's husband had called me to her bedside sooner. Hester Jackson might never have been hanged, and the horrible aftermath would have been avoided. But what use is there in such vain thoughts? Perhaps it was God's will.

According to Sarah's gossips, a few days after the Asquiths buried their son, Sarah and William were sitting at supper when Sarah was taken by a gripping pain in her side. She took to bed and for a time she seemed to improve. But the pain returned, and this time it was accompanied by vomiting and a fever similar to the one that had carried off her son. She demanded water, but no matter how much she drank she could not be satisfied. When her belly became stretched, William summoned a physician, but he could no more help Sarah than he had little Peter. He said that Sarah's illness was unlike any he'd ever seen, and that he doubted it was natural. It was this physician who, perhaps because he could find no cure, suggested that Sarah might have been bewitched.

Once that seed had been planted in Sarah's and William's minds, it did not take long to grow. Desperate to break the curse, they sought remedies wherever they might be found. William rode out of the city and hired a blesser who tried to counter-check the curse that had been laid on Sarah. The blesser did his best, but he had no more success than the physician. He told William that unless he discovered the witch who had cursed his wife, she surely would die. Sarah's condition grew worse, and death hovered over her. With every passing moment, William grew more frantic and racked his wits for the name of someone—*anyone*—who might have bewitched his wife.

Finally he found an answer: Hester Jackson.

The previous month, just a few days before Peter had fallen ill, William had been in his shop when Hester entered and begged of him a little food. She was a poor old woman, she said, and with bread so dear she had nothing to eat. When William turned her away, Hester had muttered something under her breath. He thought nothing of it at the time, but with all that had happened since, he was convinced that Hester had taken her revenge by bewitching both Peter and Sarah. If we lived in some country hamlet, William might have broken the curse by burning a bit of thatch from her house, but Hester's home, like so many in fire-frighted York, had a tiled roof. On such small happenings do men's lives turn.

Desperate to save his wife, William went to the Justices and accused Hester of witchcraft. Some said that if a witch were taken by the law, her curses would be broken. I do not know if this was William's hope, but if so, he was disappointed. Hester utterly denied that she was a witch and said she could not lift a curse that she had not cast. Because William stood alone against her, the Justices refused to make an arrest. Sick with fear and grief, William hurried home, only to discover that even as he'd stood before the Justices accusing Hester, Sarah had died.

With his wife and child newly dead, William found himself alone with his anger and sorrow. Though he never said as much, I think he blamed himself for the death of his family. If he had not denied Hester Jackson a pennyworth of charity, she would not have bewitched Peter and Sarah. But no man can bear such guilt for long, and soon William began his quest to avenge the destruction of his family. He found allies among his neighbors, who said that Hester had always been a bad neighbor and that they had long suspected her of witchery. One woman claimed that Hester had bewitched her churn so she could no longer make butter. Another said she so corrupted a cow that it would not give milk. People remembered that Hester's mother had long been accounted a witch, and that her aunt (or was it some other relation?) had been hanged as a witch in Lancashire (or was it Cheshire?) some twenty years before.

After the Justices arrested Hester, the rumors and gossip took on lives of their own, and on some days it seemed that York talked of little else. And while the town might disagree on some of the details or challenge the more extravagant claims, no one denied her guilt.

"I heard that the devil came to her in the shape of a handsome young man," Hannah confided to Martha and me one evening. "And he left her an imp, a mouse named Mousnier, to work evil for her."

Martha did not even attempt to suppress her snort of disgust. "What, is the devil now a Frenchman? Or does he just employ French mice as his imps? Once their tongues start wagging, the people of this city are crack-brained fools."

"Who are we to judge Satan?" Hannah replied, offended by Martha's scorn. "They say that a company of devils traveled with the Queen from France when she came to marry His Majesty."

"And the devils brought their own devil-mouse with them?" Martha shook her head in disbelief and stalked out of the room.

While Martha could mock the idea of devils and their mice crossing the Channel on a boat, I knew that once people began to gossip about devils and Hester's imp, I could look forward to a visit from a Justice of the Peace.

As I expected, two days later a note arrived calling me to the Castle to search Hester's body for the Witch's Mark. While the summons did not come as a surprise, I was sorry all the same.

"You'll do that?" Martha asked.

"I have little choice," I replied. "If Hester had an imp, she must have a teat from which he sucked. And who better to find it than a midwife?"

"Will I accompany you?" Martha asked. I could hear the uncertainty in her voice. She'd become my apprentice to learn the art of midwifery, not to search old women for signs of witchcraft.

"It is a part of being a midwife," I replied. "But remember this: Examining a witch is a delicate thing, and we must tread carefully. So many in the city are convinced that Hester is a witch—" I paused, trying to find the right words.

"That if we don't find the Witch's Mark they will turn their anger on us?" she asked.

I nodded. "Since she is already known to be a witch, they

would wonder why we couldn't find the Mark. After all, it must be there."

"They wouldn't accuse us, would they?" Martha asked.

"No, they never would," I replied with a laugh. "Midwives are the *last* ones to be called witches. Who is more trusted by their neighbors? No, we are the women who send witches to the gallows, not the women who are sent."

"I do not like such work," Martha said.

"Nor do I," I replied. "But it must be done."

"And if you find the Mark you'll send Hester to her death?"

I paused before answering. A few years earlier I would not have hesitated to perform this duty. But in the time since Martha had come to my house, I'd had a hand in more deaths than I cared to count. And while none could be counted as murder, my appetite for blood, even the blood of the guilty, had long been sated.

"If I must," I said at last. I could hear the doubt in my voice.

I decided to wait until morning before sending a reply to the summons, and that night I petitioned the Lord to take the cup from my lips.

To my surprise, God answered my prayers in the affirmative. The next morning, hours before sunrise, I heard a knocking at my door. Hannah answered, and by the time she came upstairs to get me I'd already started to dress. There was only one reason for someone to come to my house so early.

"Jane Morris is in travail," Hannah said as she helped me finish dressing. "Martha is gathering the necessary herbs and your valise."

"Thank you, Hannah," I said. "Send a note to the Castle telling them I won't be able to examine Hester Jackson. They should find someone else." I paused for a moment to thank God for His mercy. Had I known that a more poisonous draught would follow, I would not have been so fervent in my prayer.

Martha and I had only a few minutes to talk as we walked to St. Wilfred's parish, where Jane lived.

"I delivered Jane twice before you came to the city," I said. "And she's reached her time, so the child should be a strong one."

"Were there any problems with the earlier births?" Martha asked.

"None at all," I said. "Perhaps you should take the lead today?" A smile lit up Martha's face, making it even more beautiful than it ordinarily was.

"I was hoping you'd ask," she said.

As I'd anticipated, Jane's travail was quick and without any problems. Martha acquitted herself marvelously.

But the next afternoon it became clear that when I refused to examine Hester Jackson I had called a storm upon the city. Though the initial breeze seemed harmless enough, it was followed by winds and torrents powerful enough to overturn all good order and wash away many lives, including my own.

I was in the dining room helping Elizabeth with her writing when I heard the front door open and then the telltale gait of my nephew Will Hodgson. Elizabeth recognized it as well, dropping her quill and racing to greet him.

"Elizabeth, your hands are covered in ink!" I cried out as I righted the inkpot she'd knocked over in her haste. Will shouted out in mock horror as Elizabeth approached, and I found them tussling in the entry hall. Will held fast to her wrists while Elizabeth insisted that she wanted to draw a mustache on his face. Since coming to my house, Elizabeth had become especially fond of Will, and I could not help thinking that it was because they had been orphaned within days of each other. While separated by years, they were bound by death.

After I shooed Elizabeth off to find a basin and towel for her hands, Will retrieved his cane from where he had dropped it and came to embrace me. He had been born with a clubfoot, and he spent all his life trying to overcome this deformity. Other children had teased him relentlessly, of course, and Will had learned to defend himself with his fists. When his own father rejected him because of his misshapen body, Will seemed bound for a life of drink and violence. He had been pulled back into a respectable life by my good offices, but more by his love for Martha. They had not yet declared their affection to me, but I had seen and heard enough to know that they intended to marry once Will had established himself.

For a time, such a match had seemed unlikely, if only because Will's father, Phineas's brother Edward, would never have allowed his son—even one with a club foot—to marry a maidservant. But the terrible bloodletting that had visited York the previous summer ultimately freed Will from such constraints. The first step in this strange journey was the return of Will's older brother Joseph to the city after a time in the wars. Joseph proved to be zealous for the Puritan cause and unceasing in his pursuit of power. His return led to the deaths of half a dozen men and women, including Edward. In the aftermath, Joseph drove Will from their childhood home and seized their father's wealth. While some men doubted Will's guilt, none were willing declare his innocence in public; Joseph's power and ruthlessness were too great, and the consequences of angering him too dire. Will mourned his father, of course, but realized that while he'd lost his wealth, he now had the freedom to marry whomever he chose.

Will's fortunes within the city took an unexpected turn for the better when, in the wake of Edward's death, his godfather took an interest in him. George Breary had been Edward Hodgson's friend and rival since they had been youths, competing first for the affection of York's women, and then in business and in government. When the wars had started, Edward favored Parliament, while George remained loyal to the King. Despite all this, the two remained friends, bound by their love for Will and York. To my great pleasure, George recognized Will's plight after Edward's death and took him into his service. In the past months George had given Will greater responsibility for his business, even sending him to London in search of silk he could trade to the Scots. If Will's fortunes continued to improve, he could hope to match his brother's power *and* to marry Martha. That is what I begged of God, at least.

Once Will and I had settled in the parlor, Martha brought three glasses of wine and sat with us. An outsider might have considered us an odd little family—a gentlewoman, her deputy and maidservant, and her club-footed nephew—but the love we felt for each other overcame the strangeness.

"So tell us the gossip of the town," Martha said. A mischievous lilt crept into her voice, but Will, who could sometimes fall into fits of pomposity, missed it entirely.

"'Tis not gossip," Will objected. "It is news."

Martha and I burst out laughing, and Will joined in once he realized that he'd been the butt of Martha's joke. We talked for a time of the city's business, and just as we emptied our glasses, Will brought us back to a more serious matter.

"And did you hear the news of Hester Jackson?" he asked at last. "Joseph has taken the lead in the investigation. The

Searcher they called in to replace you discovered what she called 'a most unnatural and fiendish teat.'"

"Poor woman," I said. Her hanging now seemed inevitable.

"That is not all," Will said. "The Searcher was Rebecca Hooke."

My stomach lurched, for I knew without a doubt that for me and mine, the city had just become a much more dangerous place.

Chapter 3

"Rebecca Hooke?" I cried. "How so?" I felt myself pulled between the Scylla of fury and the Charybdis of despair. It had been over a year since I had last spoken to her, but she and the evil she had done still haunted my dreams.

Before my arrival in York, Rebecca had been the most famous midwife in the city, but one who violated her oath with astonishing regularity. She would assist the poor only if it was convenient and if she could see an advantage in it for herself. In the delivery room she was a horror, bullying the gossips and threatening the mothers that they would die if they did not follow her every command. She was no better after the delivery, as she used the secrets she learned to terrify women and men alike into doing her bidding. When Henry Perkins sued Rebecca's husband over a business matter, Rebecca announced that he was a whoremaster and had put the French Pox on his wife. She should know, she said, for she had seen the sores with her own eyes. And when Elizabeth Stoppard offered Rebecca some slight—to this day, I know not what it was—Rebecca told all who would listen that

Elizabeth's stillborn child had been born as black as trash and smelled of a turd. Of course, she was not the midwife anyone wanted, but the women of York quickly learned that she would have her revenge on anyone who spoke against her or went to another. Soon Rebecca had the choicest clients in the city.

It was not until I convinced a handful of my neighbors that my wealth and name could protect them from Rebecca that they began to abandon her, and soon others followed. Rebecca's fury knew no bounds, and she swore she'd see me out of the practice. I had no choice but to have her license taken. She never forgave me for that insult. Ultimately, what little sympathy I'd had for her—there was no denying she'd led a hard life—died when I discovered that she was guilty of a crime that would break even the hardest of hearts. Now my only regret was that I'd not been able to see her hanged.

"How is this possible?" Martha demanded. She looked as pale as I felt. "Who in the city would want her to have such power?"

"My brother Joseph," Will admitted. "He is behind it."

"But why?" Martha asked. "She is so malicious, what good could come of it?"

"He is concerned with power, not guilt or innocence," I replied. "He requires a Searcher who will find witches where she is told, no matter the circumstances."

"And that is Rebecca," Martha said.

"She would welcome the opportunity to judge women guilty of witchcraft," I said. "She loved the authority of a midwife, and a position as a Searcher would bring her even more. Now she can threaten death itself."

"And you think she found the Witch's Mark on Hester Jackson?" Martha asked.

"If it would be to her advantage, she would have found such a mark on a new sheet of paper," I replied. "Joseph didn't make her Searcher so she could find Hester innocent."

"But why is he hunting witches at all?" Martha persisted. "What advantage does it bring him?" Martha and I had long ago realized that like too many of the Puritan faction, Joseph's love of God was matched only by his love of power. The fact that doing God's will also served his own interests would strike Joseph as another example of God's goodness.

"He wants to show the city what a good and godly ruler he would be if only they would invest him with *more* authority. And if he has an unscrupulous Searcher on his side, they would be a powerful pair. There is no end to the mischief they could make. We shall have to tread carefully until we know the nature of their scheme."

Together, Joseph and Rebecca brought death, of course. We knew they would bring death for Hester; there could be no avoiding that. But if I had known how many would follow Hester to the grave, or that those I loved would find themselves in Joseph and Rebecca's path, I would have taken my family, fled the city, and never looked back.

Once Rebecca Hooke had found the Witch's Mark on Hester, the City Council had to determine how to try her. Before the war, we would have waited for the Assizes, the court that tried all felonies. But the King could hardly send judges into a city held by Parliament, so the city had to handle such matters itself. During the previous year, York's governors had tried felons themselves, with disastrous results. Now they were more cautious, and the City Council tried to create formal courts with judges who had served in the office before; they called these courts Special Assizes.

And so it was that Hester languished in York Castle for weeks before her trial. I hated to think how she suffered, for I had seen the low gaol where the city put its worst criminals. These poor souls resided in darkness and filth so complete that many prisoners welcomed their hanging if only for the few moments of sunlight and fresh air that preceded it.

When the judges of the Assizes came, the city put itself on display. Musicians and a platoon of the Town Watch met the Earl of Lancashire when he arrived at the gate, and with his judges trailing behind him he rode from Micklegate Bar to the Castle. After a few days of preliminaries, the trials began with their usual pageantry and the slow parade of criminals. Some marched from the court to freedom, others to the stocks, and a few to the gallows. There was no reason for me to attend any of the trials, so I did my best to ignore the entire process. In my youth, I would have found myself caught up in the majesty of the occasion and embraced the Court's decisions without question, full of confidence that they offered justice. But in recent years I had seen the law go astray too many times to keep my faith in the Court. To my eyes, the law seemed to be a weapon the powerful used to plunder from the weak or to destroy their enemies. Perhaps things had been different before the war. Or perhaps I'd learned to see the corruption that had always been there.

The Special Assizes were still in session when I received an invitation to dine with George Breary. Since Will had entered George's service such invitations had become more common, and as I dressed for supper I assumed that it would be a social visit. Will accompanied me as we made our way through the city, heads bowed against the rain that the wind whipped into our faces. I said a prayer of thanks that George lived near me in one of the city's northern wards, rather than across the river in Micklegate. Will and I weaved back and forth across the cobbled streets to avoid the puddles, most of which now had a thin layer of ice across the top. One misstep would mean a cold and unpleasant evening.

When we arrived at George's stately home, we found him hard at work on some business matter, but he put that aside and we retired to the parlor. He was perhaps fifteen years my senior—I would have put him at around fifty—and had the air of a man comfortable with the authority that God had given him. His clothes were of fine wool and like many who had stood by the King, he wore his hair to his collar. I sometimes wondered what would have happened if I'd married a man such as George rather than so weak a specimen as Phineas. But what use are such fantasies? As I settled into my chair I noticed the richness of the fabric. The poor were suffering from the wars, but George was doing well enough. We talked for a time of the news of the town, especially the rain and cold that fall had brought, before George suddenly turned our conversation to more serious matters.

"Lady Bridget, I must speak to you of your nephew Joseph," he said.

"What is it?" I asked. "I have not seen him since Edward died." I glanced at Will, unsure how much he had told George of our suspicions about Joseph's true nature. The previous summer, a prisoner had died in York Castle. Though we could not prove it, we had good reason to think Joseph was behind the death.

"I believe that Joseph soon will make another attempt to drive all manner of sin and sinners out of the city. Last summer it was drunkenness and fornication; now it is witchcraft. It is all of a piece."

"Will and I already discussed this," I replied. "We shall have to be careful indeed."

"As soon as Hester Jackson was arrested, Joseph asked the Council to hire Rebecca Hooke as the Searcher," George continued as if I had not spoken.

I sighed impatiently. "Yes, yes," I said. "We know all this."

"There is more," he said. "I had hoped that you would be a part of our defense against Joseph's scheme. I had hoped you would play a role in the hunt for witches."

"What do you mean?" I asked. I did not like where George's fancy was taking him.

"When Joseph proposed hiring Rebecca, I thwarted him by telling the Council that *you* had agreed to act as our Searcher in this and all other cases that might arise."

"You did what?" I cried. "You told them this without speaking with me first?"

George seemed surprised by my anger.

"I had no choice," he complained. "I could not stand idly by and let Joseph Hodgson and Rebecca Hooke seize such power for themselves. If Hester Jackson is guilty, then let her be hanged. But Joseph and Rebecca have no interest in guilt or innocence, only in making the city their own. I thought my plan was quite brilliant. At least until I learned that you had chosen a woman in travail over the search of Hester Jackson's body."

I heard a note of reproach in his voice, as if I had somehow betrayed him by going to a labor. I would have none of it.

"You did not consult me beforehand, and you know I cannot abandon my clients." I gave my anger free rein, for he had far overstepped his bounds. "I've done enough business with the city to expect such ill-treatment from most men, but I expect more from you. That kind of stupidity drives me mad."

George hung his head for a moment in a show of contrition before continuing as if I'd said nothing of consequence. "My fear is that they have more ambitious plans than the hanging of one old woman. I think they are conspiring against me and others who are not zealous enough for Parliament."

I nodded. "Again, that is no news. He means to make York his own, as he always has. He will use the law to rid York of its sinners, whether whores or witches, and once he's done so he will turn it against his enemies. If a few old women are hanged along the way, so be it; you are right to be afraid."

"The danger is imminent, and we cannot wait to act," George said. "They say that Suffolk has hanged hundreds of witches. If Joseph were to make himself a Witch Finder . . ." We fell silent at the prospect of Joseph presiding over scores of hangings.

"Give me a writ to question Hester Jackson," I said at last.

"What? Why?" George asked. "What good will that do? She is to be hanged."

"If Rebecca and Joseph are scheming to see her executed, there must be a reason, and she may know what it is. If I speak to her, I might be able to discover their next move." In truth, I was not convinced that such a strategy would work—Joseph and Rebecca were far too careful to tip their hand to a woman such as Hester Jackson—but it could do no harm.

George nodded. "She is to be hanged on Friday, so you will have to go tomorrow. I will send a letter to the Castle's Warden ensuring that you are allowed to see her. Will your deputy accompany you?"

"If I am going as a spy, there is nobody I would rather have at my side," I replied. George did not know of Martha's past as a cutpurse and burglar, but the truth was that when our work drew us across the border between the lawful and the criminal, I was *her* deputy.

After that, I steered the evening's conversation onto subjects more comfortable than witchcraft and executions, and we had a pleasant time of it. When I arrived at my home, I acquainted Martha with the task that lay before us. As I expected she warmed to the challenge, but she recognized that we could not enter the fray without some danger to ourselves.

"Mr. Hodgson and Mrs. Hooke will know that we've visited Hester Jackson," she said, "and they'll not be pleased."

I nodded in agreement. Rebecca was as smart as she was malevolent, and I knew that if she saw the opportunity to destroy me she would take it, particularly if she thought I was opposing her plans to regain her power within the city.

"Once the battle has been joined we shall have to act quickly," I replied. "For we will surely hazard all."

Martha and I rose early the next morning and made our way to the Castle. Clouds hung low overhead and the wind still tore at our cloaks, but the rain had stopped and I gave thanks for that. The Special Assizes would be in session two more days, so even at that hour, a steady stream of people joined us in our journey. When I looked toward the Thursday Market I could see workmen assembling the three-legged mare for the hangings that would begin the next day. I imagined that Hester would be among the first to die.

As we neared the edge of the city, the stone keep known as Lord Clifford's Tower came into view, standing watch over the city as it had for centuries. We passed around the Tower and approached the drawbridge. Like many visitors, Martha had been disappointed the first time she saw the Castle, for it was hardly worthy of the name. No lord would deign to live there, for it was little more than a wall surrounding a courtyard, with towers at the corners. During the siege of 1644, it had been at the heart of the King's defenses, but now it served only as the city's prison.

Our progress slowed as the crowd squeezed through the narrow gate into the Castle yard. "Let us see Samuel first," I suggested. Martha nodded, and we crossed to the small tower where Samuel Short lived and worked as one of the Castle's jailors. When I rapped on the tower door, a small window opened and Tree's face appeared. He grinned when he saw us, and let us in.

"Lady Bridget," Tree cried as we entered, and Samuel bade us sit. I had met Samuel when a friend of mine had been taken for murder and imprisoned in his tower. The Warden saw to it that most women sent to the Castle found themselves in Samuel's care. He thought that because Samuel was a dwarf, he was less likely to take advantage of the women in his charge. I do not know if he was right, but I had never heard anything to the contrary. Unfortunately, Hester Jackson was too poor and her crime too heinous to receive such courtesy, so she would be in one of the lower dungeons. If the jailors abused her, what of it? She had rebelled against God and deserved her fate.

"Welcome, Lady Bridget," Samuel said as we joined him around his rough-hewn table. Samuel and Tree lived in two rooms in the tower, with the luckier (and wealthier) prisoners above, and the poor or unlucky in cells belowground. "I heard you would be coming to us. The other jailors wonder how you will top the commotion that accompanied your last visit."

"I imagine so," I replied with a tight smile. The *commotion*, as he called it, had ended in four deaths.

Samuel must have recognized that he'd stepped out of line, for he moved on as quickly as he could. "What business brings you to the Castle?"

"I wondered what you might know of Hester Jackson."

"Yes, yes, the witch," Samuel replied. "Not very much, I'm afraid. The Warden put her in the Castle's lowest dungeon. Her keeper's surprised she hasn't died of gaol-fever. Nobody down there lasts for long. She was lucky to live to see her trial."

"Lucky?" asked Martha. "She'll be hanged tomorrow!"

"Better a quick death at the end of a rope than a slow one by the fever," Samuel replied flatly. "Believe me, I know whereof I speak."

"Do you hear anything of her interrogation?" I asked.

"Ah, that's why you're here. Anything that brings Joseph Hodgson and Rebecca Hooke together must give you fits of the night-mare."

"It is not the friendship I most hoped for," I admitted. "And I must know what they are planning. Have you heard anything?"

"Nothing of interest to you, I don't think," Samuel replied. "Mr. Hodgson and some of the other Justices questioned her, and she confessed. When Mrs. Hooke found the teat, there was little left to do except wait for the judge and the hangman." He must have read the disappointment on my face. "If I hear that anything untoward happened, I'll pass it along," he added.

"No," I replied, "I did not think they would be bold enough to announce their scheme so plainly, but one can hope. Where are they keeping her?"

"She's in the tower nearest the Ouse," he replied. "I will take you there." The three of us crossed the Castle yard to the tower where Hester Jackson was being held.

While few of the Castle's jailors could match Samuel in the strangeness of their appearance, Hester's was quite a sight all the same. He could have been anywhere between forty and seventy years of age, and his wizened face had been slashed in two by a scar that ran through what used to be his left eye.

"Good morning, my lady," he said with an exaggerated bow. "I have been awaiting your arrival with the same anticipation I await the return of Jesus Christ himself." I did not know whether all jailors spoke so impudently to their betters, but he already lived in a gaol overseeing the worst prisoners in the Castle. What else could I do to him? "My name is Benjamin Hunter. Welcome to my tower." A ghost of a smile flitted across Martha's lips at Hunter's performance.

"Thank you," I replied. "We are here to see Hester Jackson."

"Yes, yes," he replied. "The Warden said you would come today. Not a moment too soon, either, for on the morrow her only visitor will be the hangman, and after that she'll be of no use at all, except for the anatomists." He stared at me for a moment, but he made no move to unlock the door that led to the cells. I glanced at Martha, utterly confused as to the jailor's game.

"You can imagine the number of people who have come here in hope of seeing a witch," Hunter said at last. "Hundreds have paid their money."

Ah, I thought, he just wants his bribe. I slipped him a few pennies, and he led us down the spiral stairs to the lowest room in the tower. When we reached the last cell, Hunter handed me a lantern and unlocked Hester's door.

"Here you are, my lady," he said. "I introduce to you, Hester Jackson, widow and witch."

Chapter 4

As I stepped into Hester's cell, my mouth went dry and my heart began to race. It was said that arresting a witch broke her power, but if a woman could kill with words, why would prison walls make a difference? I glanced at Martha, hoping to draw some courage from her, but fear shone in her eyes as well.

Hester Jackson sat on the edge of the rough wood pallet that served as her bed, staring at the floor before her. When she looked up, it was as if we were staring at the face of death itself. In the guttering light of the jailor's lantern, Hester's cheeks were all hollows and bone, as if time and rot refused to wait for her death before they stripped her skull of its skin and flesh. She stared at us with empty sockets, and for a moment I wondered if her eyes had been put out. Strands of hair hung on either side of her face, deepening the shadows of her sunken cheeks. I had not known Hester well, but at that moment I would have sworn that she was a witch and I wanted nothing more than to run from the cell as fast as I could.

When she tried to stand, the entire illusion fell away. She

was halfway to her feet when her breath caught and she began to cough great body-shaking coughs. She fell back on her bed and drew her knees to her chest. By the time she finished coughing, Hester was weeping. When she could finally sit up I saw that chains bound both her hands and feet.

"You laid her in double irons?" I asked Hunter incredulously. "To what end?"

"To the end of keeping my place," the jailor replied. "The Warden tells me to do something, I do it. And after the madness of last summer, I'd be a fool to take chances. I don't need to tell you that, do I?"

I thought back to the previous summer, when a prisoner had slipped from his irons and hanged himself. How many deaths had that caused? Two? Three? I did not know when to stop counting. Perhaps I had not yet finished.

"Have you come to take my bucket?" Hester asked the jailor. She pointed at a small wooden bucket in the corner; the smell that rose from it made clear its purpose.

"I'll take it in the evening like I always do," Hunter growled. "Ask again before then and you'll be wearing it." To emphasize his point, he tipped it partway with his foot, threatening to spill its contents into the filthy rushes that covered the floor.

"Take the bucket," I commanded. "I'll not have it in here when I speak to her."

Hunter looked at me in surprise. His mouth flopped open for a moment before he snapped it shut. "Yes, my lady," he replied at last.

"Now, leave us be," I said. "I will let you know when we are finished."

Hunter nodded, picked up the bucket, and shuffled back up the stairs.

"Hester, I am Lady Bridget Hodgson," I said. "Do you know me?"

"My mind's not so far gone yet," the old woman replied. "I know you. But who is she?" she thrust her jaw in Martha's direction.

"She is my deputy."

Hester nodded and turned back to me.

"What do you want then?" she challenged. I supposed the prospect of hanging had freed her of the need for common courtesy.

"I need to speak with you about your case."

"Why? I'm convicted and sentenced. Tomorrow I'll hang, won't I?"

I nodded. "Yes, you will. There is nothing I can do about that, even if I wished." I peered into Hester's eyes, trying to find a sign of a woman who would kill a child over a crust of bread. In the end I gave up: She seemed no different than a hundred other ancient widows and spinsters who lived in the city.

"Well, all right then," she said. "What is it?"

"I need to know about your interrogation by Mr. Hodgson and Mrs. Hooke."

Hester looked confused. "What for? There was little to it. They asked me what I'd done, and I told them."

"You told them that you bewitched the Asquiths?" Martha blurted out. "How could you have?"

Hester offered a toothless smile.

"You want to learn how to witch *your* neighbors?" she asked with a bitter laugh. "You see where it will get you." Hester's manacles rattled when she held up her hands.

"That's not what I meant," Martha replied.

"I know what you meant," Hester said. "You are wondering

38

how an old woman became a witch, and why I would kill a young mother and her innocent babe."

Martha nodded.

"God's truth, I don't know how it happened." Hester shook her head at the mystery. "I went to Mr. Asquith's door, begged some bread of him. When he denied me, I told him that he would suffer for refusing me simple Christian charity. The next day his boy fell ill, after that his wife," she concluded.

"So you *did* curse them?" I asked.

Hester shook her head. "If I did, I didn't mean to. I never said a word to curse the boy or his mother, not on purpose. They were innocent. They had none of Mr. Asquith's sin on them. I wanted *him* to suffer. But not them, not like this. If Satan heard my words and killed them at my urging, I . . . I . . . I never meant to do it. I am sorry."

A single tear shimmered in the lantern light. I fought against the sorrow that welled up in my belly. I did not know what to make of Hester's confession. Had she truly bewitched the Asquiths? Or did her guilt grow out of some overheated imaginings? Could Satan have twisted her words as she claimed? Could he have acted without her knowledge or permission? We could never know the truth, of course; indeed, even she did not seem to know it. But on this day the truth did not much matter, and now was not the time to think melancholy thoughts about a child and mother bewitched to death or the woman who would be hanged for the crime. No matter what I did, Hester Jackson would die the next day, but Rebecca and Joseph would remain a threat to me and my family long after she was in the ground.

"And the imp?" I asked. "You told them about your familiar?" I'd never interrogated a confessed witch before, and I wanted to learn as much as I could. God only knew how many more witches Rebecca could find if she set her mind to it.

"What, the French mouse they keep talking about?" Hester asked. "What do they call him, Mousnier?"

I nodded.

"The mouse came from their fevered brains," she said. "Satan might have killed the Asquiths, but I never saw an imp whether mouse, cat, or mole."

"And you told all this to Mr. Hodgson?" I asked.

Hester nodded. "But after I told him about the curse I laid, it did not matter what I said." She paused and stared into my eyes. I could still see a flicker of life in her. Not much, but it was there. "Lady Hodgson, I will tell you now that I did not mean for them two to die, but I said the killing words. And I'm sorry for it."

I nodded. I could not help feeling that she wanted some sort of absolution for her crime, but that was something I could not give.

"Did Mr. Hodgson ask you anything else?" I pressed. "Did he ask about any other witches?"

Hester shook her head. "Nay, he never did. Once I told him what I'd done, he called in the Searcher."

"Mrs. Hooke?" I asked.

"Aye. She was a rough one, poking around my privities like that. I'm glad she'll not be doing the hanging tomorrow."

"But if you didn't have an imp, how could she have found a teat?" Martha asked.

Hester shrugged. "I don't know. I cannot say I care either. Perhaps I have an imp who suckles at night without me knowing. Who can say how Satan does his work?"

"Did *she* ask you about other witches?" I asked.

"Aye, and she was not pleased when I told her that I did not know of any. She threatened to have me swum if I did not tell the truth. But I knew she couldn't do that, not by herself. I kept my peace."

Martha and I bid farewell to Hester and I pounded on the door to summon the jailor.

"Lady Hodgson?" Hester said as we waited. For the first time she sounded uncertain. "Will you be there tomorrow?" I turned to face her. Her eyes shone in the lamplight, and I realized that she'd invited me to her execution.

For a moment I wondered why she would ask such a favor. What comfort could I offer to such a wretched creature?

And then I knew.

For as long as she could remember, Hester Jackson had lived on the edge of the parish. She had no husband, no children, no family. Nobody in the city loved or cared for her. In the best of times her neighbors viewed her as a parasite, taking bread from the mouths of their children, and with all of England at war, we hardly lived in the best of times. When William Asquith accused Hester of witchcraft and murder, whatever friends she'd had would have abandoned her. Indeed, they'd probably been crueler than most, if only to distance themselves from an accused witch. Hester Jackson had nobody.

I nodded, and she thanked me.

As soon as Benjamin Hunter returned to let us out of the cell, it was clear that the black mood into which I'd cast him had subsided. When Martha and I reached the top of the stairs we saw the reason. A dozen or more people stood outside the tower door, eagerly waiting the chance to see a witch before she was hanged, and each would have to pay Hunter for the privilege. As we left, I prayed that Hester would not suffer at Hunter's hands, and that her visitors would not mistreat her, although with less than a day to live, what further indignity could they offer?

Martha and I found the road into the city far busier than it had been on our way out, and we had to fight against the crowds to cross the Castle drawbridge. The mass of people eased once we reentered the city, and we could talk without having to shout over the hubbub. By now the shopkeepers had set up their stalls along the street, and boys, wrapped in layer upon layer of cloth, cried their wares as the north wind whipped the brightly colored awnings.

"That was not what I expected," Martha said.

"What do you mean?"

"I didn't expect her to say that she had killed the Asquiths. I didn't think she would admit to being a witch."

"Once the guilty have been condemned, they often *want* to tell the truth," I replied. "We saw it ourselves not so long ago."

"Yes," she replied. But I could tell that something else bothered her.

Martha tried again. "I didn't think she would say she had bewitched them. How could she have?"

Then I understood.

"You don't believe witchcraft is real!" I cried. I knew there were some who denied the reality of witchcraft, and I had heard of Reginald Scot's infamous book, but had not thought to count Martha among the skeptics.

Martha shrugged. "I don't know what to think. But I can't help noticing that most women accounted as witches are like Hester: Poor and old, with no family to save them."

"Such women are all the more easily tempted by Satan," I replied.

Martha laughed coarsely. "Yes, yes, I've heard the sermons. Witches are no different than other women. We are weak willed and so inclined to lust that Satan can lead us astray with little trouble. No wonder men must keep us leashed."

"It's not just that," I replied. "He offers women like Hester everything they lack, everything they could dream of: money, protection from the world, and the power to take revenge on their enemies. For some women, especially those inclined to malice, it could be a difficult offer to resist. Hester says she did not mean to hurt the Asquiths, but even so she fell into witchcraft. You heard her admit it."

"I suppose," Martha said. "I told myself I'd believe in witchcraft when the Justices started hanging men for the crime."

"Do you believe in it now?" I asked.

Martha's doubts about God and the supernatural were not new, of course. From her first weeks in my service, Martha and I argued over the place of God in the world. She had long abandoned any belief in His goodness or the usefulness of prayer. In her mind, if God existed at all, He was an absent parent who had left His children to engage in whatever petty cruelties they could imagine. For a time I endeavored to convince her otherwise, but in truth she had turned me more to her opinion than I had turned her to mine. Or perhaps she was just finishing the work that Michael's and Birdy's deaths had begun. I would be lying if I said that I did not question God's goodness when I cast a handful of dirt on the corpse of my last surviving child.

"What did *you* make of Hester?" Martha asked.

"She is a confessed witch, and she will hang," I replied. "But

I cannot believe that Joseph and Rebecca came together to hang one woman."

Martha nodded. "There *must* be more to their scheming than that."

"And until we find out what it is we will have to watch them both as best we can."

When we got home, I wrote a letter to George Breary describing our visit to the Castle, and advising him to beware. *I do not know what game Mr. Hodgson and Mrs. Hooke are playing,* I concluded, *but I feel sure that it is far from over.*

That night I took my time putting Elizabeth to bed. To her great pleasure, I drew out every moment, making sure the water for her face and hands was neither too hot nor too cold, and spending extra time cleaning her teeth. We lay in her bed and read from a horn book, one that Birdy had used when she was learning her letters. I doubted that Elizabeth's mother had been able to read—what whore could do so?—so it was no great surprise that Elizabeth knew only a few of her letters when she came to me. When I'd proposed she learn to read, she laughed in delight as if I'd suggested teaching her to fly. In the few months that she'd been in my house she'd proven herself a quick study, and constantly begged me, Martha, and especially Will to read to her.

"Ma?" Elizabeth asked suddenly. Only then did I realize that my mind had drifted.

"Yes, little one?"

"I heard they will hang a witch tomorrow." She looked up at me, her blue eyes filled with apprehension.

"Yes," I said.

"Did she really bewitch a little boy?"

"Yes, she did."

"And he died?"

"I'm afraid so. And now he is with God."

"Why did she bewitch him?" Elizabeth asked. "Was he wicked?"

"No, he did nothing wrong," I said. "She was angry at the boy's father and cursed him. But the boy died instead."

Elizabeth nodded solemnly. "Did you know the witch?"

Though she'd only been with me for a short time, Elizabeth had realized I was well-known within York. Over the years I had delivered hundreds of women before thousands of their gossips, so such a question was not strange in the least.

"I saw her today," I replied. "Why do you ask?"

"I wondered if she was frightening," she replied. "Is she going to bewitch other children?"

I thought about that day's visit to the Castle and shook my head. "No, she is not frightening," I said. "Not anymore. She is old, sad, and frightened."

"Then she can't hurt any more children?"

"No," I replied. "She is past that."

"And tomorrow she'll be hanged," Elizabeth concluded, clearly satisfied with Hester's fate.

"And tomorrow she'll be hanged," I agreed, and dimmed the lamp. Elizabeth snuggled into my side and wrapped her arms around me. We prayed for our household, our city, and the King. I added a silent prayer that God would be a fair and impartial judge when Hester Jackson stood before Him, and then said a prayer of thanks for Elizabeth.

But even as I prayed, I worried for the future. Elizabeth delighted in talk of the sprites that lived in the city's orchards and sometimes took the shape of mice or moles. If she saw our cat Sugar stalking some creature or another in our garden, she would cry out, *Beware, beware, it could be a sprite. If you get too close, he will turn your whiskers into daisies!* Until Hester's arrest, I delighted in such talk. But now the idea of a magical animal chilled me to the bone. It was but a short step from Elizabeth's sprites to Hester's Satanical imp.

I could not imagine anyone accusing Elizabeth of witch-craft, but what if I was wrong?

Chapter 5

On the morning after Hester Jackson's execution, the December wind brought nearly a foot of snow. While I had seen snow before, not even York's oldest residents could remember seeing such a storm, and many worried what it might portend. The city's Puritans, Joseph chief among them, cried out that God's fury at England's sinful ways had not yet run its course. They put their spurs into the constables and beadles, ordering them to redouble their efforts to suppress sin. By the time the storm ended, dozens of whores and drunkards found themselves in the city's gaols. I was amazed the City Council would tolerate Joseph's campaign—they had tried the same thing the previous summer and it had ended in a sea of blood. Had they learned nothing?

Elizabeth, of course, had never before seen so much snow, and begged with such fervency for me to take her out that I could not deny her. I worried that the cold would leave her phlegmatic, but she skipped gaily along, not minding it in the least. When we entered the Thursday Market I was relieved to see that the gallows had been taken down. I did not want Elizabeth to be reminded of Hester's fate.

"Good morning, my lady!" a voice called out. I turned to find Peter Newcome, the chapman I had met at Hester's hanging, still crying up his pamphlets. Elizabeth dashed over to his board, and stared intently at the lurid pictures that he'd pasted there. "Have you given any more thought to my offer?" he asked. "A little book on last summer's murders would sell in prodigious numbers, but your story won't remain fresh forever."

"Some new horror will overtake it?" I asked sharply.

Newcome shrugged. "I do not tell people what to read, my lady. I simply sell books that people want to buy."

I looked down at his board and the parade of murders, monsters, prodigies, and witches that it offered. One title caught my eye: *A Wonderful Discovery of Witches in the Town of Bolton, Lancashire*. The picture on the front showed four women being hanged together before a massive crowd. Beneath this were the words *Thou shalt not suffer a witch to live*. It seemed that witch-hunts had come to the North at last. Then I noticed the print at the bottom of the page, and my jaw fell open. It read, *Printed by order of the Lord Mayor and Aldermen of the City of York*.

"This was printed here in the city?" I asked Newcome.

"Aye," he said. "I bought them today at a ha'penny each. After yesterday's hanging, they'll be gone in hours, and I'll have a tidy profit."

"So you know the printer?"

"Of course, I do," he replied with a smile. "And if you think the three of us can make a deal for *your* story, you're right."

"My story will remain my own," I replied, unable to suppress a smile. "But I'll buy this book from you, and if you'll take me to the printer I'll give you a penny on top of that."

Newcome nodded and shouted for his boy. A lad about Elizabeth's age—the same one who had accosted me the day before—crossed the street and looked up at Newcome. On top of his coat he wore an apron stuffed with pamphlets he'd been selling on Newcome's behalf.

"Take Lady Hodgson to Mr. Williams's shop," Newcome told him. "She'll give you a tuppence, plus another penny for the book."

I started to object to the price, but before the words escaped my lips the boy dashed toward the Minster. I glared at Newcome, who gave me a wolf's smile in return, and Elizabeth and I hurried after the boy. He led us to a courtyard on the north side of the cathedral and stopped.

"Which door?" I asked.

The boy gave me a smile distinctly similar to his master's.

"Ah, your tuppence," I said.

"And the penny for the book," he said, smiling wider at the prospect of payment.

I handed him the coins and he pointed down an alley.

"It's there. There's a sign above the door." He nodded at Elizabeth and hurried back the way we'd come.

I took Elizabeth by the hand, and we entered the alley. As the boy had promised, a roughly painted sign hung above the printer's door. I knocked, and the door opened to reveal a young man wearing an ink-stained apron.

He looked at the two of us for a moment before speaking. "This is a printer's shop," he said uncertainly.

"And I am here to see the printer," I replied. "Is he in?"

He recovered himself and bowed. "I am sorry, my lady. It isn't often that gentlewomen or children come to the shop. I assumed you had lost your way."

"Is your master in?" I asked again.

"I am the printer," he replied. "My master fled with the King's men, and I've been here alone ever since."

I looked into the shop and saw a huge wood press, boxes of type, and piles of paper waiting to be made into books.

"You are here by yourself?" I asked.

"I have a boy to set the type, but I cannot trust him to check the text. I must do that myself. We print the sheets together. How can I help you, my lady?"

"I am here about a book you printed recently. The one about the witches in Lancashire."

The lad nodded. "Aye, a rushed job if ever I had one. The boy and I stayed up half the night, but I was well paid, so I cannot complain."

He stopped, and a worried look appeared on his face.

"Is there a problem with my work?" he asked. "I have a license signed by the Lord Mayor."

"No, it's not that," I said. "I need to know who sent the pamphlet to you."

"Oh, thank the Lord." He was visibly relieved. "In these times, I can never know who my books will offend. People will blame the printer when they can't find the author. But I'm afraid I can't help you."

I felt my heart sink. "What do you mean?"

"The man who brought me the pamphlet never said his name. He gave me the script and the money, and went on his way. He didn't even want copies for himself. He just made me promise to sell them all . . . as if I'd keep them." He shook his head in wonder.

"What did he look like?" I asked.

The lad furrowed his brow in thought. "He was a soldier,

I suppose. He had that air about him. And he had just three fingers on one hand."

My heart quickened at this, and I could feel the blood rising in my cheeks. "Three fingers?" I asked. "Which three?"

"He had his first two fingers and his thumb. He'd lost his little finger and his leech-finger. And a bit of his hand had been cut away as well."

My face must have reflected my distress at the news.

"What is it, my lady?" he asked. "Do you know him?"

"Aye," I replied. "All too well."

I offered the printer my thanks, took Elizabeth's hand, and started home at a trot.

"What is it, Ma?" Elizabeth asked as we rounded the east end of the Minster. "Did you find the man you were looking for?"

"Yes, my love, I did," I replied. When Stonegate was in sight, I stopped and took Elizabeth by her hands. "I need you to go straight home," I told her. "Tell Martha and Hannah I'll be along shortly, but I must see Mr. Breary."

The girl nodded solemnly and threw her arms around my neck. "You'll be back tonight?"

"I will," I said. "I promise."

I watched Elizabeth as she raced across High Petergate and down Stonegate, wisps of red hair trailing behind her, and felt an ache in my heart. For the first time since Birdy died, I'd begun to feel the hope and fear that is part of being a parent in this fallen world. We could love our little ones with all our hearts, but love could not protect them from a God who took the young so often and without any warning. I took a breath to gather myself and began the walk to George Breary's house.

When I arrived, George's servant ushered me into his

office right away. He and Will sat at a large table surrounded by sheets of figures and piles of letters. They both stood when I entered, and they greeted me warmly. George sent his servant for spiced wine to warm me from the cold, and I handed him the pamphlet. He and Will read it while I drank my wine. I sighed in contentment as the warmth spread through my body.

After a few minutes, Will looked back at the cover and noticed the imprimatur. "Printed by order of the Lord Mayor and Aldermen?"

"I'm an Alderman, and I knew nothing of it," George said, answering the first question on my mind. "What does this mean?"

"This is part of Joseph's scheme," I said. "I questioned the printer, and he said a man with three fingers brought him the book for printing."

"Mark Preston," Will and George said simultaneously.

I nodded. Preston had fought with Joseph in the wars and then had followed him to York after each of them had been wounded. Before Edward died, Preston had spent a few months in his service, but now he was Joseph's dog, and a vicious one at that. Only the Lord knew how many men Preston had killed at Joseph's behest, either in the wars or after.

George furrowed his brow in thought. "So Joseph is behind this pamphlet, but to what end?"

"He intends to bring a witch-hunt to York," I replied. "But he is as careful now as he was when he fought with Cromwell's cavalry. He knows to test the enemy before attacking, and that is what he has done with the city. Hester Jackson was his stalking horse, for her case would tell him whether the citizens would hang an ill-mannered old woman as a witch. When Hester's neighbors turned against her, he had his answer."

"And the pamphlet?" George asked.

"It is the first cannon-shot of the battle itself. He wants to be sure the citizens' blood is boiling when the hunt begins. Nothing is left to chance. He is being as deliberate as the devil himself."

"That makes sense," George said. "Joseph has called for a special meeting of the Council tonight. He's not said what it concerns, except that it is an urgent and secret matter."

"He is going to call for a witch-hunt," I said.

George nodded. "The battle is joined."

"I should like to be at the meeting," I said.

George looked at me in surprise. "Why?"

"If Joseph is intent on bringing a witch-hunt to York, it concerns me. The fate of the city's women is my business—it always has been."

George started to respond, but I held up my hand to silence him.

"There is more," I said. "Rebecca Hooke will have a place in Joseph's plan, and she has compassed my destruction for years. I am in as much danger as anyone."

George nodded. "The Council will gather tonight at seven. Meet me at the hall at six, and we will find you a hiding place. It might not be comfortable, but you should be able to hear well enough."

I thanked George for his assistance and started for home. Though I would not have imagined it possible, the wind seemed to blow even harder, and it cut through my cloak as if the garment were made of delicate silk rather than heavy Yorkshire wool. As I passed by some of the city's poorer tenements, I marveled at the suffering of those living within. Between ill-fitting doors and crumbling plaster, the buildings would provide as little warmth as my cloak. Such thoughts took my mind to Elizabeth's life before she'd come to live with me, for she had lived in just such a tenement. I wondered what she would remember of her childhood when she was grown, and whether she would recall the decaying house in which she'd lived, or her mother's illicit profession. Or would she simply put the past behind her and live the life of a gentlewoman's daughter?

In truth, I did not know which would be best. I did not want Elizabeth to forget her past entirely, but it was so terrible, what parts would I have her keep? She should remember her mother's love, of course. And I wanted her to see the struggles of the poor, for how else could she love them as God intended? If my work as a midwife did nothing else, it showed me how the lower sort lived, and I felt I was a better Christian for it.

By the time I reached my house, my bones ached from the cold, and I hurried to the warmth of the kitchen, where I found Hannah and Martha teaching Elizabeth how to make bread. I immediately joined in, and soon the four of us were covered with enough flour to make yet another loaf. When Hannah opened the oven door, the firelight shone through Elizabeth's golden-red hair, and for a moment it seemed as if she were the sun itself.

As we did our best to knock the flour from our clothes, Martha looked at me with a raised eyebrow, asking where I'd been. I inclined my head toward the dining room, and we withdrew from the kitchen.

"Elizabeth told you about the printer and the three-fingered man?" I asked.

Martha nodded. "Aye. What's that mongrel Preston got to do with a pamphlet?"

I explained what I'd learned from the printer.

"And you think Joseph is priming the pump for more witch hangings," she said.

"Aye," I replied. I crossed to the window and looked past my reflection. We were just a few days from the brumal solstice, and even at this early hour the street was cloaked in shadows. "I think the pump is already well primed. The question is when Joseph and Rebecca will start to work the handle."

Martha rarely showed signs of fear, but I could see that the prospect of a witch-hunt coming to York unnerved her.

"Why in God's name is he doing this?" she asked. "What profit is there in starting down this road?"

We both knew the answer to these questions; indeed she had answered one even as she asked it. Joseph's brutality was matched only by his righteousness. While some men sought power for its own sake, or for the wealth it would bring, Joseph wanted it in order to do the Lord's work. The previous summer (how long ago it seemed!) Joseph had become constable and used his office to suppress all manner of sin. His goal, the goal of all the city's Puritans, was to turn York into a "city upon a hill." In his mind, the minister and the magistrate should work together to drive the city's residents away from their sinful habits.

"It's no different than when he harried the city's doxies," I said. "He believes that he is doing God's bidding by ridding York of Satan's handmaidens. That he is also gathering power to himself is almost an accident."

"It is a dangerous scheme, this business of witch-hunting,"

Martha said. "Once the hangings start, who is to say he will be able to control its course?"

"He is at war with the devil, and there can be no victory without risk," I said. "But that is also why he needs Rebecca Hooke. So long as she is his Searcher and does his bidding, he will decide who will hang and who will not."

Martha swore. "So they will find witches only among their enemies. And you are chief among them."

"Precisely," I replied. "That is why we must be on our guard. Joseph and Rebecca have cast an incendiary into the city, and there is no telling which way the wind will take the fires once they start."

After supper, Martha and I set out into the darkness, walking south toward the Ouse Bridge and the hall where the Council would meet. The full moon shone down on us, painting York's streets a shimmering silver. Were it not so breathtakingly cold we might have paused to admire the scene; instead we pulled our cloaks tight, lowered our heads, and pushed forward. Within moments I was shivering, and I could hear Martha's teeth chattering together.

As we neared the bridge we caught a glimpse of the river, and we both stopped, shocked at the sight that greeted us.

"The river has frozen over," Martha said at last. Neither of us had ever seen—or even imagined!—such a thing. York relied on the Ouse to bring food in and send goods out; if trade came to a halt we all would suffer.

"Perhaps it will thaw in the morning," I said. But neither of us believed it. God had not yet shown Himself to be a merciful Father, and I had no reason to think He would start now.

When we reached the hall we found two men standing outside. Will (or the man I took to be Will, for I could hardly see him under his coats and heavy wool muffler) held a lantern and waved when he saw us. The other man—George Breary, I assumed—unlocked the door and ushered us inside.

The meeting would not start for an hour, and we had the room to ourselves. By the light of day it was nearly as impressive as the Merchant Adventurers' Hall, with vaulted ceilings and richly covered oak furniture. But at night and without its torches lit, the shadows above seemed ominous rather than awe inspiring.

George hurried over to the large fireplace, added wood, and fanned the embers into flame. Only then did he begin to unwrap himself. "I sent the keeper home," he said. "The fewer people who know you are here, the less chance that Joseph will find out." I nodded my thanks. Will took a torch from the wall and lit it from the fire. While Martha and I huddled next to the hearth, he walked around the room lighting the remaining torches. Soon the lower portion of the hall had a pleasant glow about it.

"Come with me," George said when Will had finished. "I know a place for you to stay during the meeting." He led us up a set of stairs to a balcony overlooking the room. A few chairs and other odd bits of furniture had been stored up there, but the space was mostly empty. I peered over the edge and saw the large table where the Council would sit.

"Will, can you see us?" I called down.

Will looked up from his seat at the table. "Take one step back," he replied. We did, and he nodded. "Nobody will see you if you stay still," he said.

I started to respond, but I swallowed my words when we heard the hall door creak open. I nodded to George, and he disappeared down the stairs to meet whoever had arrived. By ones and twos, the members of the Council and their followers arrived at the hall, and soon the sounds of their conversation bubbled up to us. I envied them their nearness to the hearth, for I could feel the cold seeping into my bones.

I peered into the growing crowd, occasionally catching a glimpse of friends and more distant family. When I married a Hodgson, I had married most of York. After what seemed an eternity, the Sergeant of the Mace called the Council into session, and we heard the sound of chairs scraping on the floor as the Councilmen took their seats. A minister offered a short prayer, and then the Lord Mayor stood to speak.

Matthew Greenbury had been elected Lord Mayor some months before, and it was the fourth time that he had held the office. As it happened it was also his fourth decade on the Council, and every year was etched on his ancient face. Despite his advanced age, Greenbury remained sound in body and retained every bit of the authority he must have had in his youth. Even before the war between King and Parliament had begun, Greenbury had refused to choose one side over the other, wearing the title "neutralist" as a badge. While it endeared him to no one, once the fighting broke out it made him the most logical choice to lead the city.

"As most of you know, we are here at the request of Mr. Joseph Hodgson," Greenbury announced. "So without further delay I will turn the meeting over to him."

When Joseph began to speak, I leaned forward hoping to catch a view of him. I caught my breath when I saw Mark Preston's familiar and entirely unwelcome face. He stood against the far wall, facing us, and when I glanced down at his ruined hand a shiver ran through me. While Joseph and Rebecca were the architects of the scheme to rid York of its witches, it would be a mistake to forget about so dangerous a man as Preston, and I vowed not to do so.

Joseph sat with his back to us, but in my mind I could see the hard lines of his face and his cold, clear eyes. When he'd left to fight in the wars, he'd been a kind young man, a bit aloof perhaps, but not a bad sort at all. He'd returned from Cromwell's side soaked in blood and well schooled in the ruthlessness necessary to succeed in politics. When Edward died, Joseph stepped into his place without a moment's hesitation, and he made it his business to purge the city of sin—and of his enemies.

Joseph's chair scraped back as he stood to speak. "It is no secret that York has suffered, and continues to suffer at God's hands," he said. "Summer heat has turned to the iron cold of winter, and many in the city know not where to turn for relief. The answer, of course, is that they should turn to the Lord, but too many have not seen this simple truth, and even to this day they wallow in their sin." Joseph continued in this vein for some time, and had I not known who was speaking, I would have thought it was a godly minister preaching to his flock. Joseph dropped his voice to a whisper, drawing in his listeners, and then shouted about God's law or God's glory, overwhelming the Council with the power of his voice and the sheer force of his will.

"Good and learned ministers of the gospel have shown us that the End of Days is upon us," Joseph continued. "Soon, very soon, the Risen Christ will do battle with the fallen Antichrist, and all men will have to choose whether they are among God's people or Satan's. Even now, the battle is joined, as the hanging of the witch Hester Jackson has shown." At this Martha and I stood a little straighter. This was why we'd come.

"In years past, learned men have amply proved that witches—these handmaidens of the devil himself—never work alone. In this, witches are like the rats that so often suckle from their hideous teats. If one rat is found in the kitchen, there must be more within the walls. And if one witch is in the city, there must be more within *its* walls." I could hear members of the Council murmuring in agreement with Joseph's logic.

"Although it is unusual, I should like now to bring an expert on witches and their evil ways before the Council." Martha and I looked at each other in alarm. "I am sure you all know Mrs. Rebecca Hooke," Joseph continued. "She was born and bred in the city, and worked for many years as a midwife. Indeed, the wives of more than a few Councilmen benefitted from her care. Mrs. Hooke examined Hester Jackson and found the Witch's Mark on her body. And she knows far more about witches and witchcraft than any one of us."

When none on the Council objected, the clerk called for Rebecca Hooke. Confidence and cruelty echoed through the hall each time her heel struck the rough wood floor. I could not resist peering over the edge of the balcony to watch Rebecca's performance. She stood at the head of the table and looked around the room. Once she was sure that she had the attention of every Alderman she began to speak.

Chapter 6

"Gentlemen," Rebecca Hooke said, "no good man would deny that Satan is active in the world, more now than at any time since Jesus Christ walked the earth. We hear daily of witches acting on behalf of the King to destroy godly religion and hasten the fall of all men into perdition."

Such pious words from such a harridan were absurd, of course. When the King had held York, Rebecca had been as strong a royalist as you'd care to meet, but once Parliament had taken power she donned the garb of the Puritan and became a reformer. I had no doubt that if the King returned to the city, so too would her love of monarchy. As best I could judge, Rebecca was a bit older than me, nearing her fortieth year. And while men assured me of my comeliness, she far surpassed me in beauty. Her high cheeks and ice-blue eyes seemed perfectly suited to the winter's cold. The Councilmen couldn't look away.

"When Hester Jackson was arrested as a witch, Mr. Hodgson summoned me to search her body for unnatural teats." Rebecca's voice echoed through the chamber. "I found just such teats near her fundament. She confessed her guilt to me, to Mr. Hodgson, and to the court of Special Assizes. There can be no doubt of her guilt, or the justice of her hanging. This you know already."

The Councilmen nodded in agreement.

As much as I hated Rebecca, I could not help admiring her strength and how far she had come in this life. While I had the privilege of an ancient name and estates, Rebecca had made her way from nothing. Some said that she was the bastard daughter of a maidservant, while others claimed that she had deliberately gotten with child so she could force the man of her choosing into marriage. None dared say such things anymore, for Rebecca had made it her business to exact terrible revenge on those who trafficked in such news. Her favored weapon was gossip, and she spread rumors so vicious they drove entire families from the city. After marrying Richard Hooke, she had become merciless in her pursuit of power and money, harrying the poor man into great wealth and a seat on the City Council. If he had not been every bit as weak as my own Phineas, Richard Hooke might have been able to resist his wife's base nature, but in the end she bent him to her will.

"But there are things you do not know," Rebecca continued, "things Mr. Hodgson and I have kept in the greatest confidence for fear of exciting tumult within the city."

The Councilmen feared disorder more than anything else, and they leaned forward in their seats, unwilling to miss a single word.

"As Mr. Hodgson said, it is not in a witch's nature to labor alone in the vineyards of Satan. And before she died, Hester swore to us that she was not the only witch in the city. There are others, many others." The Councilmen looked at each other in alarm and began to whisper among themselves. I glanced at Martha and saw the surprise on her face, for Hester has denied knowing of other witches in the city. I was not surprised that Rebecca would lie, of course, but I could not help being struck by her audacity in doing so before the Council. At the same time I realized that it was a brilliant stroke: With Hester dead, who could gainsay Rebecca's words?

"Mrs. Hooke," the Lord Mayor said. "Did the witch Hester Jackson tell you who these other witches are?"

"No, my Lord Mayor," Rebecca said. "I am afraid she would not go so far as that. It seems even Satan's handmaidens have a sense of loyalty."

"Well then, Mr. Hodgson, what can we do?" the Lord Mayor asked Joseph. "Surely you did not ask us here simply to tell us of the danger."

"My Lord Mayor," Joseph said as he rose once again to his feet. "This is why I called the Council into session. I have a solution." The murmuring stopped and all eyes settled on Joseph. He and Rebecca could not have planned the meeting any better.

I stole a glance at Will to see his reaction to his brother's words, but his face remained a mask.

"Many of you have heard of witch hangings in other parts of England," Joseph continued. "Most have been to the south, but today word reached us of witches found in Lancashire." He passed around copies of the book I'd bought from Newcome, the book that he himself had paid to have printed.

"It is well known that witches thrive in times of disorder such as those in which we now live. And it is common knowledge that Satan has sent his imps to aid the King's faction. And now it seems that the devil has sent his witches here in hope of overthrowing this very Council. Why would he do this? Why would he single out York from all the cities in England? Because Satan cannot tolerate our efforts to root out sin and build York into a shining city upon a hill. Gentlemen, Satan has challenged us, and if we do not accept the challenge we shall be defeated. If we do not drive these witches, the devil's own waiting-women, out from the city, then God will have no more mercy on us than he did on Sodom. If we do not act, God will loose Satan's hand. We will be destroyed—and rightly so."

"Mr. Hodgson, how do you propose we pay for this hunt?" George Breary rose to his feet as he spoke. "We will have to pay the jailors, the Searchers, the lawyers . . . the expense you are asking the city to bear is no small thing." Some of the Councilmen were notorious for their parsimony, and I think George hoped to give them pause. If so, he was disappointed, for Joseph was prepared for this line of opposition.

"Mr. Breary, what price would you put on defending the city against Satan's assaults?" Joseph's voice rose as he spoke, making his outrage at George's words clear to all. "If news came that the King's armies approached, would we not strengthen the city walls? Would we not build up our store of cannonshot and gunpowder? Of course we would. The horrible truth is that the enemy is not approaching, no. He is already here; he is already within the city walls. Witches already have murdered a mother and her child. You have no wife, no small children, so you may be safe. But others among us have families. And I must ask you, Mr. Breary, how many of *our* wives and children must die before you say, *I wish we had spent a few shillings to defend the city?*"

George opened his mouth to reply, but Rebecca interrupted. "Members of the Council." Her voice was as clear and loud as any man's. "As you know, Richard, my late and beloved husband, had the singular honor of serving on this august body."

I suppressed a laugh at her description of her husband. While he was alive, he was never beloved of anyone, least of all her, and his service to the city consisted of sleeping through meetings and voting as she instructed him.

Rebecca continued, her voice ringing through the hall with no less authority than Joseph's had. "I would be doing his memory a terrible injustice if I did not take up his standard and defend his city, *your* city, against the assaults of these devils. Witches are not just murderers; they are rebels against God Himself. In Exodus the Lord commands, *Thou shalt not suffer a witch to live.* Shall we now—even as God makes clear his hatred of England's sinful ways—turn our backs on His commandments? As His vice-regents on earth, you will be called to account if you fail to do your duty. You must protect the city against these witches just as you would defend it against the Irish horde. Indeed the danger of witches is greater than this, for even now they are within the city, doing the devil's work."

She paused and looked around the table, making sure that she had every Alderman's attention. She needn't have worried—they were spellbound.

"I will not presume to tell you how to act in this matter. But I have seen what witches can do to a child's body, and I have seen what trafficking with the devil did to Hester Jackson. Because of this I know all too well the depths of the devil's depravity. But all is not lost, for I also know that you will do God's will. I know that you will do the right thing for York." As the Council stared at her in awe, Rebecca turned from the table and strode from the room, her cloak billowing behind her.

After such a performance, the Council's vote was a mere

formality. Even George voted in favor of beginning the hunt; else he would have been the only one to dissent. Martha and I remained in our hiding place until only George and Will were left in the hall. When we descended the steps, George had an air of resignation about him.

"There was little you could have done," I assured him. "Rebecca and Joseph planned that meeting with exquisite care."

George nodded. "Perhaps. But I should not have been taken so completely unawares. They are doing battle against Antichrist, and I am counting pennies? Of course the Council voted for Joseph's motion!"

George and I said our farewells, and then Will, Martha, and I started for home. I slowed a bit so Will and Martha could walk alone for a while. I heard snatches of conversation and the low laughter that new lovers shared. I remembered such longing from my own youth and smiled.

The north wind had calmed, and an eerie silence settled over the city as its residents huddled indoors, doing their best to keep safe from the killing cold. The sound of our heels striking the cobbled street reminded me of nothing so much as gunshots echoing off the surrounding buildings. None of us spoke the rest of the way home.

Hannah met us at the door and started clucking over us like a hen over her chicks. She herded us into the parlor, timbered the fire, and went to the kitchen for spiced wine. Once we'd warmed ourselves, our conversation turned to the night's events.

"It seems we were right about Joseph's scheme," I said. "The question now is how we can best protect ourselves."

Will nodded. "It's the same as always with Joseph. He sees himself as doing God's work, and he will not be denied. If we oppose him in any way, he will cast us as enemies both of God and of the city. *There can be no opposing the will of God,* he'll say. And after today's performance, I have no doubt he could turn the Council against us."

"So we must tread carefully," Martha said. "Once the hunt begins in earnest, there is no telling how events will fall."

"But with his seat on the Council and her position as Searcher we can be sure that they will fall in Joseph's and Rebecca's favor, at least at the outset," I replied. I shuddered at the havoc such a malign pair could wreak. The three of us talked for an hour or more, until the fire was reduced to embers and the cold had begun to seep into the room. We found no answers to our dilemma. Though it galled each of us, we would simply have to wait for Joseph and Rebecca's assault, and respond as best we could.

Although the Council made no proclamation about their plans to rid the city of witches, the next day York buzzed in anticipation. Soon it became impossible to go to the market without hearing the word *witch* or seeing a pamphlet about hangings elsewhere in England. Some had been printed in London or Hull, but I felt sure that a few had sprung from Joseph's pen as he prepared the city for his bloody scheme.

The Saturday after the Council meeting, Martha and I passed Peter Newcome as he cried his wares in front of the Minster, and while he still had a variety of coversheets on his board, he shouted up witchcraft more than anything else. He raised his hand in greeting when he saw us, and bowed as we approached.

"My lady, how goes it today?" he called. Before I could answer, an elderly woman stepped in between us and peered at the board.

"Have you still got this one?" she asked. "The one about

the witches?" She pointed at a pamphlet called *The Seven Women Confessors, or A Discovery of the Seven White Devils.*

"Of course, of course," Newcome said. He nodded at his boy, who dug into their pack and produced the pamphlet. The woman handed the boy two pennies and hurried off, her eyes already glued to the book.

Newcome smiled at me. "I do apologize, my lady, but when business calls I must answer."

"I understand," I said. "Were I summoned by a mother, I would abandon you in a moment."

Newcome laughed at the comparison. "It's been like this for days," he said, shaking his head in wonder. "I've got stacks of murder books I can't give away, but if it's about witches, it sells in an instant. The printer has hired another boy, but even so, he can hardly keep up. I can't imagine what it will be like once the hangings start."

I could not help noticing that he did not say *if the hangings start.* A gust of wind flew through Bootham Bar and rattled the pages on Newcome's board. One pamphlet escaped from his pack, and Newcome's boy scampered after it. I pulled my cloak a little tighter, bid Newcome farewell, and started for home.

Sunday morning came, cold and dark. I stayed in my bed as long as I could, knowing that however cold I might be under my blankets, it would be worse when I climbed out. As the watery winter sun began to chase the shadows from my chamber, Elizabeth slipped into my bed and curled up beside me.

"Must we go to church?" she asked.

Elizabeth's mother had never been a regular churchgoer, and like so many children Elizabeth found the ceremonies and sermons tedious at best and vexing at worst.

"It is the law," I said. "And it is good to pray to the Lord. He shall be very pleased to see you."

"But it's so *cold*," she said. "Hannah says that God is in all places. If that is true, He can see me even if I am in the parlor next to the fire."

I bit my lip to keep from laughing.

"We'll be no colder than anyone else," I said. "And it is best that all the parish shivers together. If we do not, we might forget the poor entirely, and if that happens, where will the nation be?"

Will had spent the previous night at Mr. Breary's, and sent word that he would attend church with him. As a result, Martha, Hannah, Elizabeth, and I had my pew to ourselves for the service. A few months earlier we'd buried old Mr. Wilson, who had served the parish for decades, and since that time we'd been visited by a variety of ministers. Those who came to us from neighboring parishes were not so bad, but most had travelled north from Cambridge with godly zeal boiling their blood. On this day, our minister was one of these. He was not much more than a youth by the look of him, but what he lacked in years he made up for in enthusiasm and volume. From his first words, he roared and shook, moaned and cried. Elizabeth grasped my hand as she stared in apprehension at the spectacle. I glanced at Martha from time to time, and I could see her growing impatient with the preacher, particularly when he finished the second hour of his sermon without showing signs of fatigue. He continued on for another half hour before setting us free.

"My God, I thought he would never finish," Martha whispered once we were safely on our way home. Elizabeth delighted in such blasphemy, of course, and even I had to suppress a smile when the two of them took to aping the preacher's frantic arm waving, each one trying to surpass the other in outrageousness.

When we returned for the afternoon service, we discovered that the same minister would preach again, and their smiles vanished. Martha moaned as he strode down the aisle and whispered that she hoped to get home before dark. And while none in the congregation was so vocal as she, I did not have to look far to find expressions of dismay on my neighbors' faces. At the outset, his sermon seemed little different than the one he'd delivered that morning, full of hellfire and sin, but of little interest to any who were not already among the godly. I sat back in my pew and began to compose a list of medicines I would need from the apothecary.

"All men know that God has revealed himself to man through his prophets, his patriarchs, and his apostles," the preacher bellowed. "Today He reveals Himself through the Ministers of the Gospel. And because he is God's opposite in every way, just as God has his preachers and prophets, Satan has his soothsayers, his pythonesses, and his witches. Where Ministers of the Gospel provide council to the weak and succor to the weary, witches provide only deceit, damnation, and death."

At the mention of witches I sat up in my seat and glanced at Martha. She had heard him as well and stared raptly at the preacher. To my relief, Elizabeth paid him no more mind than she had in the morning, choosing instead to play with the ribbons on her dress.

"If any man in York thinks it merely a curiosity that such evil creatures have come to so godly a city, he is mistaken. Such visitations are never mere happenstance. Rather, we must take it as a sign from God Himself. By permitting the devilish sin of witchcraft, He means to rouse the godly from their slumber. He means to tell us that our work is not yet done, that man still wallows in his sinful nature. God has set a question before us. Will we cleave to Him and His Word, or will we seek comfort in Satan and his wicked spirits? In Exodus, the Lord God tells us, *Thou shalt not suffer a witch to live.* Will we heed Him? Or will we show ourselves to be rebels of the worst kind?"

When the preacher paused to let his audience consider the question, I realized that Joseph had commissioned this sermon as surely as he had commissioned the pamphlets that now flooded the city. Together the pamphlets and sermons would drive the city into a state of alarm, and once the fear had reached its peak, Joseph would begin his witch-hunt. He would offer the people a fire that would cleanse the city of all malignancy.

As I looked at the crowd around me, I prayed that my friends and neighbors would not fall under this mountebank's spell. But by the look on their fevered faces and the angry glint in their eyes, I knew that the minister's words had done their job. York's residents would do the minister's bidding. The only question was, what would he demand of them?

"I can tell from looking at you, my dear people, that you see the threat that lies within the city, and for this I am glad. But you must now wonder how you can discover these witches, women of supreme cunning who—with Satan's aid—have hidden themselves in the city."

A few in the audience nodded their heads.

"I must tell you, the discovery of witches is no easy thing," the minister continued. "And it is not to be entered into lightly. Nor is it the duty of the common man to punish witches. If you find one, you must stay your hand from action."

The preacher paused, and I could see looks of puzzlement

on his listeners' faces. If they could not act, then what *could* they do?

"While you shall not punish the witches yourselves, it is your duty, yea your sacred obligation, to find them out and to acquaint the Justices of the Peace with their names. And once you have done your part, you may be assured that your city's magistrates will do theirs. Once you have found Satan's sirens, his temptresses, his murderesses, the Justices will see them tried and punished. The Lord would not have it otherwise."

Cries of *Amen! Amen!* echoed through the rafters of the church, but to my ears the parishoners were crying up not the glory of God but the shameful ambition of sinful men.

"And as to the punishment, there can be no doubt." The minister's voice fell to a whisper, and all the parishioners leaned forward in their seats, desperate to hear every word. "The Lord demands that every witch, truly convicted, is to be punished with death."

Heads nodded in grim determination. They would follow the minister's instructions to the letter. When the service finally ended, the four of us hurried up Stonegate fighting the wind with each step. Elizabeth skipped ahead with Hannah close behind, while Martha and I trailed after so we could talk.

"It seems that Joseph is building a solid foundation for his witch-hunt," Martha said.

"I can't imagine ours is the only parish to which he has gifted such a sermon," I said. "By the time he is done, Joseph will have made the entire city into his deputies. The people will find the witches, and he will hang them."

"He's making the people into his allies," Martha agreed.

"Once they have joined with him in hunting and hanging witches, what power will they deny him?"

I did not reply. Rather, I wondered how we might escape the coming storm.

Chapter 7

The next morning Martha and I were called to the travail of Lucy Pierce, and my mind thus was blessedly drawn from witchcraft and death to childbirth and new life. Lucy lived just outside the city in Upper Poppleton where her husband owned a few acres of land and rented some more. All told, he was able to provide well enough for his young wife, and the two of them lived in a small, well-built house north of the city wall.

In Lucy's chamber, heavy curtains covered the windows, keeping out the worst of the wind, and with a fire roaring in the hearth we were more than warm enough. When Martha and I entered, the women greeted us and then fell silent as I examined Lucy. I found that her labor had not yet begun in earnest, so the half dozen women who had gathered in the birthing room returned to gossiping.

When the talk turned to witches, witch-hunting, and the previous day's sermons, it became clear that Joseph had indeed paid for sermons to be preached against witches throughout the city; the women came from different parishes, but all had heard the same sermon. No less disturbing was the fact that Joseph's plan seemed to be working. While a few women were apprehensive about the hunt, most seemed eager to have it.

"Mr. Hodgson and Mrs. Hooke will rid us of the scourge of witches, they will," said Sarah Crompton.

"By the time they are finished, Mother Lee won't trouble us any longer," Grace Hewitt replied.

"Aye," said another woman. "And if any woman can find the Devil's Mark, it's Rebecca Hooke."

I marveled at how quickly they had forgotten Rebecca's cruelty in the delivery room, but after a moment's consideration I realized that they knew the situation better than I. If Joseph were to succeed in extirpating York's witches root and branch, his Searcher would have to be utterly merciless. Rebecca was the perfect choice.

"You're going to accuse Mrs. Lee of witchcraft?" I asked carefully.

Several women nodded, and Sarah Crompton spoke for them all. "She's vexed us for years. Any time we deny her demands for a little coal or a pound of cheese, she sees that we pay for it. She bewitched my churn so I couldn't make butter, killed two of Grace's piglets, and kept Goodwife Butler's ale from brewing."

"We're lucky she's not done worse," Grace Hewitt added. "But we'll not take the chance that she might. If we stand together against her, Mr. Hodgson will see her hanged."

As I considered the situation, I realized that Joseph's scheme to make the town his own had succeeded, at least with these women. Once he'd rid the neighborhood of a witch, what would they deny him? He could ask for money, for power, for anything at all, and the people would rush to give it to him. Worse, as Joseph gained power, Rebecca would be at his side, perfectly positioned to take her revenge on me for all I'd done.

"What if she doesn't hang?" Lucy Pierce asked. A note of fear crept into her voice. "What if the jury acquits her? What will she do to us then?"

The women looked warily at one another.

"We cannot dwell on that," Grace Hewitt said doubtfully.

"Those are strong words from a woman whose children are grown," Lucy replied. "If we accuse her and she's not hanged, she'll have her revenge on all of us, won't she? I'll not have her bewitch my child."

An uneasy silence settled over the room. While nobody thought witches made for good neighbors, thus far Mrs. Lee had not proven herself anything worse than a nuisance; nobody died if butter wouldn't churn or if beer turned sour. But if they charged Mrs. Lee as a witch and she *didn't* hang? It would be a declaration of war against one of Satan's own, and only the Lord knew what evil she would unleash upon her accusers.

"If we stand together, we cannot fail," Grace Hewitt repeated. "We have read the books and heard the sermons. Mr. Hodgson will not let her escape justice." A few women nodded, but others seemed more concerned at the prospect of failure.

"What if she bewitches my child?" Lucy asked. The women fell quiet.

I did not know Mrs. Lee well enough to say whether she was a witch, but I did not envy the women the terrible decision that lay before them.

Rap, rap, rap!

A harsh knocking at the window broke the silence.

Grace gasped, and we all stared at the curtain.

Rap, rap!

A cry escaped from Lucy's lips, and she looked wildly about the room. I felt my heart hammering in my chest as I strode to the window and threw back the curtain to find a cracked window, but nothing else. I peered through the frosted glass as best I could but saw neither man nor beast.

"It was just the wind," I said, though I could not explain how the wind could knock on a window or crack the glass. No doubt the women could hear the hollowness in my voice, but none challenged me, for they, too, wanted it to be the wind.

I drew the curtain and tried to turn the conversation to a topic other than witches, but with little effect. A darkening mood settled over the gathering as the women returned to the question of what to do about Mother Lee. I wished that Lucy's child would come, if only to hurry the day along.

A bit before midnight, Lucy's final travail began, and we gathered around her. Lucy sipped caudle between labor pangs, and all seemed to be in order until the child began to make his way into the world. As his head appeared I saw that it was grey and hairless, and the skin peeled away at the gentlest touch. While Lucy could not see the child from her perch on the birthing stool, she could read the faces of her gossips.

"What is wrong?" she cried, looking down at me.

"Nothing yet," I said. I glared furiously over my shoulder at the women. They should be a help, not a hindrance. "Let us have the child into the world." I prepared myself to work as quickly as I could, but only a few moments later, the smell of death and decay assaulted me. I could not say why or when, but the child had died in Lucy's womb. A soul-tearing sorrow welled up inside me as I looked up at Lucy. There were few things I dreaded more than telling a mother that her child would not live. I could see the horrible combination of desperate hope and knowing fear on Lucy's face. She knew what had happened, but she prayed that I would tell her she was wrong, that her child was not dead.

"I am sorry, Lucy," I said. "Your child has died. There is nothing to be done."

Grief creased her face, and she clamped her eyes shut as a moan welled up within her. "Ah, God," she cried as another labor pain struck. Even in death the child demanded to be born. Lucy's gossips held her tight and cried along with her as I brought the child into a world he would never know.

"Do you want me to baptize him?" I asked. Most churchmen would fly into a rage at the question, but at times such as this I worried less about the Church's law than the women in my care. I did not know what baptism might mean for the child's soul, but I knew that it mattered to his mother. Lucy nodded, and I whispered a prayer over the water I poured on his head. I dipped my fingers in oil and made the sign of the cross, and it was done. Afterward, I swaddled his tiny, shriveled body just as I would a living child, and gave him to his mother. I left Martha with the women and slipped out of the delivery room. It was my sad duty to tell Lucy's husband what had happened.

Henry Pierce took the news as well as any husband and father could, nodding slowly and wiping away a tear. A friend who had joined him for the evening put his hand on Henry's shoulder, and the two men embraced. Henry turned back to me. "What about my Lucy?" he asked. Relief spread across his face when I assured him that she was in fine health.

"You may go in when Martha has finished binding her," I told him. "It should not be long."

The moment I returned to the delivery room, I knew that the women had transformed their sorrow into fury, and I did not need to ask who was the object of their rage.

"It was Mother Lee who did this," hissed Sarah Crompton. "She bewitched the child to death, and that knocking on the window was her. She *wanted* us to know what she'd done." The other women nodded.

I marveled at the dark magic that the grieving women had worked on themselves. In mere minutes their love for Lucy had become hatred for Mother Lee.

"We'll have our justice," Sarah said. "She'll hang for what she's done."

Martha and I stayed with Lucy until the next morning when the vicar arrived. He was a kindly man, and I knew he would care for the Pierces as best he could. I was more worried what would come of the gossips' fury toward Mother Lee. The death of Lucy's baby had convinced even the most timid of her neighbors that they must act, and since I had delivered the child I certainly would be called to testify about his condition when he was born and the cause of his death.

As Martha and I walked home, our breath hung before us in the still morning air. The cloud of the night's events seemed to follow us even as the sun sat cold and distant in the early morning sky. Could it be the same orb that had threatened to burn the city to ashes just a few months before?

"How long had the child been dead?" Martha asked as we passed through Bootham Bar.

"There is no way to know," I replied. "He was not newly dead, but fingernails had come in, so he was not long from being born. Around a week, but it is a hard thing to judge."

"So the knocking at the window wasn't Mother Lee bewitching the child."

"No, the child was long dead by then," I said. "But such observations won't turn aside the matrons' wrath."

"Do you think that Mother Lee bewitched Lucy?"

I considered the question for a time before answering. "I don't know," I said at last. "I've seen such deaths before. They are extraordinary and troubling, but not necessarily unnatural. It could have been the work of a witch or the devil. Or it could have been that the child died. Sometimes children die."

We walked in silence down High Petergate before turning onto Stonegate.

"When I was a girl," Martha said at last, "there was a woman—Mother Hawthorne, we called her—who lived in our village. She was one of the poorer sort, and she often came to our door in hope of a little bread or a few pennies. But she was also a cunning-woman. When one of our neighbors lost her purse, Mother Hawthorne, would look in a glass to find out who had taken it. Other times maidens asked her to look in a pan of water to see who they would marry, and later to cast bones to discover whether their child would be a boy or a girl."

"Every village has such a one," I replied.

"When I was just a girl, perhaps Elizabeth's age, my brother was bewitched." Martha continued as if I hadn't spoken. The mention of her brother took me by surprise. She'd not spoken of him since his death over a year before.

"One morning he awoke, and his leg could not bend," she said. "We didn't know who had done it, but nobody doubted it was witchcraft. He dragged himself around the village screaming that he would have his revenge. I'd never seen him so afraid. Mother Hawthorne took him in, laid him on her table, and said a blessing over his knee. The next day he was fit as could be. He was the cruelest boy in the village, and she took him in and healed him. And do you know what the strangest thing was?"

I shook my head.

"In all the time she helped her neighbors, she never asked for a penny. If someone was kind enough to offer, she accepted it, but she never set a price or demanded to be paid after she finished. She was just trying to be neighborly in the best way she knew how. The only way she knew how."

We walked in silence. I did not think she'd finished her story.

"Of course I don't think much of her work was magic," she said at last. "She just knew enough of village business to figure things out. When my father lost two shillings, and John Parker appeared in a new shirt, she knew to blame him. And when Sairy Smith asked who would marry her? Everyone in the village knew that Nehemiah Shaw had eyes for none but her. It wasn't magic, it wasn't the devil, it was just that she knew things, and she knew what people wanted to hear."

By now we'd gotten home and settled in the parlor. I could hear footsteps above, and I knew Elizabeth would soon join us.

"What about your brother's leg?" I asked.

Martha laughed. "Healing him *might* have been the work of the devil. He'd not have caused such trouble with a bad leg, would he?" She paused. "I don't know how she healed his leg, just as I don't know what happened to Lucy's son. But some things are counted as magic that are nothing more than common sense or happenstance. And these seem a thin rope with which to hang a woman."

"There was a cunning-woman in a village near our manor," I said. "Widow Rugge. But she dealt more in vinegar than sugar.

My parents told our servants that if she came to the door in search of food or wood for her fire, she should not be denied."

"They believed her to be a witch?" Martha asked.

"They never said as much," I answered. "I think they decided it was better to give her a few pennies than to lose a sow or have a cow run mad."

"Or worse," Martha said. "She could have taken you."

"Aye, she could have." I did not relish the idea that Widow Rugge had used me as a lever to move my parents to charity.

"What became of her?" Martha asked.

"She died in her sleep just before I married Luke," I answered.

A look of surprise crossed Martha's face. Just as she rarely mentioned her brother Tom, I did not often speak of my first husband.

"I don't think Mother Lee will enjoy the same quiet death," Martha said.

"No," I replied. "I don't think she will."

For the rest of the week all of York held its breath in anticipation of the witch-hunt. The city vibrated with the same mixture of excitement and dread that precedes a terrible storm. We all knew there would be blood and some would suffer terribly. But the hope was that the slaughter of York's witches would appease God, and that His wrath against the city—wrath made visible by the icy river and audible by the howling winter wind—would abate.

One of the more pleasing effects of the December wind had been to drive Tree down from the Castle for days at a time, which gave me the chance to mother him and Elizabeth both. Elizabeth was no less pleased by Tree's arrival, and the two of them soon were joined in the excitation of the coming witch-hunt. I found them one afternoon peering out the parlor window trying to guess which passersby might be witches. Whenever anyone looked in their direction, they would cry out in horror and seek shelter behind the curtains until the danger had passed. Martha and I looked on their antics with amusement, but I heard Hannah reprimanding both of them.

"And what do you think a witch would do to the two of you if she thought you were mocking her?" she demanded. Elizabeth and Tree—wisely, I thought—stayed silent. "Why, she could bewitch you with a glance or a word, and there'd be naught that anyone could do to save you."

I thought she had gone too far in scaring the children and stepped in.

"Hannah, that is enough. There's no need to frighten them so."

If Hannah heard me, she gave no sign of it.

"And if anyone offers you food or seeks to pinch your cheek, you must flee from them, for that is how children are bewitched," she continued. "The day of reckoning is upon us, and the evil ones will not give up their place in the city so easily." She looked at me. "If the city troubles the witches, the witches will trouble the city, for they will not be hanged without a fight. We'd best be prepared."

I shooed the children upstairs where, I was quite sure, they would continue their game, but Hannah would not harry them so long as they were out of sight. I considered her claim that if the city's witches feared extermination they might be driven to do even more evil. It was one thing to hang a frail old woman like Hester Jackson, one who had fallen into witchcraft by accident. But what if the magistrates threatened a genuinely powerful witch? What revenge would she exact on the city? Even worse, what if there truly were an entire company of witches in York and they acted together? I said a prayer that God would have mercy on us, and pushed such fearful thoughts from my head.

That afternoon, just as we were sitting down for dinner, I heard the front door open and a few moments later Will entered the dining room.

"We did not expect you," I said. "Why aren't you at the hall with Mr. Breary?" I had heard that the Council was meeting again to discuss the witch-hunt.

"The meeting is nearly over," he said. "And I wanted to give you the latest news. The first witches will soon be taken."

"Will Mother Lee be among them?" I had told him about Lucy Pierce's labor and asked him to keep his ears pricked for any news from Upper Poppleton.

"Probably in the morning," Will replied. "Joseph has been collecting the names of witches and will give the beadles their orders this afternoon." I could not hide my surprise at the speed with which Joseph had moved. But I supposed there could be no dallying once the battle against Satan had begun.

"And then what?" Martha asked.

"They'll be taken to the Castle, and Joseph will interrogate them there."

"Is Mr. Breary still at the hall?" I asked.

Will nodded. "He said he'd be there a while longer, but he asked that you join us tonight for supper. He wishes to discuss the witch-hunt, but he said he has other business for you as well. I suggested that Martha should join us, and he agreed."

"Thank you, Will," I said. "Are you returning to Mr. Breary now?" He'd not removed his coat, and he seemed anxious to go.

"Aye, I will see you this evening." He stepped forward as if to give Martha a kiss before recovering himself. His ears were bright pink by the time he made it to the door.

"Supper with an Alderman!" Hannah teased Martha. "Soon enough you'll be the Lord Mayor's guest!"

Martha's ears pinked, and I could not help laughing along. "It's the lot of a midwife," I said. "Rich silks, fine wines, and sumptuous meals."

"And bastard births, blood, and death," Martha added. I could see she regretted her words, but it was too late, and they cast a shadow over the meal.

I nodded. "Those, too. And soon enough, witches and hangings."

Chapter 8

That afternoon, as Martha and I turned from High Petergate onto George Breary's street, it occurred to me that the city hardly needed a night watch; only fools such as ourselves would venture abroad, and we moved as quickly as we could. If someone were lying in wait, he would be frozen before he found his prey. Though George's home was just a few minutes' walk from my own, Martha and I were both shivering by the time we arrived.

"Thank God," Martha sighed as we stepped into George's parlor, shed our cloaks, and allowed the heat from his hearth to wash over us.

George and Will stood when we entered, and George crossed the room to embrace me. Over his shoulder, I could see Will and Martha looking into each other's eyes, and they clasped hands briefly. George called for spiced wine, and soon the cold had been banished from our bones.

For a time we talked of the smaller news of the city and nation, avoiding the darker developments that plagued York of late. Of course the brutal winter was near the top of everyone's concerns.

"This afternoon a boy walked across the Ouse," Will said. "He went all the way from the King's Staith to the Queen's. He said he heard the ice crack once, but it held firm."

George nodded. "And I heard the Thames has frozen as well. You should think such happenings would warn the Parliament-men that the Lord does not own their cause. The closer they come to overthrowing His Majesty, the more terrible God's wrath becomes."

I could tell from the expression on her face that Martha was about to argue the point, and I shook my head slightly. Such arguments could be found in both of our warring factions, as both the King's men and Parliament's believed God had a hand in everyday affairs. The victor in every battle took it as proof that God fought on their side. Strangely enough, the losers never interpreted defeat as God's rejection of their cause: They simply claimed that the Lord was testing them as He had tested Israel.

Of course Martha rejected all such arguments, and I could see that she wanted nothing more than to dispute them with George. But this was hardly the time or place for her to contest the finer points of theology with a gentleman. I might tolerate—or even welcome—such tussles, but serious men such as George never would.

When we made our way into the dining hall I marveled at the wealth it displayed. The chair coverings and tablecloth were of a rich red silk, and the golden candle-branch held a dozen or more tapers, which set the room to glowing. The servants refilled our glasses with red wine and we settled into a marvelous meal of roast fowl, beef, and other spiced meats. As we ate, I asked George how the Council meeting had gone.

A sly smile spread across his lips, and he nodded triumphantly. "I was going to save the sweetest news for dessert, but you have forced my hand. We have won, I think. I have bested both your brother Joseph and that harpy Rebecca Hooke. We have nothing to fear from them."

The three of us stared at George in amazement.

"How is this possible?" I managed at last. "This is wonderful. What did you do?"

George settled back in his chair, clearly pleased by our reaction and enjoying his moment as cock of all the city. "Well, it cost me more money and favors than I'd care to recount, but I convinced a majority of the Aldermen to support a measure against Joseph."

"What do you mean?" Will seemed no less shocked than I. Could our problems have been solved by a few well-placed bribes?

"I simply offered a new motion to the Council. I agreed that the city faced a dire threat from witches, but pointed out that until we discovered Hester Jackson, neither Joseph nor Rebecca had ever interrogated a witch." George stopped and smiled beatifically.

"And?" I demanded.

"I suggested that we look outside the city for someone with more experience hunting witches. I convinced the Council to send for a man named Matthew Hopkins. He has led the witch-hunts in the south, and had great success."

"So Joseph will not oversee the search?" I asked. "And Rebecca is no longer Searcher?" My heart thrilled at the news.

"Aye," George replied. "And there is more. I had them name

you as the city's Chief Witch Searcher. When Mr. Hopkins arrives, you will be his assistant. You will search the city's women for the Witch's Mark."

Silence settled across the table as George smiled broadly and awaited further praise. Martha and Will looked at me awaiting my reaction. After a moment George's smile faded and his triumph turned to puzzlement.

"What is it?" he asked. "I should have thought you'd welcome the change."

"You had me named the city's Chief Witch Searcher—whatever that is—and you did not see fit to consult me beforehand?" Anger rose within me as I spoke.

"Well, yes," he said. "But . . ."

"But nothing. I did not want the position before and I do not want it now. What is more, I do not want you acting on my behalf without consulting me!"

"I did not think you'd object."

"Obviously not," I said through clenched teeth. "Obviously you did not think about my wishes at all. Why would I want to become involved in such a bloody business? I am a midwife, George, my work is to bring young souls into the world. I did not learn the art and mystery of that craft so that I could see a gaggle of old women hanged."

"But you've done it before," George objected.

"No, I haven't," I cried. "I questioned Hester Jackson *after* she'd been convicted. And there is many a mile between talking to a lone witch who cursed her neighbor, and the slaughter that Joseph has proposed. Do you really believe that the city has been overrun by witches? Or that hanging a few dozen old women will convince the Lord to welcome us back into His good graces?"

George stared at me in astonishment. "But you were worried about Joseph and Rebecca." he said. "And with one shot I felled them both from their perches. I thought you would be grateful." He said the last of these words with the petulance of child unused to reprimand.

"Grateful that you purchased me a terrible office, George?" I asked. I felt my anger turning to exasperation. "Have I not earned my place in the city through honest work as a midwife? Have I ever traded on my name in such a blatant fashion? Have I ever said that I wanted to be a part of such a hunt?"

George said nothing, choosing instead to stare at the candlelight refracting in crimson through the crystal of his glass.

At that moment I became aware that Martha and Will had witnessed the entire conversation, and I found them staring at us, aghast and unable to speak. We sat in silence for far too long, each of us in desperate search of words that might temper the embarrassment I'd just caused.

"Now, George, why don't you call for the sweetmeats?" I asked at last, and joined him in staring at my wine.

After we had finished dessert and forgotten, for the moment at least, George's importunity, Martha, Will, and I prepared to walk home. While we waited for the servant to bring our cloaks, George joined us in the entry hall and cleared his throat.

"Lady Bridget, might I speak to you in the parlor?" He opened the door, and I followed him through.

"George, there is no need for you to apologize," I said before he could speak. "You were trying to help me, and did what you thought was best. It is what friends do for each other. We will find a solution in the morning, but now it is quite late."

"Er, that is not what I wanted to talk to you about." He shifted from foot to foot as if he were anxious to use the jakes.

"What is it then?" I could hear the edge in my voice. If he thought I'd forgotten about his audacity in making me the city's Witch Searcher, he was wrong.

"Lady Bridget, you know that I have admired you ever since you came to York. I have always held you in the highest esteem, and value your friendship above that of any other woman. And I do not think I am overstepping my bounds if I say that you truly are a handsome woman."

I felt the bottom drop out of my stomach, and suddenly I was the one who needed to use the jakes. "George . . . ," I started to interrupt, but he would not be stopped.

"Under the best of circumstances, we would make a powerful couple, and I would still make this proposal," he continued. "But even if my maneuver against Joseph and Rebecca is successful, the circumstances remain most dire, for they will not give up so easily."

He paused for a moment, and I steeled myself for what I knew he would say next.

"I think it would be best for both of us if we were to marry," he said at last. "You, Martha, Elizabeth, and even Hannah would benefit from my protection. And I would . . ." He trailed off as he tried to think what benefit — beyond my wealth of course — that he would reap from such an arrangement.

"George," I repeated, but once again he ignored me.

"I will not have an answer tonight," he said. "Whether it is yea or nay, I will wait until you have had the chance to think about my offer at length. Please tell me you will consider it."

I could only nod in response.

"And in the event you decline," he said, "I trust you will

keep the matter between us." He nodded curtly and hurried from the room as if he were a guest who had pocketed the silver plate from supper.

Martha poked her head into the parlor, a puzzled look on her face.

"Later," I said before she could even ask the question. "Outside."

Once we were outside, however, we found conversation to be nearly impossible, for the evening had brought a gale-wind that threatened to tear the clothes from our bodies. We would have had to shout in order to be heard. We bent before the snow and wind, and trudged toward our home.

Just before we reached St. Michael le Belfrey, I thought I heard a cry from behind us, and stopped to look back. I could tell from Will's and Martha's reactions that they had heard it as well, and the three of us peered into the dark.

"What was that?" Will shouted over the wind. I shook my head.

"It must have been the wind," Martha replied. "When it passes through the belfries it moans something strange. And what bloody-minded fool would be out in this if he could help it?"

I cast my eyes behind us one more time, but nothing moved save the blowing snow. "Let's go," I said at last, and we hurried home.

The three of us tumbled through the door, eager to put the cold wind and the terrible, distant cry—if that is what it was—behind us. Hannah took our cloaks and hurried us into the parlor where a fire burned bright and warm. "I'll be back with some chocolate," she said, and bustled off to the kitchen.

"So what did he need to speak to you about?" Will asked. I studied his face before I spoke, wondering if he'd known about George's proposal before I did. It did not take him long to confess.

"I warned him not to ask you," Will said desperately. "Not in that way."

Martha looked between us in utter confusion. "What are you talking about, Will? What happened?"

"Mr. Breary had a second proposal for me, didn't he, Will?" I said. "And when you came to me this afternoon, you knew what he would ask me but you said nothing."

"Aunt Bridget, please," he cried. "I told him he should not ask you, but he would not be deterred. There was nothing I could do!"

In truth I was not angry with Will, for I knew he was right: He could not have dissuaded George from his offer. Like so many men who found success in business, once George settled on a course, there would be no changing his mind regardless of what contras presented themselves; challenges were to be overcome, not yielded to. Finally I released Will from my gaze and turned to Martha.

"Mr. Breary asked me to marry him," I said.

"What?" Martha cried, her face the very picture of alarm and astonishment. "You didn't . . . What did you say?"

"He wouldn't have an answer," I replied. "He wanted me to reflect on it until tomorrow."

A look of uncertainty crossed Martha's face. She had an opinion on the matter—and I had a good sense of what it was—but did not want to overstep her bounds. Though it undoubtedly took a heroic effort for her to hold her tongue, she managed admirably.

"He said he could better protect us from Joseph and Rebecca," I said. "And I suppose he might be right."

Of course I had no intention of marrying George, but I *had* said I would consider the matter. Martha stared at me with ill-disguised surprise, but before she could speak her mind, a knock came at the door.

"Who is out on a night such as this?" Hannah asked as she carried a tray of steaming chocolate into the parlor. "Are you expecting a mother's call, my lady?"

"I'll see who it is," Martha said, and slipped out of the parlor.

She returned a moment later, a look of concern on her face. "There's a lad here who says he's Mr. Breary's footman," she said. "He has brought Mr. Breary's cloak."

Will and I hurried to the door, and found a young man waiting. He held a heavy wool cloak in his arms and looked at us expectantly.

"Why have you brought Mr. Breary's cloak?" I demanded. "Did someone tell you he was here?"

"After you left, my lady, he dashed after you," the lad replied. "I called to him, and said it was too cold, but he would not stop. I thought he must be following you, so I came here." Martha, Will, and I exchanged worried glances. I think we all remembered the cry we'd heard as we neared St. Michael's.

"Is he not here?" George's servant asked at last.

"Get lanterns," I said to Martha. "One for each of us. We must search for him."

We hurried up Stonegate to St. Michael le Belfrey where we'd heard the cry. I prayed that the sound had indeed been the wind, and that George had ducked into an alehouse to escape the cold. It would have been the sensible thing to do, and (except for his marriage proposal) George was nothing if not sensible. I could only hope that his desire for my hand had not driven him to some new idiocy. Within a few minutes we arrived at a point where four narrow streets came into Petergate. We stopped and peered into the darkness each street offered. Miraculously, the wind hadn't blown out any of the lanterns, and we huddled together as we considered our options.

"It could have come from any one of these streets," Will said.

"Let's search in pairs," I said. I knew Will had a sword hidden in his cane, and I took some comfort from that, but it appeared that George's servant was unarmed. "Will and Martha, you start there." I indicated the nearest street. "The lad and I will look in the next one over. Don't go too far in. We'll meet back here. And if you hear anything, cry out." I was not sure we would hear anything in the wind, but we had no other recourse.

Will and Martha nodded then disappeared into the darkness. The servant followed me into the second alley, and we held our lanterns high in an effort to dispel the shadows. The close-built houses crowded us from the sides and the eaves loomed above. George's servant seemed a timid creature, and he began to fall behind. At that moment I realized that despite my frequent visits to George's house, I'd never seen the boy before and had no idea if he truly was George's man. Was it possible that I'd fallen into some sort of trap?

I whirled to face the lad and found him just a few yards behind, lantern held high, his hands otherwise empty. In the guttering light I could not read his face.

"You should take the lead," I said. I would rather have a clear path back to Petergate if I needed to escape.

As he passed me, me we heard a voice cry out three times—there could be no mistaking this for the wind. I raced back to Petergate. I could hear George's servant behind me as I tore down the street toward Will and Martha. I found them crouched over something—or someone. When I arrived, my fear was made real.

"Oh God, no," I cried out.

George Breary lay against the side of a building, and it was clear that he'd been beaten terribly. The left side of his face was covered in blood. I knelt by his side and took his head in my hands.

"Is he alive?" Will asked.

"I think so," I said. "We must get him to my house."

I took George's cloak from his servant, and laid it over him. Will and the servant took George by his shoulders, while Martha and I lifted his legs, and together we carried him back to Petergate and toward my house.

Hannah cried out when she saw our grim burden and hurried to find towels and blankets. We laid George on the couch in the parlor, his head on a pillow. His skin had taken on a bluish tinge, and Martha added more wood to the fire. We wrapped George in a blanket, and I washed the blood from his face. As I did so, it became clear just how terrible the beating had been. His skull was broken in several places. I could not see how he could survive such grievous wounds.

"Martha, take George's servant, and fetch Dr. Baxter," I said. I did not think that binding George's wounds would make a difference, but I could not simply let him die in my parlor.

Martha nodded and began to wrap herself against the cold.

"Wait," I said. I placed my hand on George's chest but felt no movement. "Get me a mirror."

Hannah handed me a small glass, and I held it close to George's nose and mouth. The glass stayed clear.

"Ah, God," I said softly. "Never mind Dr. Baxter. Find the vicar and fetch a Justice of the Peace."

George Breary was dead.

Chapter 9

In the hours that followed, a parade of city officials marched through my parlor. Some came to pay their respects, others to question us about George's murder. Mercifully, Joseph saw fit to absent himself on this occasion, though other Aldermen assured me that he knew of George's death and would not rest until his murderer had been hanged. Given Joseph's antipathy for George such assurances rang hollow, but I held my tongue.

It was three in the morn when my guests finally left and only George's body remained. It awaited the arrival of the Lord Mayor's men, who would take it to his church for burial. I sat for a moment and looked at my friend's face, allowing sorrow to wash over me for the first time that night. George could play the part of a fool, to be sure, but after Edward's death he had remained true to me and, more important, had helped Will regain his feet. In short, he had proven himself to be a kind man and a loyal friend at a time when few seemed inclined to these virtues. While I would not have married him, he *had* been my friend, and in a way I did love him. I did not know who had killed George Breary, but I was determined to find out and see him hang.

A soft knock came, and Martha admitted the Lord Mayor's men. They wrapped George's body in a wool shroud and disappeared into the night. Will, Martha, and I returned to the parlor. I settled in my chair while Will and Martha eased themselves onto the couch. Hannah had disposed of the bloody pillow, and now there was no sign that a man had so recently breathed his last on the very spot. Martha leaned against Will, laid her head on his shoulder, and closed her eyes. I allowed them that rare moment of intimacy before I brought them back to the terrible events that had just played out.

"How are you, Will?" I asked.

He looked at me, his eyes bloodshot from fatigue and sorrow. I knew that he recognized the ramifications of George Breary's death. He had lost a friend and mentor, of course, but also his last best chance to obtain the power and prestige that his ancestors had enjoyed. From his youth Will had dreamed of following his father into city government, and while the road had been far from smooth, George Breary had been ready to guide him. Now Will was naught but a wealthy man's impoverished son, dependent for his survival on the goodwill of his twice-widowed aunt.

"What do you think happened?" I asked.

"I don't know," Will replied.

"It might have been Joseph," I ventured. "We have to consider it."

Will stood and began to pace the room, unwilling to meet my gaze.

"No," he replied. "It's not Joseph. I'll not deny that he is a hard man, but he is not a murderer."

"If Mr. Breary really had summoned another Witch Finder to replace him, it would make sense," I persisted. I was not sure how far to push Will in this matter. No matter how turbulent their relationship had become, it was no easy thing for him to accuse his brother of murder.

Will started to reply, but Martha spoke first.

"It might have been Mark Preston without Joseph's knowledge," Martha said. An image of Preston's deformed hand flashed through my mind. He might not be able to charge a pistol anymore, but he could certainly wield a club.

Will considered this for a moment and gave me a curt nod.

"That is possible," he said. "If Joseph spoke ill of Mr. Breary, Preston might have killed him without asking permission."

"Very well, Mark Preston," I said. This concession seemed enough for the moment, so I left well enough alone.

"Is there anyone else?" Martha asked. "Can you think of anyone who might have profited from his death? Who might have been jealous of his success?"

Will pondered the question for a moment and, to my surprise, his ears pinked as if he'd thought of something unseemly.

"What is it?" Martha asked. She had noticed the change as well.

"It is nothing, I'm sure," Will said. "It could not be."

"Obviously it *could* be, or else you wouldn't have thought of it," Martha replied. "What is it? You must tell us."

Will hesitated yet again.

"Will, the man is dead," I said. "He has no more secrets. If he had some unsavory business dealings he would not be the only one in the city."

Will shook his head, as if hoping to drive the thought from his mind. "It is not business," he said. A pained look crossed his face, and I knew he could not hold out much longer.

"You must tell us," Martha said.

After a moment, Will looked me in the eyes. "I'm sorry, Aunt Bridget. I could not tell you earlier. I would have said something if you had agreed to marry him."

This threw me into confusion. "Will, why must you apologize to me? What is it?" I could not imagine a sin—in business or otherwise—that would have hurt me.

"Mr. Breary was a good man in many ways." Will sounded as if the words were being ripped from his chest, and for the first time that evening he began to weep. "And he took me in when no other man in the city would even speak to me. He believed me, not Joseph's lies. He defended me when nobody else would."

"But there was more to him." Martha took his hand.

Will nodded as the tears coursed down his cheeks. "Mr. Breary had taken a paramour of late," he said at last. "I do not know who she was, but the signs could not be missed. I saw cryptic notes on his desk, listing only a time and place. When the time came, he would disappear for a few hours. He never told me where he went, and I knew I should not ask."

"It could have been anything," I replied. "A business dealing he could not yet share with you, or something to do with the city."

Will shook his head. "I wish it were. But he hid nothing of his business from me. And when he came back he seemed more relaxed and vibrant than I'd ever seen him. A meeting for business would hardly do that to a man."

I considered Will's point for a moment before I realized why he'd been so reluctant to tell me of his suspicions.

"Will," I said, my voice rising. "You knew that he was mired in such sinful courses, *and* that he intended to marry me, yet you said nothing of it?"

"I know," he said. "I was going to tell you tonight, but it's not the sort of thing I could bring up during supper."

"Perhaps after he served the sweetmeats?" Martha said, trying to ease the tension in the room. "Mr. Breary could have presented the delicacy and let Will present the debauchery."

Will and I smiled despite ourselves. I knew that he had done his best under difficult circumstances, and he seemed so miserable that I had to release my anger.

"Well, you did no harm," I said at last. "And now we must consider our best course of action."

Will and Martha agreed.

"Mark Preston seems the most likely culprit," Martha said. "But how could we prove it?"

"What about Rebecca Hooke?" Will asked. "She had even more to lose than Joseph. Joseph would remain an Alderman even if he lost control of the witch-hunt. But if Rebecca lost her place as the Searcher, she would be as powerless as before."

I nodded in agreement. "It is possible. The thought of losing yet another office to me—first that of a midwife then of a Witch Searcher—would drive her mad. But she is hardly strong enough to beat a man to death. And I cannot see her lying in wait for Mr. Breary on a night such as this." The wind rattled the windows, as if to underscore my point.

"She would have hired someone," Will said. "There are ruffians enough in the city."

"Might she have sent James?" Martha asked.

Will and I shook our heads simultaneously.

"Not James," Will said. "A fool such as he could never change his spots."

I nodded in agreement. James Hooke was Rebecca's only son, and if he'd taken after his mother, he would have been an imposing figure indeed. However, while he had his mother's clear blue eyes, he also had his father's kindly soul and weak mind. Twice in the past, he'd become embroiled in evil schemes, but never as the prime mover. He simply was too stupid to avoid the trouble that the world brought in his direction.

"Mark Preston is the most likely suspect, and he knows it," I said. "We would have to approach him with caution."

"Then let's begin somewhere less dangerous," Martha suggested. "We could start with Mr. Breary's mistress and see where she takes us."

I nodded in agreement. "Preston will think we're letting the constables do their jobs. If we are discreet, he may not realize that he is our quarry. At least not right away."

With that matter decided, Will climbed the stairs to his chamber, leaving Martha and me alone.

"You don't believe Mark Preston killed Mr. Breary," Martha said. It was not a question.

"He may have, but only with Joseph's permission," I said. "But you saw Will's face. If I persisted in accusing Joseph, he would have rebelled entirely. But Preston is so close to Joseph that stalking him will do, at least for the moment."

"But how will we find Mr. Breary's mistress?" Martha asked. "I've heard no gossip about it, and if Will doesn't know, who does?"

"We can fight that battle in the morning," I said. "But I think I know who to ask."

Our search for George Breary's mistress got off to a slow start when Tree appeared at my door, eager for breakfast and Elizabeth's company.

"I'm going to walk across the river," he announced. "Other boys have done it, and they're no braver than me!"

Elizabeth, of course, was enraptured by the idea, and imagined Tree to be as heroic as David had been when he took the field against Goliath. By the time we'd finished our pottage, Tree and Elizabeth were so ardent for their adventure, I could hardly deny them. So Will, Martha, and I trailed after the children as they raced down to the King's Staith on the north side of the river.

"It is a wondrous sight," Will said. "I've lived here all my life, and I've never seen it like this."

"Is it safe to cross?" I asked.

Will hopped off the staith onto the ice and stomped his feet. "Solid as stone," he replied.

A group of children had gathered at the edge of the river, and some of the braver boys had ventured out onto the ice, arguing over who would be the first one to cross. Tree joined them and, with his chest thrust forward, announced his intention to lead the way. No other boy volunteered, so to my trepidation—and to Elizabeth's delight—Tree tiptoed further onto the river. Every few steps he looked back over his shoulder at us, his face shining with excitement.

His expression turned to horror when the ice gave a terrific *crack*. He turned to face us, his mouth a tiny *O* as he realized what was about to happen. Then the ice opened up, and in an instant he disappeared.

At that moment the world around me slowed to a crawl.

As if in a dream, I heard Will and Martha crying out in horror, the other boys shouting, and Elizabeth wailing in fear. After a terrible moment, Tree's head and shoulders reappeared. I could see his mouth moving as he cried out for help, his hands scrabbling for purchase on the ice. As if guided by another hand—God's, perhaps—I jumped down to the ice and took a few tentative steps toward Tree, as though treading softly would lessen my weight.

As I drew near him, the ice began to creak and crackle beneath my feet, and soon these sounds were all I could hear. I took another step, heard another *crack*, and stopped. If I retreated, Tree would die. If I continued toward him, I would join him in the river and we both would die.

As I gazed into Tree's eyes, I became aware that another boy had come out onto the ice, and that he was shouting at me.

"Lie down!" he shouted at me in accented English. "You must lie down!"

I stared at him. What could he mean?

"You must crawl out to him on your . . . your *buik*," he cried, patting his stomach. "Your belly!"

Then I understood. As slowly as I could, I lowered myself onto my stomach. The ice seemed to quiet a bit, and I took a shallow breath. I hardly felt the cold as I pushed myself inch by terrible inch toward Tree. Our fingertips just touched once, and with one more push forward I held his hands in mine.

His teeth chattered madly as I pulled myself backward and he slowly emerged from the river. His lips had turned a frightening blue and his breath came only in fits. I continued to crawl backward until I felt someone (Will, it turned out) grasp my ankles and pull both Tree and me to safety.

Without a word, we bundled Tree in our cloaks and raced

toward my home. I counted it as a blessing, perhaps even a miracle, that despite our haste we did not slip on the ice-covered stones. Within minutes, we had buried Tree in goose-down quilts, and Hannah brought him a hot bowl of pottage. Once his chattering had slowed enough for him to talk, he began to tell an enraptured Elizabeth his account of the morning's adventures. The fact that he had nearly died seemed not to matter to either one of them.

I later learned that the boy who had told me to lie on my belly was a Hollander who'd come to York with his father and been trapped in the city when the river froze. I thanked the Lord for the boy and the good he'd done us. After a time, Elizabeth climbed under the covers with Tree and the two of them drifted off to sleep.

With that fright behind us, I sought Will and Martha so that we could begin our search for George Breary's mistress and, through her, his murderer.

Helen Wright was often described as a *bawd*, a *pimp*, or a *putour*, but such terms hardly did her justice. While she *did* secure whores for any man who would pay her price, this was only the start of her work. If there was an illicit need in York, she would find a way to meet it. She owned alehouses that specialized more in doxies than drink, and if a whore needed a tenement for her work, Helen would rent her a room. She provided "wives" for merchants who came to York for a trading season, and if anyone in the city required a secret room for an adulterous tryst, Helen could provide it. It was the last service that gave us hope she might help us find George's mistress, for he did not bring her to his home, and he was too well known to rent a room at one of York's inns.

In order to avoid the unwelcome attention of city officials, Helen lived just outside the city walls, so Will, Martha, and I began the long walk to York's southern gate. As we crossed the Ouse Bridge I looked down at the hole in the ice that Tree had made, and I said a prayer of thanks that God had not seen fit to take another of my little ones.

We crossed the bridge into Micklegate, the southernmost of the city's wards. South of the river, the streets were wider and the houses far larger. And while I had to make do with a small courtyard behind my house, Micklegate's more substantial residents enjoyed large and carefully tended gardens. Will had grown up here, and when I looked down St. Martin's Lane, I could just make out the house where he had lived, the house that he had thought might someday be his. I glanced at his face and found him staring resolutely ahead, unwilling to look upon on his former home. My heart ached for him, and I took his arm. Martha must have seen the same thing, for she reached over and squeezed his hand. He ignored both of us.

Within a few minutes, the massive stone gate called Micklegate Bar appeared before us, and the street became more crowded as travellers and merchants made their way in and out of the city. During Parliament's siege, the King's men had patrolled the city walls, but now they served more as a road for people making their way around the city than as a defense. We slipped in behind a southbound carriage and followed it through the gate. Though it had been nearly eighteen months since the King's men had burned the suburbs, few of the houses had been rebuilt. Who would spend so much money while the war still raged? We all knew that if the war returned to York, so too would the burning.

Helen Wright, of course, was an exception to this rule. She

had enough money to buy nearly any house inside the city, but every reason to live beyond the walls. Her house stood three stories tall, and it was every bit as grand as I remembered. I could not help feeling apprehensive as we approached, not because of her wealth and the way she'd earned it (or at least not *only* because of those things), but because during my last visit, in the midst of that terrible and bloody summer, I had accused her of murder. I did not know what kind of reception we would receive.

Martha had been thinking the same thing. "She'll be happy to see you," she murmured as we approached the door.

"Perhaps you should speak for us," I replied, only half in jest. While Helen and I often fought, she had developed a certain fondness for Martha. This was born, I think, out of a sense that they had much in common. And perhaps they did, for Martha had narrowly escaped a life not unlike Helen's, and there could be no doubting that they were both whip smart and had learned how to survive on their own. The only difference was that while Martha had escaped from criminality to midwifery, Helen had risen from whore to bawd.

Will knocked on the door, and within a few moments Helen's man, Stephen Daniels, appeared. He smiled when he saw us, and a chill ran through me. While he'd never threatened me or mine, violence hung about him as surely as it did about Joseph's man Mark Preston. Daniels stood nearly half a foot taller than Will, and there was no mistaking his strength.

"Lady Bridget," Daniels said with a bow. "I am quite sure that Mrs. Wright will be pleased to see you. Can I tell her what this concerns?"

"We are here about a murder." Only then did I realize I'd said almost exactly the same words the first time I'd visited.

Stephen remembered as well, and he laughed out loud. "Of course you are! You should come in, then." He opened the door and led us into Helen's parlor. As on my last visit, the room announced Helen's wealth and elegance: Rich fabric covered finely wrought furniture, and splendid paintings adorned the walls. It was not what I'd originally expected from a country girl who found herself awash in cash, but Helen had surprised me in many ways.

On this visit, she did not make us wait for long. She swept into the parlor, resplendent in silk and lace, and I felt my old prejudices come roaring back. Will had once pointed out that she and I had much in common: We both dealt in the city's secrets and matters of the body, and through our own efforts we each had gained a measure of power within the city. Whatever the merits of his argument I had no interest in dwelling upon it, and I pushed it from my mind.

Helen smiled at Will and Martha, and—to my surprise— at me as well. I felt quite sure that any happiness she felt grew from the fact that, once again, I'd come to her for help. Nothing would give her more pleasure than to see me beg.

"Lady Hodgson, it is good of you to visit. Tell me what you need." She nearly laughed as she spoke, and I could feel anger rising within me. I took a deep breath to cool my blood. This was not the time to vent my spleen.

"Thank you," I said. I knew she wanted me to add *Mrs. Wright*, but I would not do her that honor, no matter how much we needed her help. "Once again, it is tragedy that brings me to your door, and I can only hope that you will be as helpful as you were last summer."

"I assume you are here about Mr. Breary's murder."

"We are," I said. "We have heard . . ." I paused. "We have

reason to believe that Mr. Breary . . ." I stopped again. I could not defame my friend to such a woman.

"Mr. Breary had a mistress," Martha blurted out. "And since he never brought her to his home, we thought he might have rented a room from you. We need to find her."

Helen nodded. "You don't think the Justices will find her on their own?"

"They don't know she exists," Martha replied. "And even if they did, they would hesitate before parading his sins before all the city."

"Fair enough," Helen conceded. "And you have indeed come to the right place. Mr. Breary had a head for government and an eye for business, but his pillock led him nowhere but astray."

I stared at Helen for a moment, surprised by her forthrightness—I'd expected minutes, if not hours, of denials. I could not help wondering what her motive might be.

"You know who his mistress was?" I asked.

"Aye," she said, the smile returning to her face. "I rented him a room from time to time, and had Stephen watch his comings and goings. He saw her regularly."

"And you'll tell us?" I could not help worrying that Helen was simply toying with me or that she would announce some new and extravagant demand in exchange for the woman's name.

"Aye, I'll tell you," she said. "She's Agnes Greenbury, the Lord Mayor's wife."

Chapter 10

"Agnes Greenbury," I repeated. My mind worked furiously to make sense of Helen's words. "She is but a girl."

Will could hardly hide his smile. "She might be a girl, but she's as comely as any in the city." Martha stared daggers at him, but he paid her no mind. "When she came to York, the alehouses would talk of little else. Many of the lads wondered how long it would be until she wandered away from that old toad, but none thought it would be so soon."

"Or that she'd choose yet another ancient," Martha remarked.

As distasteful as it was to consider, I had to admit that Will's memory matched my own. When Matthew Greenbury, the Lord Mayor, had been widowed two summers before, the whole town assumed he would remarry within a few months; it was the way of the world. But, led by his pintle rather than common sense, Greenbury had chosen a girl of no more than seventeen years, younger even than several of his grandchildren. So strange was the match that when Agnes first appeared at his side, many took her for his stepdaughter rather than his be-trothed. The Lord Mayor showered his bride with the finest silks and jewelry, and soon became the town laughingstock. But behind the laughter was envy, for every man in York wished that *he* were the one bedding down with Agnes each night.

"Why are you telling us this?" Martha's eyes narrowed and bore into Helen's. I recognized the look—it was the one she gave to bastard-bearers whom she suspected of lying about the true father of their child. "You don't make a habit of announc-ing your clients' business to the world."

"A valid point," Helen conceded. "If you had asked about nearly anyone else, I would have told you to pike off. But today our interests coincide."

"You haven't answered the question," Martha replied. "And you'll have to explain yourself before we go charging into the Lord Mayor's parlor accusing his wife of adultery, and perhaps of murder."

A look of annoyance passed across Helen's face, and I counted it as a small victory. After a moment she replied. "Since last summer's killings, the beadles and Justices have been nothing but a hair in my neck. They've arrested my doxies and closed my alehouses. As if my girls were the cause of all the trouble! Things cannot get much worse for my business, and if you bring down the Lord Mayor they might get better. Besides, I've never had much use for that miserly old cuff."

I wasn't entirely convinced that Helen had told us the truth, but at least we had a name. We managed to take our leave with-out further exchange of insults (no small achievement there), and began the journey back through Micklegate to our side of the city. We now walked into the wind, and our cloaks billowed behind us.

"Why should we believe her?" I asked as we passed through the bar and into the city. I was being peevish, but I could not help myself.

"Aunt Bridget, if you weren't going to accept her answer, why did we come all this way?" Will demanded.

"She admitted that she wanted to see the Lord Mayor fall," I replied. "And she would have no problem lying if it would serve her needs."

"You asked her who Mr. Breary's mistress was, and she told us," Martha cried. She could not hide her exasperation with me any better than Will. "We should follow the scent and see where it takes us. If for some reason Helen Wright has deceived us, so be it. We discover Agnes's innocence and move on."

I knew I could not allow my antipathy for Helen to obstruct my better judgment and grumbled my agreement.

"Why don't we call on her right now?" Martha asked. "They're on this side of the river, aren't they?"

"They're on the same street as my brother's house," Will replied. "And if Agnes is innocent, we could pop in at my brother's for dinner and ask Mark Preston whether *he* murdered Mr. Breary."

I smiled a little at the image and said a prayer of thanks that Will could attempt such a jest. For some time after his father's death Will was loath to even mention his brother. I agreed with the plan, and we turned toward the Lord Mayor's home.

"How will you get her to see you?" Will asked. "She's not one of your clients."

He was right, of course. Why would a newly married girl want to meet with a midwife? I considered the question and felt a smile play across my lips. "I think I have the answer for that." By the time we arrived at the Greenbury's home, my plan was complete.

The Lord Mayor's footman bowed when we approached and admitted us to the entry hall where another servant greeted us. He was dressed in fine silks that announced the Lord Mayor's wealth, and he had a haughty air about him. As soon as I laid eyes on him, I knew my plan would work.

"Lady Hodgson, how are you this morning?" he asked. "I am afraid the Lord Mayor is not in. Would you like to leave him a message? I will be sure that he receives it today."

"Thank you, but I am here to see Mrs. Greenbury," I replied. "It concerns . . . a private matter." I allowed my voice to trail off and cast my eyes to the floor.

"I'm afraid it is impossible," he replied. "Mrs. Greenbury does not like unexpected visitors. Perhaps you would tell me what this concerns."

"Very well," I said. "Please tell her that I have come to discuss her menstrual discharges, and the best course for retention or restoration."

In a welcome irony, the blood drained from the servant's face and he stared at me, mouth open but unable to speak.

I smiled and waited as his Adam's morsel bobbed up and down.

"I will see if she will speak to you," he said at last. "I will take you to the drawing room and have her meet you there. Your gentleman will have to wait here, of course."

"Of course," I said.

Will looked annoyed, but he could hardly object. A man could not be a part of the conversation I'd proposed.

Martha smiled approvingly as we followed the servant into the drawing room, and why not? I'd learned such tricks from her, after all. It seemed strange how naturally deception came to me, but we lived in strange times.

Agnes Greenbury flew into the drawing room, a tornado of silk, lace, hair, and fury. She strode past Martha without a glance in her direction and stopped with her face mere inches from mine. Despite, or perhaps because of, the fury that burst from every pore, I could see why Matthew Greenbury had risked universal scorn to marry this girl. She was astonishingly beautiful, and she exuded so much energy that even I found it a bit unnerving. What man—especially one nearing the end of his life—could refuse such a combination? Marrying this girl would be akin to seizing lightning in his hand.

"You have ten seconds to explain yourself before I have you thrown into the street, you whore." Her dress was made from the richest silk and cut in the latest fashion, but her voice shouted of the northern moors. I doubted if she'd seen a paved road before she came to York. Where had the Lord Mayor found such a girl, and what must she make of her new life?

Such coarse language from so gorgeous a creature left me speechless, but as so often happened, Martha came to my rescue.

"George Breary," she said.

Agnes's face twitched, and I knew that Martha's shot had found its mark.

"I don't know who that is," Agnes said to Martha, though her eyes never left mine.

"Of course you do," Martha replied, circling behind Agnes. She knew she'd found one crack in Agnes's armor, and now she sought another. "You've been jumbling him for God knows how long. It's the talk of all the town, or it will be soon enough."

Agnes looked briefly in Martha's direction before returning her eyes to me. A thin sheen of sweat had appeared on her forehead. Though she'd only been in the Lord Mayor's house for a few months, she'd learned how to get her way. She could not understand why her fit of ill humor had not convinced us to leave her be.

"What do you want?" she asked at last. "Why are you here?"

"Last night George Breary was murdered," I replied.

She didn't even blink.

"What, no tears for your paramour?" I asked. "He was beaten and left to die in an alley, and you have nothing to say?"

"They brought the news last night," she replied. "I knew he was dead before you did."

"I doubt it." I could tell that the scorn I felt for this girl had crept into my voice, and to put her on her heels I decided to give it free rein. "I doubt you know half so much as you think. You haven't the slightest grasp of the world around you, or of what the future holds for light-skirted queans like you. If you did, you'd not play the harlot so thoughtlessly."

"Not that you'll be playing that role for long." Martha continued as if we were one. "Your future holds naught but the hangman's rope."

Agnes's eyes flashed in Martha's direction again, and her tongue darted out to wet her lips. She did not answer.

"We don't think you killed him yourself," I said. "But surely a girl like you would have no trouble finding some fool to do it on your behalf."

"But why would she bother, Lady Bridget?" asked Martha. "If he was a mere dalliance, he'd hardly be worth the trouble."

"Ah, but what if *he* had fallen in love with *her*?" I said. "Tell me Agnes, was he trying to convince you to abandon your husband? Perhaps Mr. Breary threatened to tell him about your wanton ways, and you killed him to keep your secrets."

"No!" The word burst from Agnes's lips, and her regret was both immediate and clear.

"You'd have no trouble at all finding someone to commit murder," I said. "If you made the right promises and lifted your skirts at just the right time, you could convince a man to do nearly anything. Was it one of your servants? A soldier from the garrison? Who did this for you?"

For a moment it seemed as if Agnes intended to answer, to confess that we were right, that she had arranged George's murder. But without warning she broke my gaze and started for the door. Martha blocked her path. With no way out, she turned to face me.

"I'll scream," she said. "The servants will be here in moments."

"Yes, they would," I agreed. "And what would you tell them? That a gentlewoman detained you in your own house and accused you of murder?"

"Not even your gossips would believe such gabbing," Martha said. "Then you'd be counted a foul slattern *and* a lunatic."

Tears sprang to Agnes's eyes. I imagine she hoped they would melt my heart, but they did no such thing. I had little doubt she kept tears at the ready in the way a sentry keeps his pistol charged. Where bluster and flirtation failed, weeping might find a way.

"I did nothing wrong," she cried.

Martha barked with laughter.

"Nothing wrong?" I cried, joining in the derision. "You could not even remain faithful to your husband for half a year!"

"But I did not kill anyone," she said.

"How does your husband feel about your shameless living?" Martha asked. "Surely he expected better of you."

Agnes's eyes became hard and, as if by impulse, she cradled her forearm.

Agnes cried out in surprise when I stepped toward her and pulled up her sleeve. I knew what I would find before I saw it: Bruises covered her arm from wrist to elbow.

"Take your hands off me," she hissed as she pulled her sleeve back in place. But the damage had been done.

"Your husband did that?" Martha asked. "Not so surprising, I suppose. He can't have been happy to learn you'd cuckolded him with one of his Aldermen."

"Or perhaps he found out that you plotted to kill Mr. Breary," I said. "If you're merely a wanton strumpet, he'd be mocked throughout the city. If you're a murderess, he'd find himself expelled from the council."

"Which is it, girl? Are you a whore or a killer?" Martha had crept up behind Agnes, and hissed these last words in her ear. "Or are you both?" For a moment I regretted our cruelty, but I knew that we had little choice, and that she deserved little better.

Then the tears began again, this time in earnest, and Agnes Greenbury collapsed against me. As if by their own volition, my arms wrapped around her. The scornful expression on Martha's face made clear that she was having none of it.

"He is so cruel," Agnes gasped at last. "You must help me."

"You have to tell me the truth," I replied. Martha disguised her snort of disgust as a cough, but I could read her expression well enough.

"You are right," the girl—and at that moment she did seem to be a girl—moaned into my chest. "You are right about everything. My husband found out about George and did this to me. He said that he'd not be made a fool of by so fresh a whore, and that George would suffer for debauching me. *He* must have done it."

"You think your husband killed Mr. Breary?" I asked.

The girl looked up at me, her clear blue eyes now red with crying. "What else could he have meant?" she asked. "I did not kill George, I . . . I . . ." Agnes's voice trailed off.

"You loved him?" Martha asked, not even bothering to hide the contempt in her voice.

Agnes slipped from my arms and sat in one of the lavishly covered chairs. "Of course I didn't love him." She wiped her nose on her sleeve, leaving a trail of snot from elbow to wrist. You could put a country girl in a silk dress, but teaching her manners was a different matter entirely. "But he was nice enough. I didn't kill him."

Though I knew it was a hopeless task, I gazed at the girl's face, trying to find a sign of the soul within. She seemed as sincere as any girl could be, but I'd heard too many lies to give her much credit.

"You didn't, but your husband might have?" I asked.

Agnes looked down at her hands as they fiddled with a ribbon on her dress. "I don't know. Maybe. He was angry enough. I've never seen a man so furious."

I looked up at Martha, and she inclined her head toward the door. She'd seen enough of the girl.

Martha and I slipped from the drawing room into the parlor where Will waited for us. I did not know how much of our conversation he'd heard, but the expression on his face told me that the sound of the girl's wails had escaped.

Before we stepped outside the three of us wrapped ourselves as best we could, with Will stealing glances in our direction, anxious to hear what we'd discovered. Once we were away from the Lord Mayor's house, Martha and I took turns telling Will what Agnes had said to us.

"Do you believe her?" he asked. We'd reached the Ouse Bridge and paused to watch as the children ventured back out on the ice. They avoided the spot where Tree had fallen through, but otherwise showed no fear.

"About what?" Martha shrugged. "That her husband gave her those bruises and swore revenge? Or that she didn't want Mr. Breary killed? We know she's a liar and a adulteress, so we can't believe much of what she says."

"She didn't give herself the bruises," I said. "And I cannot imagine Matthew Greenbury would tolerate such behavior in his wife."

"Well, he couldn't have killed Mr. Breary himself," Martha said. "He is so old he can spit into his own grave."

"He could have hired a man," I replied. In these times of war, even respectable gentlemen kept killers close by. That was why Joseph, and Edward before him, tolerated Mark Preston. "But would he kill one of his own Aldermen for committing adultery?"

"Not for adultery, but perhaps for making his new wife a whore, and giving him the cuckold's horns," Will said. "There's many a man who would kill to avenge that wrong."

"But Mr. Breary's murder also could have been *her* doing," Martha said. "She's a thoughtless trollop. Who knows what she might have done in a moment of anger? Mr. Breary crosses her, she flatters a soldier, and the next thing we know he's dying in an alleyway."

"So either of them could be behind the murder," I said.

"Or neither of them," Will said. "Mark Preston had reason enough to kill. And we know he's capable of doing so."

I did not add, *And your brother as well.* I sighed in resignation. We now held four people suspect in George's murder. Just where had our day's work gotten us?

When we reached my home, Elizabeth met us at the door, vibrant and full of life. She wanted to know where we'd gone, whom we'd seen, and when she would be allowed out on the ice like Tree. She burst into tears when I denied her.

"But I'm *littler* than he is," she wailed. "And I'm not afraid." She picked up Sugar—who meowed loudly at the indignity— and gazed up at me, her eyes overflowing with tears.

"Come, let us read," I said, scooping both Elizabeth and Sugar into my arms and carrying them to the parlor. I was determined to spend the time before dinner reading a book that had nothing at all to do with murder, adultery, or witches. For an hour, the Lord left us in peace, and I convinced myself that nothing, not even the winter wind, would disturb us so long as we kept the doors and windows locked tight.

The problem, of course, is that there is no way to keep the world from your door, and even as we finished our dinner a knock announced that our retreat had ended.

Hannah answered the door, and moments later Tree bounded into the dining room. His eyes lit up when he saw that we'd not yet finished the roasted capon, and he helped himself to meat and bread.

"Samuel sent me down," he said between mouthfuls. "He wanted me to tell you that Mr. Hodgson and Mrs. Hooke have started taking witches."

"Mother Lee, no doubt," I replied. A sense of dread settled in the pit of my stomach. Where would this end?

Tree shrugged in response. "Might be. They've taken so many it's hard to tell."

Will, Martha, and I stared at Tree, our mouths agape.

"What do you mean, *They've taken so many?*" Will asked.

"Witches," the boy replied. "When I left they'd locked up two dozen, and the Castle Warden was shouting to make room for more. I have no idea how many there will be when I get back."

Chapter 11

Although my first thought was to hurry out to the Castle, I hesitated when I saw the darkening sky and the light snow that had begun to fall. Who could say how long we would be gone? I did not relish the prospect of a late-night walk home through the city, not after what had happened to George.

I awoke well before sunrise to a clear, cold sky. The moon had set, so the only light came from the shimmering stars, which made the cold all the more dreadful. After a few moments my breath so fogged the window that I could not see. I lowered my head and said a hopeless prayer that God would relent in His judgment against the nation. When I looked up again, the darkness behind the stars was so complete, for a moment I wondered if there might be nothing more to our existence than this world and the stars above. I recoiled at the thought, begged God for forgiveness, and hurried downstairs. Martha and Hannah were already at work in the kitchen, and I joined them hoping to share in the oven's warmth and escape my own blasphemous thoughts.

A few minutes later, Elizabeth came clattering down the stairs, hair flowing behind her, and began her morning ritual of chasing Sugar through the house. As was his habit, Will was the last to rise, joining us as the sun began its reluctant journey across the morning sky. After breakfast, Hannah took Elizabeth upstairs to dress, while Martha, Will, and I met in the dining hall.

"I should like to go up to the Castle," I said. "We must find out just how bad the witch-hunt has become. Then we will better know what it means for the city and how we can defend ourselves."

Will shook his head in despair. "With Mr. Breary dead, there is nothing we can do."

I had no reply that would change his mind, so I did not try. "Will, do you think Mr. Breary's servants will grant you access to his papers?" I asked.

Will nodded. "He has no family in York, so nobody else will claim them. If need be, I can tell them I am in search of his will. I am family enough to do that."

"Good," I said. "You search for any evidence that might help us unravel his murder. Letters, a diary, anything at all. Martha and I will walk to the Castle and see if we can learn the lay of the land. If we don't see each other before, we'll meet here for dinner."

Will and Martha nodded in agreement, and after wrapping ourselves against the cold, we parted ways and set out into the city.

Martha and I trudged silently along Coney Street, each alone with our thoughts. I tried to prepare myself for the sights and sounds we would find when we reached the Castle. If Joseph had indeed filled the gaol with witches, the conditions would be dire, though not so bad as they would soon become. When we reached the crossroads with High Ousegate we found a cart trying to turn toward the Castle. The driver had badly misjudged the angle of the crossroads, and the cart would not make the turn. Even from a distance we could hear the driver swearing as he hauled on the reins. The horses were not inclined to comply.

Martha and I stopped, in part to watch the spectacle, but more out of fear of being trampled should the horses suddenly become more compliant. Our prudence was rewarded when the cart darted forward, nearly crushing an unwary passerby under its iron-rimmed wheels. Martha's gasp echoed my own when she saw the cart's terrible cargo: the wagon had been transformed into a rolling cage filled with people. I counted a dozen figures, mostly women, but I thought I saw an aged man as well. The prisoners grasped the bars to keep from being tossed about. I winced as one poor woman lost her grip and was hurled facefirst into the side of the cage. Blood ran from a cut on her cheek as she struggled back to her feet. A few children ran along side the cart, hurling stones and pieces of ice at the prisoners. One boy missed the mark and struck the driver in the head, provoking another round of curses.

"Joseph is not limiting his search to the city itself," Martha said. "Those are country folk."

"Such arrests might not be his doing," I replied. "Perhaps the country Justices have caught the fever for hunting witches as well."

We fell silent at this grim thought, and in my mind I saw the witch-hunts spreading across the north. How many hundreds would die if they did? I prayed that God would not allow such a thing to pass. We followed the cart to the Castle.

Each of us kept our eyes on the road rather than the sorry figures before us.

As we passed through the Castle gate, it became clear just how far Joseph's fever had spread. Dozens of prisoners were scattered around the Castle yard waiting to be taken to their cells. Nearly all had been laid in double irons, and their fear and misery filled the air. Martha and I hurried to Samuel's tower. When we approached the door, his voice echoed into the yard as he swore loudly at some poor soul.

"This is *my* tower, and you'll not tell me how to manage it," he shouted. A moment later, the Castle Warden scurried through the door. If he'd had a tail, it would have been tucked well between his legs. He glanced about to see who might have witnessed his humiliation before hurrying off in search of a more malleable jailor.

When we entered the tower, Samuel continued shouting at the Warden's back even as he nodded a greeting to us. "Keep *more* women in my cells? Who do you think will clean up after them? Me, that's who! I've got too many down there already. Adding even a few more will turn this place into York's largest privy!" He ended his philippic with one of the most spectacularly foul oaths I'd ever heard, sending Martha and me into fits of laughter.

Samuel leaned against the tower wall, red-faced and winded from his cursing.

"You won't believe the number of witches they've brought here," he wheezed after a moment.

"I think I might," I responded. "We passed through the gate with another prisoner cart."

"God's blood, what do they intend us to do?" Samuel asked.

"We can't hold them all until they are tried. In the time it takes to gather a court, half will be dead!"

Samuel was right of course. Under the best of circumstances, the Castle's cells were pestilential, and more than a few accused felons died while awaiting trial. When it happened in ones and twos, nobody troubled themselves overmuch, but what would happen when prisoners started dying by the dozens, and the occasional burial became a long funeral procession? I started to give voice to my concerns, but Samuel had not yet finished his diatribe.

"I mean, who is going to pay to feed these people?" he moaned. "The women all are paupers. I'll wring water from stone before I get even a penny from them."

"Surely the city will pay," Martha said.

Samuel snorted at the suggestion. "Those nithing bastards? They'd sooner pay for their own hanging rope than to feed so many prisoners. No, I'll be selling my shirt before these trials are done." He paused for a moment, now fully recovered from his shouting. "What is it that brings you up here?" he asked. "You've not been coopted into this terrible business, have you?"

I shook my head. "I don't see Joseph having me on as a Searcher, even if I wanted the duty. We're simply trying to find out as much about his scheme as we can. The city's women are my own, and I cannot stand by and see them suffer at his hands." I did not mention my fear that Rebecca Hooke might somehow use the hunt against me and mine.

"Probably not a bad idea," Samuel replied. He knew perfectly well the evil that Joseph had done the summer before. "But I don't know much. The Justices began by scouring the city for witches, but soon enough the countryside joined in the search. I don't know if Joseph was behind that, or if it happened on its own."

I crossed the room to Samuel's desk and glanced at the list of prisoners he'd admitted that day. One caught my eye: *Mother Lee, Upper Poppleton.*

"You have Mother Lee?" I asked.

Samuel looked at me in surprise. "You know her?" he asked. "She came in with two other witches from north of the city."

"Martha and I were there when her neighbors decided to accuse her," I said. "I'll likely be called as a witness."

"She's upstairs if you want to see her," Samuel volunteered. "You're a friend, so I'll not charge you more because she's a witch. The amount other jailors are charging makes me blush, and that's no mean feat."

I looked at Martha, and she shrugged. "I suppose there's nothing to be lost by talking to her," I replied. "But I should have thought she'd be in the low dungeon."

"Don't remind me," Samuel said. "The low dungeon is full, so I had to put some of the witches above. And do you think they are paying the customary fee for such a room? Not in this world." Samuel shook his head at the injustice. "Well, come on then."

I handed Samuel his pennies, and he led us up the stone staircase.

Samuel opened the heavy door into the upper cell, and though the women had only been imprisoned for a day, a horrid stench met us at the door. Samuel cursed under his breath and pushed past us into the cell. Martha and I followed for a few steps before we stopped, awestruck at the scene before us. A dozen women had been crowded into the small room. One occupied the narrow wooden bed, and the rest sat on the rush-covered floor, or stood staring at us. If these were the conditions above, I could not imagine how those living below were faring.

Samuel had crossed the cell and now examined the figure on the bed. He swore again, more loudly this time. "Well, I've found where the smell is coming from."

I crossed the room and looked down at the woman. By my guess, she'd been dead for some hours, and when she'd died, her bowels had loosed, fouling both her skirts and the thin mattress beneath her. Her waxen flesh had taken on a bluish hue, and her toothless mouth gaped at the ceiling. None of her comrades had taken the trouble to close her eyes. With a brief prayer, I reached down and did her this small service.

"This isn't the one you wanted to see, is it?" Samuel sighed.

"I don't know." I turned to the other women. "Which of you is Mother Lee from Poppleton?"

One of the women—hardly distinguishable from those around her—stepped forward. "I am."

"Why don't you talk to her downstairs," Samuel suggested. "And, Martha, could you find a guard and tell him what's happened here? Send him to the Warden for some help fetching the body and dragging out the mattress."

Martha and I agreed and, with Mother Lee close behind, we descended the stairs. Martha stepped outside and sent a guard for help before returning. I took a moment and looked over Mother Lee. Despite the conditions in the cell above, she seemed healthy enough—she'd only been there a day, I reminded myself—but it was abundantly clear that she had lived a life of poverty and want long before her arrest. Her skirts hung loose around her waist as if she'd once been a more substantial woman, but hadn't bought new clothes as her frame shrank. I could also see that they had been mended many times over the years. There was a cruelty in her expression that I found profoundly unnerving.

"Who are you?" she asked. "And what do you want with me? I've already been searched, so there's nothing more to find."

"Rebecca Hooke searched you?" Martha asked.

Mother Lee nodded.

"And she found a teat?"

"She said she did." Mother Lee would give us no more than she had to.

"I was with Lucy Pierce when she was in travail," I said. "I delivered her of a stillborn child."

"You're a midwife then?" the old woman asked. "Makes sense. I saw you come and go."

"The neighbors say you bewitched the baby."

"Not the baby, the mother." Mother Lee spoke with barely controlled fury. "She deserved everything that happened to her, and worse. I cursed her for her want of kindness, and it killed the child. So be it."

"You murdered the child?" Martha asked, amazed by such casual cruelty.

Mother Lee smiled at the memory, and it made my skin crawl. She was a foul woman indeed.

"She invited all the neighbors except me to her travail," Mother Lee said. Poison dripped from every word. "All save me. She offered them food, drink, and a well-fired hearth, while I watched from the cold. How would you have me repay such unkindness? I threw a few stones, cracked a window, and said a few words. I had my revenge."

I was seized by the desire to escape Mother Lee's malefic

presence as quickly as I could. "Besides Mrs. Hooke, who has come to see you?" I asked.

Mother Lee shrugged. What did it matter to her?

"If you won't talk to us, we won't be able to help you," Martha said.

Mother Lee laughed high and cruel.

"You'll help me?" she cried. "You'll help me? Even if I believed you'd want to do such a thing, how would you do that? Would you go before the jury and tell them I'm a good neighbor? Tell them that the Searcher *didn't* find the Witch's Mark on me? Even if you promised me that, it wouldn't make a difference, for I said those killing words. Beside that, you've seen what it's like in my cell. I'll need the devil's own luck to live long enough to see my own trial and execution. So I'll tell you the same thing I told the others: Go to hell."

"What others?" I asked again.

She glared at me before answering. "There were two men from the city who came. Told me if I exposed other witches they'd set me free."

"And you refused them?" Martha asked.

"They were liars, weren't they," Mother Lee replied. "I could see it in their faces. They'd take the names and hang me all the same. I sent them away empty handed." She laughed to herself. "At least the one who still had both his hands." She held up a hand with the last two fingers folded down and grasped at the air with her thumb and forefinger.

"One of them had a ruined hand," I said. "He'd lost his fingers?"

Mother Lee nodded.

"It must have been Mark Preston and Mr. Hodgson," Martha said.

At that moment the door to the tower burst open and three of the Castle guards entered the room. "We're here for the body," one announced, and I pointed him up the stairs.

Without another word to us, Mother Lee followed the guards back to her cell. It seemed she had answered enough of our questions. Martha and I slipped into the Castle yard.

"She's right about dying before she's tried," Martha said as we crossed toward the gate. "Gaol-fever will carry many of them away before the hangman can begin his work. We have to do something to stop all this."

"I know," I replied, but I had few good ideas as to the best course to take.

"Where to now?" Martha asked.

"Let us go to Mr. Breary's," I suggested. "Perhaps Will has found something of use in his papers." We made our way to the Castle gate, and back into the city. Mercifully the wind had abated, though the cold still pierced my skin and made my bones feel brittle. I could not help feeling a measure of pity for the women confined in the Castle. Their cells would have been cold and uncomfortable even in the warmest of winters, but a season such as this would make their suffering unbearable.

Will answered our knock as soon as we arrived. The moment he opened the door, I knew that something was wrong.

"Someone's broken into Mr. Breary's study," Will said. "And they burned his papers."

Chapter 12

"What? How can this be?" I cried.

Will shrugged helplessly and gestured for us to enter. We went straight to George's study. Even though I knew what we'd find, I gasped when I saw the thoroughness with which the intruder had worked. Cabinet doors stood wide open, as did every drawer of his desk, yet there was hardly a scrap of paper to be found. The hearth itself completed the story of what had happened, for it was choked with ashes and a bucket sat nearby, full to overflowing. Only a few scraps had survived the conflagration, but nothing of any use—our incendiary was nothing if not complete. Curiously, George's bound books had not been burned, but had been taken down from the shelves and stacked neatly next to the hearth.

"What happened with these?" I wondered. I picked up a volume—a quarto of psalms—and fanned the pages.

"Mr. Breary would sometimes put loose paper between the pages," Will responded despondently. "Whoever did this looked

133

through every book to make sure that everything written in Mr. Breary's own hand had been burned."

"Why?" Martha asked. "It must have taken hours. Who would gain from doing this?"

Will shrugged. "That's all I've been thinking about since I arrived. It is not a short list."

"What do you mean?" I asked.

"Well, there's Agnes Greenbury. All evidence of her affair with Mr. Breary is now gone. And I know that Mr. Breary had loans out to men throughout the city—those records are burned, so his debtors are now free. His correspondence books are gone, account books gone, cargo books . . . his will . . . all are gone."

"His will is burned?" Martha asked.

Will nodded. "There might be an older one somewhere, but he wrote a new one in November and I know he kept it close to hand." He gestured at the open and entirely empty drawers of George's desk.

"Did you see it?" I asked. With George's death, a great deal of money soon would change hands; more than enough for some men to kill.

"No," Will replied. "I summoned a scribe to write it and then witnessed his signature."

"You *did* see it," Martha exclaimed.

"I saw it, but he said he dared not let me read it," Will said. Despair was etched into his face. "He told me that I would be very pleased, but I should merely sign at the bottom next to his footman. Now there is nothing."

I could find no words to comfort Will, for I knew he was right. No matter how close the two men had become, Will was in nowise George's kin, and could expect nothing out of his estate. Unless the will had somehow survived burning, some distant cousin of George's would soon receive a very pleasant surprise.

The three of us searched the room for clues that clearly were not present.

"Where were his servants?" Martha asked suddenly. "How did someone get into the study and then have the leisure to burn so much paper?"

"I thought of that as well," Will replied. "His serving-men have fled the house and taken all they owned. They may not even be in the city. The only servant left was his maid, and she said she knows nothing. Poor thing is terrified."

"And for a guess she sleeps in the garret," I said.

Will nodded. "Three stories up. If the incendiary came in the night, she wouldn't have heard a thing."

I sighed heavily and took one last look around the room. "Let's go home," I said. "There is nothing more here."

As we walked back to my house, Martha and I told Will what we'd learned at the Castle.

"Mark Preston is questioning witches?" Will said. "So we know that Joseph is indeed taking an interest in the interrogations. That's something."

I shrugged. It didn't tell us much, but after the disappointment of finding George's papers burned, it seemed like a revelation. As we approached my house, the wind rose up, and I welcomed the thought of an afternoon next to the fire reading with Elizabeth. But as soon as we stepped through the front door, I knew it was not to be. My midwife's valise and birthing stool waited in the entry hall, a sure sign that in our absence I'd been summoned to a labor. Hannah bustled in from the kitchen, Elizabeth close behind.

"Who is it?" I asked.

"A singlewoman from Goodramgate," Hannah replied. "One of the matrons just was here. She said she'd wait for you at Goodramgate church and take you there."

Martha picked up the stool and handed me the valise.

"We'll see you in a few hours," I said to Will as I embraced him.

Will started to reply when a pounding on my front door nearly frighted us from our skins.

Will swore and threw the door open to reveal a half-dozen members of the Town Watch.

I had not even opened my mouth to berate them for their impertinence when they rushed in and tried to seize Will by his arms and legs. The uproar that followed will remain with me for the rest of my days.

Will greeted the first solider through the door with the handle of his cane, and he fell to the ground, bright blood pouring from his nose. Will gave the second a terrible clout to the head, and he joined his comrade on the floor. The third and fourth threw themselves over their fallen mates, knocking Will to the ground. By now Martha had dropped my birthing stool and joined the fray, clapper-clawing one of the remaining soldiers so soundly he retreated into the street. With a roar, Hannah flew in from the kitchen wielding her rolling pin like a cudgel. She began to beat the soldiers who had tackled Will.

The sergeant in charge of the squad decided—wisely, I think—to fight the rest of the battle from afar. He stood outside and began to shout that he had a writ for Will Hodgson's arrest.

"Stop!" I bellowed, and to my surprise all the combatants did. The two soldiers who had tackled Will looked at me, and Martha halted her attack on the last soldier who remained on his feet. Hannah gave the soldiers one last stroke and then lowered her weapon. I heard a sobbing behind me, and I found Elizabeth at the top of the stairs gazing down at the tumult, scared out of her senses.

"Stop," I said again, more softly this time. "I'll not have this in my home." I climbed the stairs, sat next to Elizabeth, and took her in my arms. She buried her face in my chest and continued to cry.

"Sergeant," I called out. "You say have a warrant?"

He poked his head through the front door and cast a worried eye toward Martha and Hannah. "Yes, my lady, signed by the Lord Mayor." He held up a sheet of paper that I took to be the writ in question.

"And what is the reason for taking him?"

"For murder," the sergeant replied. Martha, Will, and I looked at each other trying to make sense of the accusation.

"Murder?" I asked. "Certainly not of George Breary." It could only be that, of course, but I still could not fathom it.

"Yes, my lady," said the Sergeant. "Mr. Breary."

"Then he will go with you," I said. "There is no need to use violence or to invade my home."

Will and Martha started to object, but I held up my hand to silence them.

"Will, I will take care of this, but you must go." I turned to the sergeant. "Are you taking him to the Castle?"

The sergeant shook his head. "With the Castle so overtaken with witches, I am to carry him to Peter's Prison."

I was surprised and not a little pleased by this news. For as long as anyone could remember, the Minster had maintained its own gaol for those who ran afoul of the law within the cathedral's grounds. Peter's Prison was much smaller than the Castle, of course, and much closer to my house. With luck—and liberal payments to his jailors—I could reasonably hope that Will would not suffer too much during his confinement.

After the soldiers led Will away, Martha turned to me, her eyes alive with fury. "How could you let them take him?" she demanded.

"We had no choice," I replied. "They had a warrant, so all was in order. Should we have tried to overpower the guards and send Will out of the city?"

"But he was with us when Mr. Breary died! Joseph is behind this."

"Or the Lord Mayor," I replied. "He signed the warrant. Whatever the case, we will see him released as soon as we can."

Martha stared at me in sullen silence.

Elizabeth had stopped crying and looked up at me. "What has happened to Will?" she asked.

"The watch has taken him," I replied. "But do not worry. He will not be far, and we will see him home soon." Elizabeth nodded. "Now go with Hannah, she'll need your help with dinner."

Elizabeth descended the stairs, and Hannah took her hand. "Don't forget the woman in travail," Hannah said. "She's waiting."

I nodded my thanks. I nearly had forgotten. I turned to retrieve my tools and my eyes lit upon Will's cane. He had dropped it during his fight with the watch. I said a prayer of thanks that he'd not drawn the sword hidden inside and spilled even more blood. I picked it up and leaned it in the corner. It would wait there until he returned.

Martha and I gathered my valise and the birthing stool,

and stepped into the cold. She maintained her silence, angry that I'd allowed Will to be taken but unable to explain what we should have done differently.

"If he is in Peter's Prison we shall be able to care for him," I said at last. "Things could be much worse."

"He is in gaol in winter," she replied. "Things will be terrible enough."

"I will do my best," I said. "And it *will* be enough." I hoped it was true.

"If Joseph is behind this, what does he mean to do?" Martha asked. By now we'd reached the top of Stonegate and turned east toward the Holy Trinity Church in Goodramgate.

"If he murdered George, this could have been his plan all along," I said. "He rids himself of a rival on the Council and sees his brother in gaol for the crime. Of course, the same could be true of the Lord Mayor if *he* ordered Will to be taken. His wife's lover is dead, and another man accused of the deed."

"Will cannot be convicted," Martha said. "We were with him when we heard Mr. Breary cry out."

"Conviction may be beside the point. Joseph may just want Will imprisoned for the time being."

"Or he may hope Will dies in gaol," Martha said.

"Or that," I admitted.

We walked in silence, each doing our best to fight back the sorrow and fear that threatened to overwhelm us. I reached out and took Martha's hand.

"We will save him," I said. "We have accomplished more difficult tasks, haven't we?"

Martha squeezed my hand. "Aye, we have."

By now we'd reached the church. The heavy, square bell

tower loomed above us, gray and threatening against the clouded sky. A lone figure stood before the church door peering in our direction. She was wrapped in layers upon layers, and she stomped her feet in hope of keeping warm. I took her to be the woman who had come to my house, for who else would be foolish enough to stand about in such cold?

"You summoned a midwife," I called out.

"Thank God you're here, my lady," a voice answered from beneath a scarf. "I feared the cold might keep you at home, and I'd have to go in search of another midwife. I am Grace Fisher. Please come this way." She turned and led us into the warren of streets behind the church. After a few twists and turns we arrived at our destination. The woman opened a low door and led us up a set of wooden stairs.

"The mother's name is Sarah Bates," Grace said as we climbed. "She is our maidservant." I could hear the anger in her voice, and I knew without asking that her husband had fathered the child. Grace led us to a small room occupied by a bed and a chest of drawers. A young woman sat on the bed. She'd drawn her knees to her chest and was breathing hard. We'd arrived in the midst of a labor pain.

"Sarah, I am Lady Hodgson," I announced. "I will be your midwife."

The girl nodded but said nothing.

"I should examine you and see how you are faring," I said. Again the girl nodded.

"Is she mute?" Martha asked Grace.

"I'm not," Sarah said. "I just didn't have anything to say."

"Good," I said, suppressing a smile. At least the girl had some spirit to her. "Now let me see where we are."

Sarah moved to the edge of the bed, and I knelt between her legs. Martha handed me a vial of oil, and I anointed my hand. To my surprise I found that the child was ready to be born.

"The child will be born soon," I announced. "But before I offer you any help, you must tell me the name of the father."

Sarah's eyes flicked over my shoulder to her mistress, and a look of uncertainty crossed her face. If I'd needed any more proof that her master had gotten her with child, I had it.

Martha stepped forward and took Sarah's hand. "We know it was your master. We just need you to say it aloud." I was pleased, though not surprised, that Martha had come to the same conclusion as I. She would need several more years as my deputy to learn the mysteries of childbirth, but she could already tell the truth from lies as readily as any woman I knew.

"Tell them the truth," a man's voice said from behind us. I whirled around, shocked both by the presence of a man in the delivery room and by the words he'd said. A man who could only be Mr. Fisher stood in the doorway behind Grace. He was handsome, appearing neither rich nor poor, and his face gave no sign of the sinful courses into which he'd fallen.

"I got her with child," he said to me. I saw Martha's brow furrow as she absorbed the words.

"This is my husband, Stephen," Grace said, her voice flat and without emotion. I could not imagine how such a situation felt. Phineas had had his faults, but a wandering pintle was not among them.

"Why are you telling us?" I asked, for I was no less puzzled than Martha. I'd attended more than my share of illegitimate births, and I'd never met a man so eager to confess his adultery.

"The sin is mine, and I will not compound my fault by denying it. It is the right thing to do."

Martha continued to stare at Mr. Fisher warily but did not give voice to whatever doubts she had.

I turned to Sarah. "Is it true that he is the father of your child?"

"Aye," she replied. "He had use of my body during the spring. Only a few times. But it was enough."

I nodded. "Mrs. Fisher, the child is so near to being born we are past the point of making caudle. We will need swaddling clothes for the child and food for Sarah."

"I'll get some linen," she said, and disappeared down the stairs.

"You've done your part," Martha declared to Mr. Fisher. "Leave us."

He nodded and slipped away as meek as could be.

Martha and I turned our attention to Sarah and, as I expected, the child did not keep us waiting for long. When Sarah's travail was at its worst I questioned her again, and she confirmed that her master had fathered the child on her. And that was that.

After we swaddled the child—a healthy and squalling baby boy—and sent for a meal, I left Martha and Sarah alone so I could speak with the Fishers. I found them in the parlor, patiently awaiting the news, though I could not tell what they hoped to hear. A stillborn child certainly would simplify their lives, and I'd known otherwise good men to give thanks to God when their bastard children died.

"Sarah has given birth to a lusty boy," I said to Mr. Fisher without preamble. "And at the height of her travail she said that you are the father."

The Fishers simply nodded. Somehow they had made their peace with the adultery that had invaded their marriage.

"You will tell the Justices?" Stephen Fisher asked. "What will they do to us, to Sarah and me?"

The question gave me pause, for I'd not yet thought about it. In the past, I would have reported the birth and the sinful behavior that preceded it to the city's authorities. Depending on their disposition, the city might have carted Sarah or simply required her to make public penance for her sin. Stephen would suffer less, at least in body. The Quarter Sessions would order him to maintain the child until he came of age, but he was wealthy enough that I did not think he would be carted or stocked.

The problem, of course, was that the present was entirely unlike the past. Now the law was dispensed by men like Joseph, godly men who took every opportunity to show off their devotion to the Lord and their power over men. I would lose no sleep over whatever they did to Stephen Fisher, but what about Sarah? She had done nothing to warrant whipping.

As I considered the choice before me, I realized that something in me had changed: I now trusted the law no more than I would a stranger on a dark street. Eighteen months before, during the siege of the city, York's governors had sought to burn a wife for murdering her husband, her innocence be damned. A year later, they had been unwilling to hang a murderer whom they knew to be guilty. And now Will sat in a cell for a crime he did not commit. In every case, the law showed itself incapable or, even worse, uninterested in doing what was just. I felt like Paul on the road to Damascus, but my revelation was not a joyful one. I now knew that when it came to the law, what was right and just mattered not one whit—there was only power and its use.

Could I turn Sarah over to the same men who were preparing to hang witches by the dozen?

"You will own the child?" I asked Stephen.

"He will," Grace answered for him. Stephen nodded.

"Good," I said. "Then I will tell nobody you are the father."

The Fishers stared at me in complete bewilderment.

"When you take the child to be christened," I continued, "tell the vicar that the father was her betrothed and that he was pressed into the army before they could marry. If he challenges you, send for me, and I will testify that she told me this at the height of her travail."

It took Stephen a moment to find his voice. "Why are you doing this?"

"Never you mind that," I replied. "Just make sure that you maintain the child as if he were your own lawful son."

Relief spread across his face, and he struggled to give voice to his gratitude.

"But know this well," I continued. "If I hear so much as a whisper that you have neglected Sarah or your son, I'll lay the next bastard I deliver at your door, and the one after that as well. Soon enough you'll be supporting a troop of bastards, and famous throughout the city for your lechery."

Blood and gratitude drained from Stephen's face. "You can't do that."

"Of course I can," I replied. "But it is entirely your choice whether I do. If you keep your word, I will keep mine."

"He will support the child," Grace said. "I give you my word as well."

I nodded. "See to it." I returned to Sarah and Martha and

found them well. The child slept in his mother's arms, and I could see that Sarah would soon join him.

"The Fishers will see that neither you nor your child want for food or shelter," I told her. "But you must never tell anyone who the true father is."

Martha and Sarah both looked at me in confusion.

"They will explain the agreement we have made," I said. "Now you should sleep." Sarah closed her eyes, and soon enough she was snoring softly, the weight of the day finally lifted from her shoulders. Martha and I slipped quietly from the room and descended the stairs. We did not see the Fishers as we left, nor did I seek them out.

"What did he promise?" Martha asked once we closed the door behind us. I described the demands I'd made of the Fishers, though not the reason behind them. While I had lost my faith in the law, I was not yet ready to say so aloud. Martha nodded in satisfaction at my decision.

As we neared St. Michael le Belfrey we both gazed in the direction of Peter's Prison, where the guards had taken Will. The sun had nearly set, and the wind tugged insistently at our cloaks, promising another chill night. Martha and I glanced at each other, each of us wondering how Will would fare.

"We'll gather blankets and food and take them to him tonight," I said. "No doubt his jailors are cold enough that they'll accept whatever aid we can offer, and let us give Will anything he needs."

"I hope so," Martha replied.

I took her arm in an attempt to comfort her, but I knew full well that only Will's safe return would end her distress.

We had just turned from Stonegate toward home when a

voice no less cold than the north wind echoed down the narrow street. "Bridget Hodgson, I have been searching for you throughout the city. I should like a word with you."

We turned to find Rebecca Hooke approaching us, a terrible and triumphant smile on her face.

Chapter 13

"Where have you been?" Rebecca crowed as she approached us. "I should have thought you'd be at Peter's Prison with your boy. Who would have thought he'd do such a thing? Well, I suppose it's not such a surprise, after what happened to his father. Perhaps the rumors are true and young Will is indeed a patricide. Now twice over, it seems."

A terrible combination of anger and fear seized me by the throat, for I knew that any turn of events that brought such joy to Rebecca Hooke could only bring sorrow to me and mine. As was her habit, Rebecca had draped herself in rich silks. When the King's men had held the city, she had favored blue—often the same blue as her eyes—and after the Parliament-men took power, she'd started wearing black. But there was no mistaking the quality of the cloth or dye.

"I imagine you've come from some birth or another," Rebecca continued. By now she stood only a few feet away. I felt my heart racing as if we were about to come to blows. Perhaps we were.

"Have you welcomed some new bastard into the world, or

uncovered yet another of the city's witches?" Rebecca's smile grew wider as she spoke. "Mr. Hodgson and I must thank you for your assistance in witch discovery. Since you uncovered Mother Lee, the women of all the suburbs have been falling over themselves to find the rest of her company."

"You know all those women aren't witches," I replied between clenched teeth. "One or two, perhaps, but not all of them."

Rebecca started to reply, but I had not finished.

"The two of you don't even care about their guilt or innocence. They're mere rungs in Joseph Hodgson's climb to power. And yours."

"Ah, now there you are mistaken, at least in part," Rebecca replied. "Joseph is a fascinating figure, for he truly believes the women are guilty. He is convinced that by God's grace he has uncovered a company of witches here in the shadows of the Minster, and that it is his duty to seek them out. It sounds mad to me, of course, but Joseph believes that the Lord preserved him during the wars so that he might pursue His enemies here in York. He believes he is God's instrument for the city's deliverance. Our Puritans are so *sure* of themselves, aren't they?"

"And what of you?" Martha spat. "You've joined with him, haven't you? How are you any better?"

A shadow passed over Rebecca's face, and she stared at Martha. Martha held her gaze far longer than I could have, but eventually looked away. Then Rebecca turned back to me. "What option did you leave for me? You came to York, waving your coat of arms and jangling the cash in your purse. And what did the mothers—*my* mothers—do? Before I knew what had happened, they started crying out *Lady Bridget* this and *Lady Hodgson* that. Soon enough it was all the fashion to be delivered by a so-called gentlewoman."

It was the first time I'd heard what might be called pain or regret in Rebecca's voice.

"And then you called on your friends in the Minster and had them take my license," she continued. "Did you think I would forget what you did to me? That you would take my place in this city, and I would let it pass as if it meant nothing at all?"

"No, Rebecca, I never thought that," I replied softly. "But you were a cruel and unforgiving midwife. I regret nothing I've done."

For some reason Rebecca laughed at this, and my heart filled with fear. What reason did she have for merriment?

"You might not regret it now, but soon you will," she said. "A Searcher has far more power than a midwife, more power than you can imagine. And as a Searcher I will enjoy more respect than you'll ever know. Bringing life is a joyful thing, and people love you for it, but now I bring death, and people fear me."

"Why have you come?" I asked. "To display your newfound authority and lord it over me? You should enjoy it, because I promise that I will see you brought low before this business is through."

"I know you think that." Rebecca spoke to me as she would a child. "But before you even consider such a scheme, I would suggest you look about you. Your nephew is in gaol, accused of murder. And that red-haired girl you call your daughter . . . I've heard she is rarely seen without her cat. Your neighbor said that she talks to it constantly." Rebecca paused. "Did you hear that in Essex they hanged a witch who was just eleven years old? Just a girl! The devil is no respecter of children, is he?"

Martha and I stared at Rebecca, unable to speak.

"You are not so cruel," Martha managed to say at last, but we both knew that she was.

Rebecca smiled. "I am simply doing the Lord's work. That is what Joseph would say. And I quite like the idea that God would make me the instrument of bringing you to your knees. So look to your own, Bridget, for you are not so safe as you think." She turned and walked away, the sound of her boot heels echoing through the street.

I watched her go, hardly daring to breathe lest she return with more threats and dangers. Once she'd passed out of sight I exhaled. "Let us go home," I said to Martha.

"Did you see James Hooke?" she asked by way of a reply.

"What do you mean? James was with her?"

"Aye," Martha replied. "He was skulking in the alley over there, peering about like he was a member of the Town Watch."

Such news was curious, and I knew not what to make of it. James had never been one to dote on Rebecca (not that she would have allowed it), preferring instead to keep his distance. I could not fault him in that.

When we arrived at my house I gazed at the door. Soon after I'd taken up midwifery I'd had it painted red so people could find me more easily, and for years I'd loved coming home to see it. But on this day, the afternoon sun bathed my street in a passing strange light that made the door seem darker than usual, the color of clotting blood. I pushed my way inside and breathed a sigh of relief when Hannah and Elizabeth greeted us.

"I've gathered all you'll need for Mr. Hodgson," Hannah announced, indicating a large basket by the door. "Blankets and a bolster for his bed, and enough food for days."

I embraced Hannah and kissed Elizabeth on the crown of her head. "I'll be back very soon," I promised. "I need to take these to Will so that he keeps warm tonight."

"I wrote him a note," Elizabeth replied. "It's in with the food. When will he be home?"

"Soon," I said. "Just as soon as we can get him."

In just the few minutes that Martha and I had been inside, the sun had disappeared below the horizon, leaving us with the merest sliver of daylight. We hurried toward High Petergate and then to the west side of the Minster to Peter's Prison. The heavy wood door loomed over us, and I felt small and ineffectual when I pounded on it. When we received no response, Martha cast about until she found a loose cobblestone. She lifted the stone above her head and hurled at the door with all her might. The crash echoed through the street. A few moments later the door groaned open a few inches.

To my amazement we were greeted not by a guard but by Will himself. A broad smile lit up his face when he saw us.

"Thank God it's you, Aunt Bridget," he whispered. "Come in quickly."

"Will, what in God's name is going on?" Martha cried.

"Keep your voice down," Will said. "You'll wake everyone." Though I'd never been called to testify in the Minster court, I knew that the floor above us served as a courtroom, the ground floor housed the jailors, and the cells—where I'd thought I'd find Will—were beneath our feet. Will ushered us inside, and I struggled to make sense of the scene before us. A fire roared in the large stone hearth, bathing the room in a warm glow, and it was clear that we'd arrived in the aftermath of a particularly unruly supper. A half dozen wine bottles stood on the rough wood table in the center of the room, surrounded by glasses, tankards, and plates of half-eaten food. The capon that had provided the main course sat in the middle of the table, stripped down to its bones. I looked around the room for the guards, but the three of us were alone.

"Will, what is going on here?" I asked.

"Don't worry, Aunt Bridget, it's fine," he said. "It turned out that I knew the jailors from my drinking days, and they were quite hospitable." In his early youth, Will had lived a far more dissolute life than I or his father would have liked, drinking and fighting with the town's lower sort. He had left that life behind (thanks in no small part to my efforts), but it seemed that his time in York's alehouses had yielded some surprising benefits.

"Where are they?" Martha asked.

"They've been asleep for some time now," Will replied, gesturing at a door that led to the jailors' quarters. "I kept pouring, and they kept drinking. Have you brought any money? I promised I'd repay them for supper and the wine if they allowed me to sleep up here rather than in the cells below. They're awful."

"We've brought you blankets and a pillow, as well as food and cash," Martha said. "If we'd known you would be living so well we would have come here for our supper rather than eating at home."

"There wouldn't have been enough for all of us," Will said with a smile. "These poor sots have to make do with so little they'd have eaten an entire goose if I'd provided it. It's lucky for me, though. The birth went well then?"

"Well enough," I replied. I considered telling him about our encounter with Rebecca Hooke, but rejected the idea. There was nothing he could do to help, and I did not want to worry him unnecessarily. "We came to make sure that you were safe and in good spirits, but I see we needn't have troubled ourselves."

"So long as I keep my hosts in beer and bread, they'll treat me well," Will said. "But we do have to find a way to get me out."

I nodded. "We will work on that."

"What is your plan?" Will asked. "My stay here is off to a fine start, but I don't much like where it might end."

"We'll find out what we can about why you were taken," I said. "If it was simply on Joseph's orders, there might be nobody to testify against you. He might merely want you out of the way for a time."

"Or he might have found someone to perjure himself," Will noted. "In which case I'm cooked." The thought—which, I had to admit, was entirely reasonable—cast a cloud over our little reunion.

Martha reached out and took his hand. "It will not come to that," she said. "We will testify on your behalf, and none could doubt us."

"A maidservant and my own aunt?" Will asked doubtfully. "I wish I had your confidence. No, if you don't free me before the Assizes, Joseph will see me convicted. I have no doubt of that."

"We will free you," I replied. "We have no other option. We will continue our inquiry into George's murder. There are others who had reason to kill him—Joseph, Mark Preston, Agnes Greenbury, or the Lord Mayor himself. It is simply a matter of finding out which one acted against him." I watched Will's face to see how he would react when I included Joseph among the suspects. He winced, but that was all.

"I hope it is so easy," Will replied.

"As do I," I said. "It is late, and we should go. I'll wait outside for a moment."

Will and Martha nodded their thanks for this gift of time alone, and I slipped into the Minster yard. It was now full dark, and the moon hung low and bright in the sky, bathing the cathedral in an eerie silver light, as if it were crafted of ice and glass rather than stone.

As I waited, I wondered what Will and Martha could be talking about. The future to be sure, but what kind of future could they expect or even dream of? Will had lost his father, then his godfather, and now he faced hanging for a murder he hadn't committed. I would try to protect him, but my encounter with Rebecca had made clear just how vulnerable those around me had become.

Not long before, I had assured Martha that midwives were safe from witchcraft accusations, but what if I was wrong? If Rebecca Hooke could make Elizabeth into a witch, we all could be charged, Hannah included. In my first years after coming to York, Phineas and I had made a family, and then I watched in horror and helplessness as death took my husband and children one by one. In the years since, I'd rebuilt my life, and now it was threatened, not by fevers or coughs, but by men. I knew there was nothing I would not do to defend my family, but as I gazed at the cathedral's majesty I realized that I had never been so powerless.

The next morning came, clear and calm. When I stepped outside, for a moment I entertained the hope that the cold had broken, but within moments the chill had worked its way beneath my cloak and begun to dig its fingers into my flesh. The only change was that the wind had died down. I thanked the Lord for this small blessing.

I left Martha, Hannah, and Elizabeth at home and retraced

the route to Peter's Prison. I wanted to visit Will, of course, but also to speak with his keepers. The previous night's bacchanal showed that they could be more agreeable than many of the city's jailors, and I wanted to impress upon them that Will was not merely their friend, but a friend who had a wealthy, powerful, and (most important) free-spending aunt.

When I entered the Minster yard I was pleased to see that Peter Newcome had set up his movable shop against the cathedral wall, for I knew that if there was any news about the witchhunts, he would have heard it first. As I crossed toward him, he raised his hand in greeting.

"Lady Hodgson," he called out. "It is a strange time to be here in York, is it not? First the city is overrun with witches, and now an Alderman is murdered as he walks the streets? I cannot but wonder what bloody crime will follow."

His tone was light—and why not? Each murder would increase his profits. I thought to reprimand him, but I realized he could not know that George had been my friend or that my nephew had been taken for the murder. No good would come from pointing out his misstep, so I did not correct him.

"And it seems the city has regained its appetite for hanging felons," Newcome continued.

This brought me up short. "What do you mean?"

Newcome smiled when he realized that, once again, he knew more than I. He drew such pleasure from spreading news, good or bad, that he truly was the perfect chapman. "Nothing is settled, but there are plans to convene another Special Assize. Too many witches, too many murders, too long to wait for the Parliament to send out judges." He held out a pamphlet. "It's all here if you read closely enough."

Bloody Murder in York, the title shouted above a crude woodcut showing a two figures, one lying on the ground, the other standing with a hammer in his hand. Beneath the picture, the title continued: *Or, an Ungrateful Son Butchers His Father.* My stomach roiled as I took the pamphlet and began to read. While it did not mention Will by name, the author claimed that George's murderer had been captured, and now awaited trial and execution. When I reached the end of the little book I found a passage that worried me all the more.

> *In a city so overrun with Satan's agents, can we delay our efforts to restore order and bring justice? If God's will is to be done, we must not tarry, but act on His behalf. Our magistrates cannot, must not, wait to do their duty or the Lord shall strike them down as He has promised to strike down all those who are lukewarm in their love of Him.*

"And from this you think that the city will start trials soon?" I asked. "How can you know this?"

"I was right about the witch-hunt, wasn't I?" Newcome replied. "And it is not just this, but what people are saying throughout the city. They say the witches must be tried and murderers must be found out and punished. As they say, *Blood cries out for blood.* What is more, the man who killed the Alderman has murdered before—his own father, if the gossip is to be believed."

"He never did," I whispered, but my words could not turn back the fear I felt within my chest. Joseph had convinced so many people that Will was to blame for their father's death, my opinions would carry no weight.

Newcome shrugged at my feeble protests. "Whatever the case, the city will not allow him to escape the hangman a second time. Besides, if the Lord Mayor did not intend to make a court, why would he allow the printing of such a pamphlet?"

I turned back to the cover of the book and saw that, like the pamphlet describing Hester Jackson's fate, it had been approved by the Lord Mayor and Aldermen. This discovery only doubled my fear, and I cursed under my breath.

"My lady!" Newcome cried in mock horror. "I'd expect such language from ... well, from myself, but not a gentlewoman."

I looked up at him, so worried for Will I could not be angry at his impudence. "The man they intend to hang for Alderman Breary's murder is my nephew. He was with me when Mr. Breary was killed, so I know he is innocent. But there are powerful men who might like to see him hanged for the crime."

To my surprise, Newcome nodded sympathetically. "My brother was hanged as a highwayman," he said. "He was guilty, of course, but it was a horrible thing all the same. They cut him down only to discover he was still alive. The bailiffs pulled him from our mother's arms and dragged him back to the gallows. I'd never heard her scream so. It is a terrible thing for a mother to watch her son hang." He forced a smile. "It seemed wrong to hang him twice for the same crime; where is the justice in that? But you should have seen the pamphlets that were written about it. They are still to be had if you care to search for them.

"If I hear anything of note," he continued, "or can do anything to help you or your nephew, I will. My business thrives on hangings, but that does not mean I wish to see more of them."

I nodded my thanks. "I wish I could think of something you can do. But ..." My voice trailed off to nothing.

"To start, I can speak against this pamphlet," Newcome

replied. "People come to me for books, but also for gossip. If I sell the book with a warning that it contains only lies, word will spread soon enough."

"Thank you," I replied. I did not think mere words could save Will, but they could not hurt, and Will needed all the friends he could find.

"Also, have you considered writing a pamphlet of your own?" Newcome continued.

"What do you mean?"

"There is no reason to let your enemies have the only word in this matter," he explained. "If the wars have shown us nothing else, it's that pens and printing presses are no less important than cannons and harquebuses. Here I can only sell works written against the King, but in the south there are just as many mocking the Parliament-men. They're much funnier, too. You should write in defense of your nephew. If enough citizens believe your nephew is innocent, he cannot be hanged."

"And you think that a book could help?" I asked.

Newcome shrugged. "It couldn't hurt, could it? So long as you are willing to pay the printer, he'll say whatever you wish. And if you give the booksellers a little on top of that, they will give the books away gratis."

"Thank you, Mr. Newcome," I said after a moment. I slipped a few coins into his hand. "I will consider it, and I may come to you for help."

Newcome bowed. "I will do whatever I can."

I looked toward Peter's Prison and decided to delay my visit to Will. There was nothing to be gained by telling him about the coming Assize. No, I needed to consult Martha, and we had to find a way to save him from the calamity that lay before him.

Chapter 14

Martha looked up in surprise when I arrived at home. She had been sweeping the parlor, but she stopped as soon as she saw my face.

"What is it?" she asked. "What has happened?"

"They intend to try Will along with the witches," I said.

Martha paled and sat on the edge of the couch. "When?"

"I don't know. They might wait until all the witches are tried. Or they might not."

"Are you sure?" Martha asked.

"Not entirely," I replied. "It is just a rumor now. I heard it from Peter Newcome, but he seems to know as much about the city as any man could."

Martha nodded. "We should have seen it coming. Is it the Lord Mayor's doing?"

"In some way, it must be," I said. "If he hired a man to kill Mr. Breary, he'd certainly want to see Will—or anyone for that matter—hanged for it, and the sooner the better."

"And if Agnes jumbled enough men she could find one to

kill Mr. Breary," Martha said. "And *that* would put the old goat in a bind."

I nodded. "If he had to choose between seeing his wife hanged, or finding someone to die in her place, there's no question which he would select. So he could hang Will in order to hide his own guilt *or* Agnes's. And that doesn't even account for Joseph . . ."

"Who would leap at any excuse to see Will on the gallows, no matter who killed Mr. Breary," Martha finished my thought.

"Lord help us, we've found ourselves in quite a web," I said.

"I'd rather we not wait for the Lord's help," Martha replied. "We must make our own way out."

As we considered our options, Sugar wandered out of the kitchen and meowed. His appearance reminded me that our problems went much further than Will, the Lord Mayor, and Joseph.

"And then there's Rebecca Hooke," I said.

"What are we going to do?" Martha asked. "There are so many threatening clouds."

"I don't know," I said.

In less troubled times, if the city were visited by the plague or some other disaster, I'd simply hire a carriage and send Elizabeth and Hannah to one of my estates. I would stay in York if I thought I could help, or go along if Elizabeth needed me. Martha could do as she wished. But either way I knew how to keep my family safe.

The problem, of course, was that a witch-hunt was not the same as the plague or a flood, and we did not live in ordinary times. Martha and I could not flee the city so long as Will remained in gaol, for without us to defend him, he would surely be hanged. And with the lawlessness that had overtaken England thanks to our civil wars, robbers and thieves haunted the roads like never before. Sending Elizabeth and Hannah away would be no less dangerous than keeping them in York. We were trapped in the city as surely as we had been during the siege of 1644.

"We must find an advantage over Joseph," I said. "He is the keystone to both the witch-hunt and Will's arrest. If we could bend him to our will or drive him from the city, the battle would soon turn in our direction." I paused for a moment. "The chapman Peter Newcome says we should write a book."

"A book?" Martha asked. She made no effort to hide her skepticism.

"He says if we turn the people against Joseph, he will have to relent."

"Or perhaps we should follow Joseph's example," Martha ventured.

"Joseph?" I asked. "What do you mean?"

Martha hesitated a moment before continuing. "When he faces a threat, he reacts like the soldier he was, with violence. We should do the same."

I stared at her for a moment, quite unable to believe what she had proposed. "You should like us to murder Joseph?" I asked at last.

"If he were dead, Rebecca would lose her power, and Will would be freed from prison."

I searched her face for some sign that she spoke in jest. She met my gaze and did not look away.

"Helen Wright's man might do it for us," she added. "Will's life would be worth the price, wouldn't it?"

I stared at Martha, struck entirely dumb. My surprise came

in part from the audacity of her proposal, but true shock lay elsewhere: My first reaction was not to reject Martha's idea but to consider the risks and benefits. Could such a plan work? If we succeeded, we would be free from the many dangers that surrounded us. But even success at killing Joseph would mean nothing if we were caught. Will might walk free, but Martha and I would take his place on the gibbet. I also knew that if we failed, Joseph's response would be to hang Martha and me alongside Will. And what then would become of Elizabeth? To my shame, it was only after weighing the worldly risks that it occured to me that murdering Joseph would be a terrible sin.

"We cannot," I replied after far too long a pause. I did not know if I rejected the scheme for the danger it presented to our bodies or to our souls. I prayed it was my fear of damnation, but I could not be sure.

Martha nodded but did not reply.

"And you will not go behind my back," I added. "I will not have you party to murder."

Martha hesitated before nodding again. She did not like my decision, but she would not disobey me.

"What then do you propose?" she asked. "We cannot write a book and leave it at that."

"Perhaps we should bring down Rebecca Hooke."

"After she threatened Elizabeth?" Martha asked in amazement. "Do you want to antagonize her?"

I had to admit that Martha had a good point. Rebecca had plenty of other witches to keep her busy. While I did not want to attract her attention I did not see any other options.

"The battle is already begun," I said. "Joseph and Rebecca are regiments in the same army. If we defeat the one, we can more easily defeat the other."

"Then we should start with James," Martha said. "He has long been Rebecca Hooke's weakest flank."

I nodded in agreement. "We will find him and talk to him alone."

When afternoon came, Martha went in search of James, starting at the alehouse nearest the house he shared with his mother. It was not long before she returned.

"He's up on Petergate," she said as we hurried toward the Minster. There was no telling how long he'd stay, and we did not want to lose track of him. "He'd just started drinking, and I sent a penny to the barman for another, so we should find him there still."

When we arrived at the alehouse I peered through the window and saw James sitting by himself in the corner. He stared at his ale, oblivious to those around him. Martha and I stepped through he door and the smell of the place washed over us, a heady mix of spilled ale, well-cooked meats, and tobacco smoke. The rough-hewn tables were crowded as the city's residents gathered together for the warmth of drink, conversation, and a roaring fire in the hearth. James was the only one sitting alone. At times like this I could not help feeling sorry for the boy. He was unloved by anyone, even his mother.

When the barman saw us enter he furrowed his brow in confusion. While his was not the most disreputable house in York (that honor went to the Black Swan), I did not imagine that women of quality often darkened his door.

"One more for the lad in the corner," I said as Martha and I crossed to James. "And ale for each of us."

James looked up when we joined him. "I've seen this play before," he said as we sat. His voice hardly rose above a whisper, and I had to lean toward him to make out his words. "You've come to me about witches and murders, haven't you?"

"I do not come to you by choice, James, but out of necessity," I replied. "I am simply trying to see that justice is done."

"By now it must be a faint hope, eh, Lady Bridget? From what I've seen, when you are involved, the innocent are condemned, and the guilty escape trial only to be hanged from the rafters." James had been a part of the previous summer's killings, and he knew as well as anyone the shortcomings of the law.

"The guilty paid for their crimes," I said. "Eventually." I could hear the doubt in my own voice.

"Some were guilty, some innocent," James replied. "You know that."

I could not meet his eyes, for he spoke the truth.

"So this is why you are here, isn't it?" he continued. "You seek an advantage over your enemies and hope that I can supply it . . . again."

I had never seen this combative side of James before, and did not know quite how to respond. In the past, he'd been a good-natured fool; now he seemed angry and watchful.

"We want to find out who killed George Breary," Martha said.

"I thought they had taken a man for that crime," James said with a cruel smile. "It was your nephew, wasn't it, Lady Bridget? It is funny how fortunes change so quickly."

"Will did not kill him," Martha said. James heard the edge in her voice and looked up.

"No, I don't imagine he did," James said, his words barely audible over the noise of the other customers. "That would not be like him at all."

"Do you know something of Mr. Breary's death?" I asked.

"That is not what you want to know," James said. "You want me to betray my mother, to play the Judas." He paused for a moment, considering his words. "I wonder . . . If I delivered her into your hands, would that make you Pilate or the Pharisees?"

At that moment the barman appeared with our drinks, and James laughed out loud. "Oh, Lady Bridget, you are as predictable as the sunrise. *Let us ply James Hooke with drink, and see if he will betray his mother!* You take me for a fool, don't you? And perhaps I was, but not any more."

"I just want to see the guilty punished," I replied. "And Will is not guilty. Tell me what you know."

"You want me to say that my mother killed him," James said. "Admit that, and I'll tell you what I have heard."

I glanced at Martha, who seemed as confused as I was by this change in James. In the space of two years, he had fallen in love twice, and twice he'd seen his beloved flee the city for fear of her life. He'd lost a father and a child, and so thoroughly disappointed his mother it was a wonder she allowed him to stay in her home. But as I gazed at him I saw something new in his eyes, something of the hardness and cruelty that made Rebecca such a dangerous woman.

"If your mother means to destroy me, I must defend myself," I replied. "Surely you can understand that."

James shrugged. "That is not my concern. But if you are looking for Mr. Breary's murderer, look to your kin, not mine."

"Tell us what you know, James," Martha said.

"Open your eyes," he said at last. "It was your nephew, Joseph. If he didn't kill Mr. Breary, he had it done."

"How do you know?" I asked.

"I'll not give you proof, if that's what you seek," James replied. "You'll have to find that on your own."

"Tell me how you know," I said. "You must."

James sighed and began to speak. "After the Council meeting, Joseph and Mark Preston came to our house. They seemed worried about their plans for the witch-hunt. Mr. Breary had arranged to hire a Witch Finder to replace Joseph. If that happened, Joseph would be in danger of losing his some of his power in the city, not to mention his ability to overwawe the other Aldermen. At least that was his fear."

"How do you know all this?" I asked.

"When he's angry he raises his voice," James replied. "And if you are standing with your ear to the door, you can hear every word."

"You heard him say he would kill Mr. Breary?" I asked.

"Not in those words. He simply said that he would stop the Witch Finder from coming no matter what the cost. He never said he'd resort to murder, but my mother knew what he meant and tried to talk him out of it. She said Mr. Breary was a citizen and Alderman, not some poor old hag. He had friends who would defend and avenge him."

"But she did not convince him?"

"Not nearly. Joseph and his man thundered out, angrier than when they came. *I know how to end our troubles*, was the last thing he said."

"What did your mother say to that?" Martha asked.

"She said if he went through with his plan, they'd both be ruined. She told him that he was a crack-brain, and that she'd not be brought down by his foolishness. But she said it to his back. If he intended to kill Mr. Breary, there was no stopping him."

"Do you think Joseph Hodgson killed Mr. Breary?" I asked.

"If he didn't, his man did," James replied. "The two of them marched out of our house as if they were going to war."

I put my hand on James's arm and squeezed. "Thank you, James," I said. "You did the right thing."

He looked at me with a thin smile. "Perhaps," he said. "God will judge me. But I'm not sure my mother would appreciate it."

"She'll not hear about it from me," I reassured him.

Martha and I stood and slipped out of the alehouse. "What do we do now?" Martha asked. We were walking west on Petergate and had nearly reached St. Michael's church and the Minster.

"Let us speak to Will," I replied. "He should know what we have discovered. He also might have an idea about how to approach Joseph."

As we passed in front of the Minster, I caught sight of Peter Newcome and his boy hawking pamphlets to passersby. For a moment I returned to his suggestion that I counter Joseph's pamphlet—the one that accused Will of murder—with a pamphlet of my own, one pointing at Joseph. Could a book save Will from execution?

On this day one of Will's jailors answered the door of Peter's Prison. "Who are you?" he snarled through the crack in the door.

"We are here to see Will Hodgson," I replied.

"You'll have to pay," he demanded. "Nothing's free." With a sigh I reached for my purse. Our transaction complete, the jailor ushered us inside. We found Will sitting on a bench against the wall reading a Bible. Martha furrowed her brow at the sight, and I must confess to my own surprise. Will favored religion more than Martha, but I'd never seen him seek out such reading. For a moment I wondered if he had heard that he would soon be tried for George Breary's murder and sought solace in God.

Will glanced at his jailor and without a word inclined his head toward the rough wood stairs leading to the prisoners' cells. I nodded, and we followed him down. The weak light provided by the small lamp Will carried showed stone walls glistening with moisture, and within moments I could feel the cold seeping deep into my flesh.

"My keepers don't read much," Will said, holding up the Bible. "If you'd bring me something else to read, I'd welcome it." I could only hope that Joseph's pamphlet would not come to Peter's Prison. If Will learned of his conviction in the press, he would lose all hope.

"Are there other prisoners here?" I asked as we made our way down the hall.

"I've got plenty of company," Will replied. "At least a dozen. But none of them can afford the payment to stay upstairs. So they're locked down here all the day." Peter's Prison included a half dozen cells, and I wondered how many of its inmates would perish before their trials. We reached the end of the hall, and an open door. We followed Will into his cell, and I shook my head in despair. The room was barely large enough for the bed it contained, and—though I'd not have thought it possible—it seemed colder than the hall outside.

"We'll keep our voices down," Will said. "The guards won't hear us, but if one of the other prisoners thinks he can trade some news for an extra blanket he'll do it."

Martha and I nodded.

"Have you any news?" he asked.

I glanced at Martha. We'd not discussed how much to tell

Will. I was reluctant to mention his impending trial. Who could know how he would react?

"We spoke to James Hooke," Martha replied. "To find out what he might know about Mr. Breary's death."

Will smiled ruefully. "Poor sot, saddled with such a mother. What did he say?"

I described the conversation that James had overheard. "Joseph and Mark Preston intended to kill George," I concluded. "And there's no reason to think that they didn't."

Will shook his head. "But why would they then burn his papers?" he asked. "What is to be gained from that? And what about the Lord Mayor? He had as much reason to kill Mr. Breary as Joseph did."

I could see that Will still clung to the faint hope that Joseph might not be so bad a man as Martha and I thought, and my heart ached for him.

"But if James is telling the truth, we know that your brother compassed Mr. Breary's death," Martha said.

I could see Will preparing to argue the point, but I interrupted. "The question of who *did* kill George is less important than the fact that you did not," I pointed out. "And our first priority is to win you your freedom, and get you out of the shadow of these suspicions."

"Well, I can't argue with that," Will said with a thin smile. "But how?"

"We'll borrow a page from Joseph," I replied. "He published books to advance his cause, we'll publish one to advance our own. If we can turn the city in your favor, the Lord Mayor will have a harder time finding a jury to convict you."

Will nodded in agreement. "Then I guess you'll have to take up the pen."

Chapter 15

After we returned home, Martha and I spent the rest of the day in the dining room planning and writing our answer to Joseph's accusations against Will. We hunched over ink-stained pages, trying different phrases and restarting our work more times than I care to remember.

"We must find a way to lay the murder at Joseph's doorstep, but still hide our hands," Martha said.

I agreed, though I did not think Joseph would be fooled for long. But what other choice did we have?

"Joseph was right in connecting George Breary's death with Edward Hodgson's," I said. "But we can put them both on Joseph rather than Will."

Martha nodded. "It was Joseph who gained power and wealth from their father's death, not Will," she replied, scribbling her ideas as she spoke. "Will has gained nothing but suffering."

"Aye," I said. "When Edward died, it was Joseph who took over his household and expelled his younger brother . . . no, his

170

crippled younger brother." I knew Will would not appreciate the reference to his misshapen foot, but our goal was to gain sympathy from the city, not appeal to his pride.

"And when Mr. Breary challenged his plans for a witch-hunt, Joseph acted as he always has—with violence," Martha concluded with a flourish.

We continued to polish our pamphlet until it shone like the stones in my favored necklace. At every turn we reminded the reader that Joseph had far more to gain from Edward's and George's deaths than Will did. As we wove together the various strands of our story, I felt increasingly confident that our plan would bear fruit. It helped, of course, that we truly believed in Joseph's guilt, and to our eyes, the indictment seemed irrefutable: Joseph had killed countless men in wartime, and he'd brought the fight back to York, killing his enemies in the city as easily as he had on the battlefield.

When we had finished our work, Martha and I hurried to the shop behind the Minster. The same young man that Elizabeth and I had met the week before answered our knock. Over his shoulder I could see a boy pulling a sheet of paper off the press and replacing it with a new one.

"Business is still good, it seems," I said by way of greeting.

The printer smiled and shook his head in wonder at his good fortune. "In troubled times, people crave news, whether it is true or not. What brings you back to my shop, my lady?"

"More business for you," I said, handing him the sheets that Martha and I had written. "I should like these printed and given to the city's chapmen."

As the printer read our work I could see the growing concern on his face. When he finished, he tried to hand them back. "My lady, I cannot print these," he said. "You know very well what Mr. Hodgson's reaction would be. He would see me out of business without a moment's hesitation."

"I'll pay you well for your trouble," I replied. "Pounds, not pence." I knew that he could not earn more than two pounds a month, and if I could buy Will's freedom for that price it would be money well spent.

"You could claim it was printed elsewhere," Martha suggested. "Put *Printed in Hull* on the cover, and then dispose of all your copies. There will be no way to prove the contrary."

The printer still seemed uncertain, but I could tell that we had his attention. I handed him a purse of coins in an effort to close the deal.

"No reason it couldn't have come from Hull," he said as he hefted the purse. "And with this I could hire another boy. I'll have it ready in a week."

I looked at him aghast. "We haven't got a week," I said. "A week would be too late." I caught a glint in his eye—a glint the color of a silver coin—and realized what he was doing. It was not often a printer could claim the upper hand in such a matter, but we both knew that he had it.

"I have far more work than time, my lady," he replied. "And I should like to keep the customers I have."

I sighed and handed him a few more coins. "This should compensate for your loss," I said.

"Yes, it should," he replied. He looked once again through the sheets we'd given him. "It's not long, so I should have the book to the chapmen by Friday." My face must have betrayed my disappointment. "Between setting the type, the cutting, and the sewing, that is the best I can do. The work takes time," he explained.

I nodded. "Very well. Friday it is." We bid the printer farewell and hurried back to my house, our shoulders hunched against the cold.

"Joseph will be furious," Martha said as we stepped inside. "And he will surely suspect that you are behind the book."

I knew this, of course, and the sound of Elizabeth clattering down the steps to greet us reminded me that my love for her was my greatest vulnerability. Rebecca Hooke had already threatened her, and I knew that the danger was real. Elizabeth threw herself into my arms, and I felt my heart overflow with love and fear. *What could I do to keep her safe from my enemies?*

This question kept me awake for hours after I climbed into my bed, but even sleep offered no respite. In my dreams, I ran pell-mell through York's streets and alleyways. Sometimes I pursued a hooded figure that I somehow knew to be George Breary's murderer. Several times I nearly caught hold of his hood and revealed his face, but at the last moment he ducked from my grasp, and my voice echoed off the cobblestone streets when I cried out in rage and frustration. In other dreams—or perhaps they were the same ones—I searched for Elizabeth as she tried desperately to escape a predator of her own. But she proved no less elusive than George's murderer. I sometimes caught glimpses of red hair as she turned down an alley, but I could never come close enough to take her in my arms.

When I awoke I wondered if *I* was the one from whom she fled. At the same time my pamphlet might save Will, it would infuriate Joseph beyond measure. And for all I knew, he would turn his rage on Elizabeth. What better way to exact his revenge?

I lay in bed telling myself that while he was a violent man, Joseph had never harmed a child. I prayed that his honor would keep him from doing so on this occasion. I then resolved to keep Elizabeth indoors until the witch-hunt had ended and George's killer had been hanged. What else could I do? I felt like a man trying to escape a maze, never knowing if my next step would take me to freedom or down another blind alley. All I could do was continue my search for an escape.

A full two hours before sunrise a boy arrived at my door and threw all our schemes into confusion. "I have a summons to the Castle, my lady," he announced. He handed me a letter held closed with an impressive seal of red wax.

As I broke the seal, Martha appeared at my side, no less worried than I was. In the past week, we'd accused the Lord Mayor's wife of murder and then written a pamphlet against the city's most powerful Alderman. It seemed unlikely that official correspondence would bring good news. It was almost a relief that the letter did nothing more than summon Martha and me to the trial of Mother Lee on charges of witchcraft.

"They've found judges for the Special Assizes," I said as I read the letter. "We're to testify against Mother Lee today."

We spent the morning gathering the food and drink needed for a day at the Castle. Victuallers would flock there, but their offerings would be better suited for the lower sort, and they'd charge a fortune. Elizabeth begged to accompany us, of course, but mindful of my dream, I denied her. Before we left, I pulled Hannah aside.

"I want you to keep Elizabeth indoors," I said. "Anything you need from the market can wait, or you can send a neighborhood boy for it. I don't want her to attract any attention at all." Between her blazing red hair and talkative habits, Elizabeth was well known throughout St. Helen's, but I had no interest in reminding my neighbors of her presence. I knew Joseph would not forget I'd brought her into my home, but the less people thought of her, the safer she would be. Hannah cast a worried look in Elizabeth's direction and agreed. Martha and I wrapped ourselves, bid farewell to Hannah and Elizabeth, and started for the Castle.

"What are you going to tell them?" Martha asked as we walked up Coney Street. The letter said the trial would be in the afternoon, but I wanted to arrive early and get a sense of the direction other trials had taken.

"Remember that we've both been called," I replied. "So you'll have to speak as well."

"That is why I asked," she said. "As midwife and deputy, we should not contradict each other."

"I'll tell the truth," I replied. I knew so vague an answer would not satisfy her in the least. "I'll tell the jury what I saw. I cannot say if the child's death was natural or if he had been bewitched." Even as I spoke, I could imagine the reaction of Lucy Pierce's gossips when I did not fully agree with their accusations. If I were not careful, the mothers in Upper Poppleton would turn to another midwife. "But in the end the trial will not hinge on my words or yours."

"It will be Rebecca Hooke's," Martha said.

"Aye," I replied. "Between the gossips, Rebecca Hooke, and her own malicious carriage, Mother Lee's fate is sealed no matter what we say."

As I expected, when we crossed the bridge into the Castle yard, we found it a hive of activity. Members of the Town Watch stood about awaiting instructions, while boys raced between buildings, wax-sealed papers in hand, cloaks billowing behind them. A few shopkeepers had already built their stalls and they cried out their wares as we passed. Martha and I fought our way through the crowd toward Samuel's tower. Since he held Mother Lee, it seemed likely that he'd know when and where she would be tried.

Tree greeted us when he opened the tower door, and he quickly relieved us of our baskets of food. I knew that they would be considerably lighter—and he would be much the fatter—by the time he returned them, but there was little in the world that I could deny him.

Samuel called out a greeting as he descended the stairs, struggling under the weight of an overfull bucket of waste. "I know you were thinking about quitting midwifery for the life of a jailor," he said, "but I should tell you that it is not all gold coins and dinner with the Lord Mayor." He put the bucket by the door and turned to Tree. "Boy, empty this in the jakes before you eat."

Tree wrinkled his nose at the smell but did not object.

Once he'd gone, Samuel turned to me. "I imagine you're here for Mother Lee," he said.

"Aye," I replied. "I received my summons this morning. They are in quite a hurry to begin the trials. Have you heard other news?"

"That is why I sent Tree out," Samuel replied. "The judges are moving forward with Will's trial. It will start within a week."

I stared at Samuel, my mouth agape. I could see the blood run from Martha's face.

"A week?" I cried. "How so?"

"It is a blessing he has that long," Samuel replied. "Joseph wanted to hold the trial today, but the judges denied him. They said they had been summoned to try witches, and would have those cases first. Thank God for small mercies."

"And thank God there will be no trials on the Sabbath," I agreed. "We have a few days at least."

"A few days?" Martha cried. "What can we accomplish in that time?" Her eyes darted about the room, as if the keys to Will's freedom were hidden somewhere within. "God only knows what evidence Joseph has conjured. You know that if Will is tried he will hang! What will we do?" She nearly shouted these last words. I tried to put my arms about her, but she shook me off and began to pace the room.

"We will save him," I replied, though in truth I did not see how we would. "We must."

"To hell with the trial," Martha replied. "I'm leaving. They can hang Mother Lee without me." She threw open the tower door and started across the Castle yard.

"If the bailiffs come looking for me, tell them you don't know where I am," I said to Samuel and raced after her.

I caught up with Martha, and together we hurried toward the gate. I did not know what she intended, but the look in her eyes told me that she would not be stopped for anything in the world. That is what I thought, at least, until Matthew Greenbury appeared before us, resplendent in the Lord Mayor's finery. To my dismay, Joseph Hodgson stood at his side and Mark Preston loomed behind them both.

"Good morning, Lady Bridget," said Greenbury with a bow. "It is a pleasure to see you." I searched the leathery contours of his face for some sign of insincerity. Despite James Hooke's belief that Joseph had arranged George Breary's murder, the sight of the Lord Mayor reminded me that he, too, had his reasons to see George dead.

"Good morning, my Lord Mayor," I replied. "I trust the winter cold is not discomforting you overmuch?"

The Lord Mayor smiled thinly. "It is hard on these old bones, but the Lord has his reasons, doesn't He, Mr. Hodgson?" He cast a glance toward Joseph, who nodded solemnly and muttered something that sounded like *Amen.* "What brings you to the Castle?" Greenbury continued.

"My deputy and I have been summoned to testify in a witchcraft trial," I replied. Even as I spoke, my mind raced to find a way to explain our hurried departure. "But it seems the trial will not be held until the afternoon. We will return then."

"Oh, dear, I am so sorry for the inconvenience," Greenbury said. His disappointment seemed genuine, but I could not be sure.

Joseph stepped forward and whispered a few words in the Lord Mayor's ear. I could not hear them, but my stomach sank, for I knew they could not work in our favor.

"Excellent idea, my boy," the Lord Mayor cried, and beckoned for one of his men. "Tell the sergeant that we will try Mother Lee first." The man nodded and hurried toward the Warden's offices. "It will take some time, but we will search out the other witnesses and try your case this morning," Greenbury announced with a smile. "Come and sit with me until we are ready to begin. It has been too long since we talked."

I risked a glance at Martha and saw panic rising within her. "Thank you, my Lord Mayor," I responded. What else could I say?

"The sooner we can dispose of this matter, the better," Greenbury continued. "And with you and Mr. Hodgson here at the Castle, nothing of import can happen in the city, can it?" The Lord Mayor chuckled at his own flattery. I could offer only the thinnest of smiles.

So Martha and I joined the crowd crossing the Castle yard to the courtroom where we would await Mother Lee's trial.

To their credit, the Lord Mayor's men gathered the witnesses against Mother Lee far more quickly than I would have thought possible, and in only an hour the witnesses, bailiffs, and jurymen gathered in the hall. Dried flowers had been strewn on the floor to prevent the spread of gaol-fever, so—for the moment at least—the room smelled curiously of spring.

The judge sat at an elevated table and peered at the crowd gathered before him. If the Lord Mayor qualified as aged, the judge was positively ancient.

"My god, where did they find such a huddle-duddle?" Martha whispered. "It'll be a miracle if he lives through the trial."

"They were in a hurry, I suppose," I replied. "And not in a position to be particular."

The judge looked around the room as if he was not entirely sure why he was there or what he should do next. Joseph apparently saw the same thing, and he crept to the judge's side to whisper something in his ear. The judge nodded his approval, picked up a small wooden silence, and knocked it on the table three times before the hammer fell from his hand. A few men glanced at the bench, but the hubbub continued unabated. Martha covered her mouth to hide a smile.

"He is a clownish one to be sure," I said. "But who do you think will be the true master of these trials?"

Martha's smile disappeared. "He'll do Joseph's bidding."

"Aye. Joseph has planned every step in his journey, from the pamphlets to hiring Rebecca as his Searcher. Of course he'll find a malleable judge to oversee the trials."

"And if he's the one who oversees Will's trial . . . ," Martha said. I could hear the fear in her voice.

I finished her dreadful thought. "He'll demand that the jury return a guilty verdict." Though I had never seen the practice myself, I had heard of judges who kept the jurymen without food for days on end until they rendered the desired verdict. While such cases were rare, I had no doubt that Joseph would bend the law to meet his ends.

"Quiet!" a voice cried. "The court is in session!"

My pulse raced as Mark Preston strode toward the jury, his mere presence threatening great violence against those who did not heed his words. The jurymen, and everyone else in the room for that matter, fell into complete silence.

The judge looked up at Preston as if surprised to see him, but he said nothing. With an exasperated sigh, Joseph crossed the room and whispered in the court clerk's ear.

"The first case we will hear is that of Mother Lee," the clerk announced. "The charge is the most damnable sin and crime of witchcraft."

A door behind the bench opened, and two bailiffs led Mother Lee, shackled hand and foot, into the courtroom to begin what would be her last day on earth.

Chapter 16

Mother Lee's time in gaol had done her no favors. Though some life remained in her eyes, she was far more pinched and gaunt than when I'd last seen her. When she entered the room she inspected the faces of the jurymen and the judge before turning her gaze on the rest of us. Perhaps she hoped to find a friend or a neighbor who had not turned against her. One of the bailiffs nudged her, and she shuffled forward, her shackles clanking and scraping as she crossed the room. I could not help noticing the cuts and scabs on her wrists where her aged flesh had been scraped raw and bleeding. Mother Lee turned to face the judge, who stared back, utterly unsure of what to do. Joseph climbed up onto the bench and gave the judge his orders.

"The clerk should charge the accused," the old man said.

The court clerk stepped forward and announced the grand jury's charges against Mother Lee, that by witchcraft she had murdered Lucy Pierce's infant son.

"What is your plea?" the clerk asked.

"Not guilty." Mother Lee's voice echoed through the hall with surprising strength.

I did not for a moment think the plea meant much. The trial was not about determining guilt or innocence. It was a play to show all the world, and God as well, that the city's magistrates had taken up arms against Satan and were marching under the Lord's standard.

"The first witness!" The judge's voice creaked like a wooden axle one turn from breaking.

The prosecutor stepped forward. His clothes made clear his wealth, and he preened before the crowd like a peacock: a fine wool cloak layered over a blue silken doublet, leather boots in the latest style, turned down just below the knee to show expensive silk stockings. He was quite a creature. The first few witnesses were Mother Lee's neighbors from Upper Poppleton. Some had been present when I delivered Lucy Pierce, and some had not, but all told the same story. Mother Lee had long been suspected of trafficking with the Devil. She had cursed her neighbors' crops, their cows, their sheep, their butter churns, their ale pans. And finally, she had bewitched Lucy Pierce's son, and he died even before he'd been born. Lucy herself told the jury of this crime, and they hung on every word as if it might be the last they'd ever hear.

And then it was my turn. I strode to the front of the room and stood next to the bench. I had no illusions that I could do anything to change the course of the proceedings, but my heart hammered in my chest all the same.

"Lady Hodgson," the prosecutor began. "You delivered Lucy Pierce of a stillborn child, did you not?"

"Yes," I replied. Better to say as little as possible, I thought.

"How would you describe the child?"

I knew the answer he sought, of course. He wanted me to say that the child's death had been unlike any I had ever seen, and thus unnatural. If he could show the jury that the child's death had been unnatural, he'd have won the day; witchcraft was the only other possible cause.

"Mrs. Pierce had reached her full term," I replied. "The child had his fingernails, which happens just before birth."

The prosecutor grimaced. He'd been hoping for a bit more cooperation from me. I could also see some of Lucy Pierce's friends looking at each other and whispering behind their hands.

"Have you ever seen a birth such as Mrs. Pierce's?" the prosecutor asked.

"A stillborn birth? Of course. I've been a midwife for many years, and attended hundreds of women in their travail. It is the Lord's will that some children live while others die." The prosecutor seemed to have developed a twitch near his left eye. He looked at Joseph, unsure how to proceed. Joseph's only reply was a slight shrug. *I warned you about her*, it seemed to say.

"Lady Hodgson, was the death of Lucy Pierce's child natural or unnatural?"

"It was the Lord's will," I replied. "The devil can do nothing on this earth without His permission."

The prosecutor furrowed his brow at my answer. While it was undoubtedly true (for who would deny God's omnipotence?), it did turn the jury's eyes away from Mother Lee. After a moment's consideration, he crossed the room to consult with Joseph. He whispered in Joseph's ear and nodded in Martha's direction.

Joseph's eyes bulged.

"No, you shouldn't call her. Not if you have a brain in your head," he hissed. "She's worse than her mistress."

I had to suppress a smile.

"Thank you, Lady Hodgson, that is all," the prosecutor said. He did not sound particularly thankful. I returned to Martha's side, and she offered a hint of a smile.

"Mrs. Rebecca Hooke!" the bailiff called out, and I felt my stomach drop. Of course she would appear—she had searched Mother Lee's body—but I had been so concerned with my own testimony I'd not thought on it.

Rebecca strode forward from the rear of the hall and took her place where I'd stood just moments before.

"You inspected the body of the accused witch, did you not?"

"Yes, my lord, I did," Rebecca replied. Her voice echoed strong and clear through the hall.

"And what did you find?"

"It was a difficult search, my lord," Rebecca replied. "At first she refused to be inspected." She paused to let the jury consider what such resistance might mean. Would an innocent woman refuse to be searched? "When we stripped her bare, I found three long teats in her secret parts. They seemed to have been sucked of late."

The prosecutor nodded in satisfaction. "And what do you think those teats were?"

"They were wholly unnatural," Rebecca said. "They could only be the teats from which her familiars suckled."

"And what did Mother Lee say when she was confronted with this evidence?"

"At first she denied it. She claimed that they were hemorrhoids and that she'd suffered from them for many years."

"What did you say to this?"

"I told her that they were no hemorrhoids, that she'd had traffic with Satan's imps. She denied it, but I pressed her further and again. I told her that such marks could only have come from the devil and that she must tell the truth. It took many hours and much pressing, but she soon saw that I spoke the truth. She told me that the imps must have come to her in her sleep and suckled then. It was the only way she could have gotten such teats."

"So she confessed to you that she is a witch?"

Rebecca nodded emphatically. "Yes, my lord, she did."

The prosecutor smiled, clearly pleased to have regained control of the trial. "Thank you, Mrs. Hooke."

The last witness was Mother Lee. The bailiffs led her to the front of the hall and left her there. She looked around the room at her neighbors, the women who had just condemned her to death. I saw no sign that she hated them for it.

The prosecutor stepped to the middle of the room and placed his hands on his hips. He sensed that victory was near and was enjoying the moment.

"When did Satan first come to you?" he asked.

"Some years ago," she replied. "Six or seven. It was about a year after my husband died. My son had gone to London in search of work."

The prosecutor strode forward and looked into Mother Lee's eyes. "And you lay with the devil when he came to you. You let that infernal creature have carnal knowledge of your body." It was less a question than a statement.

Mother Lee held his gaze. "Why do you want to know that?"

"We must have the truth," the prosecutor responded. "Tell me—did the devil have use of your body?"

"Aye," Mother Lee said at last. "He promised he would protect me, and send his imps to act as my servants. My house was in such disorder, and food was so dear. So I lay with him."

The prosecutor smiled. Mother Lee was as good as hanged. "What was the devil like? What form did he take?"

"He was tall and handsome with black hair. He was a proper gentleman, more proper than you are."

The prosecutor's smile faded for a moment as the jurymen enjoyed a laugh at his expense. Rather than risk further humiliation, the prosecutor turned to the judge and announced that he had finished. The judge nodded—or perhaps fell to napping—and the bailiff led Mother Lee from the room. The prosecutor then announced the name of the next woman to be tried. Martha and I edged toward the door and slipped into the Castle yard.

"They will find her guilty," Martha said as we hurried to the gate.

"Aye, with her confession there can be no doubt of that."

"Will all the women hang? There are so many . . ."

"It will depend on how strong they are and how far they were pressed. If they confess before the jury, they are finished to be sure."

"What are we going to do about Will?" Martha asked. "If they try him in that sort of court, he will receive the same sort of justice."

"I have been trying to find a solution. . . ." My voice trailed off.

Martha's laugh had a bitter edge. "And have you discovered a lawful escape for him?"

I shook my head. "The law is set against him, and there is no lawful thing we can do to oppose it."

"What?" Martha cried, fury visible on her face. "So we let

him try his fortune in court? Have you gone mad?" Martha made no effort to hide her anger, and passersby looked shocked that a maid would address her mistress in such a fashion. I could only image the gossip that would run through the markets after such a show.

"Of course not," I replied, taking her arm. "We will smuggle him out of the city. With a good horse and a full purse he'll have no trouble making his way to my estates in Hereford. Joseph's writ won't run so far as that. Eventually we can join him, or—if Joseph falls from power—he can safely return to York." I could see the tension run from Martha's body at my words. "Surely you didn't think I'd let him hang, did you?"

Martha thought for a moment before answering. "I know you favor the law above all else. You've caused bastard-bearers to be whipped, sent ravishers to the gallows, and felt no sorrow along the way. You love the part you play in keeping order—it is why you sided with the King even as your kin chose Parliament. Last summer you stood ready to see a murderer walk free because the law could not act."

She paused once again, perhaps wondering how far she could go. I nodded for her to continue.

"In the past you have been guided by what is lawful rather than what is right. Most often I cannot call this a fault, for I'd see ravishers hanged as soon as you would. But at times you love the law too much. It is the law that whips an unwedded mother, but exacts no such price from the man who fathered the child. There is no justice in this, but you have seen it done and thought it right. I could not help wondering if you would ever oppose the law in so open a fashion. If you help Will escape, you will become an outlaw."

By the time Martha finished speaking we had drawn to a

stop. I took her hands and looked her in the eye. "We live in a world turned upside down," I said. "Parliament has its foot on his Majesty's neck, and the true worship of God has been overthrown by plain men and their sermons. Worse, the law has become a weapon for the strong to destroy the weak."

"It has always been thus with the law. You simply closed your eyes to the truth."

"No," I replied. "The times have changed, and we must change as well. We have no choice but to pluck Will from his prison and see him out of the city. I will not let him hang for a murder he did not commit."

"Perhaps that is where we part ways," Martha said. "I would not let him hang for a murder he *did* commit."

Martha and I ate a small dinner of bread and cheese as we talked through our scheme to free Will. The guards at Peter's Prison were so loose, it would not take us long, and once he escaped, he'd simply have to find his way out of the city. It seemed absurdly easy.

We reached Peter's Prison, and Martha pounded on the door. A few moments later, one of the jailors opened it and gestured for us to enter.

"Come in, come in, before the wind does," he urged us.

Inside we found Will, his jailors, and two other prisoners sitting at a table playing at cards. If the coins before them were any measure, he jailors seemed to be doing very well for themselves. I counted this a good decision on Will's part.

"Martha, Aunt Bridget!" Will smiled when we entered the room. "You've rescued me from these conjurors. I've no idea how they do it." The jailors laughed, enjoying their success at gambling and the profits it brought.

"Might I have a word with my nephew?" I asked. "I will return him to his game shortly."

"So long as he brings his pennies, keep him as long as you want," cried one of the jailors as he waved us toward Will's cell. Will helped himself to a lantern and led the way down the stairs. The cell was no less cold than it had been on our previous visit, and I praised God that if all went according to plan Will soon would be free.

"You must escape and flee the city," Martha whispered as soon as the door shut behind us.

Will looked at us in shock. "What? What has happened? Surely things haven't become so dire so quickly!"

"I'm afraid they have," I said. "They intend to try you for Mr. Breary's murder as soon as the witch-trials are done."

Will half sat, half fell onto his pallet, his eyes suddenly wide with fear. "They said they would wait until the next Assizes. I thought we had more time. Until March."

"So did we," I replied. "But we were wrong, and we must act immediately."

Will's eyes flicked between Martha and me. I had never seen him so frightened.

"They'd not rush me to court if they intended a fair trial," Will said. "If I am tried, I'll surely be hanged."

"That is why you must escape," I said. "That you are here rather than the Castle is a stroke of luck. We've already seen that your guards are less attentive than they should be."

Will nodded. "If we supply them with sack, they'll drink themselves into a stupor. I could simply walk out the door."

"Precisely," I said. "I'll send them capons, a roast beef, and enough wine to set them spinning for days. Once they are asleep, come to my stable. I'll leave a bag of clothes and money for you there. Take one of my horses, go south to Micklegate Bar, and leave as soon as they open the gate in the morning. Your guards will still be asleep and will not have raised hue and cry. In the cold, you can cover your face and nobody will think it strange. Then it's on to Hereford. You will be safe there."

Will exhaled, and the mist of his breath rose slowly toward the cell's low ceiling. "And you will join me there?" he asked.

"As soon as we can," Martha replied.

"Moving a household takes more time," I said. "But we will come."

"Very well," Will said, rising to his feet. "The guards have all my pennies, but if I start losing shillings, they'll be in a drinking mood to be sure."

I stepped to Will and held him close. "And we will see you in Hereford."

Martha and Will locked eyes, and the pain of their impending separation filled the small room.

"I will see you soon," Will said. "I promise."

Martha nodded, and we started up the stairs. When we reached the main room, I announced my plans to send over a feast worthy of the Lord Mayor himself, and the guards cheered heartily.

"Your nephew is a welcome guest indeed," cried out one guard, clapping Will on the back. I regretted the trouble the guards would suffer for allowing Will to escape—Joseph's wrath would be tremendous indeed—but we had few options.

Martha and I had not yet reached the door when a pounding echoed through the room.

"God's blood, is someone trying to break *in* to the prison?" one of the guards shouted as he crossed to the door. "What is it? What is it?"

As soon as he pulled back the bar, the door burst open and half a dozen members of the Town Watch charged into the room. At least two had been with the squad who took Will from my house, and they still bore the marks of that skirmish. The one Will had battered the worst crossed the room and drove the butt of his musket into Will's stomach. Will crumpled to the floor without a sound. I cried out in shock, and Martha hurled herself at Will's assailant, ready to do battle. Another of the watchmen, this one bearing scratches across his face, lashed out with his fist, striking Martha on the side of her head. She joined Will on the floor.

"Sergeant, what is the meaning of this?" I shouted. "By what right do you act in such a lawless fashion?"

"By order of the Lord Mayor. And before you ask, yes, we have a warrant to take your nephew." His voice dripped with disdain. As Will struggled for breath, two of the soldiers rolled him onto his stomach and bound his hands behind him. Martha rolled onto her back and struggled to rise, but the same soldier who had struck her placed his boot on her chest. She looked at me, her eyes begging me to act. My mind raced for some way to turn the situation to our favor, for I knew that if they took Will we'd have a devil of a time getting him back.

"Good work, sergeant," a voice called out. I turned to find Mark Preston standing in the doorway. A smile crossed his lupine features when he saw me.

"There you are, my lady," he said. He did not bother to bow. "Mr. Hodgson wondered where you had gone when you left the Castle in such a hurry. He hoped you might stay to hear the witch's sentencing. She is to be hanged, of course."

"Where are you taking him?" I demanded.

"Mr. Hodgson has made room for his brother in the Ouse

Bridge gaol, and he has even arranged for a special guard. We think he will be more secure there."

My heart sank. I knew that Joseph could not have discovered our plan to sneak Will out of the city, but he had foiled it all the same.

Preston saw the look on my face, and his smile widened. "Why so sad, my lady?" he asked. "Surely one cell is as good as another. Or have we interrupted some sort of scheme?"

I said nothing.

"In any event, it does not matter what you planned," Preston continued. "Mr. Hodgson will have his trial. And then his hanging. Bring him along!"

Chapter 17

Martha fought back her tears as we hurried home. The wind had risen while we were inside, rendering useless any words of comfort that might have occurred to me. We needed time and peace in order to think of a way to save Will. Unfortunately, we had neither. By the time we slammed the front door behind us, Martha had transformed her anguish into fury.

"That son of a whore kept us at the Castle so he could summon soldiers to move Will," she said through clenched teeth. "I'll kill him myself. And that half-handed monster leading the soldiers, I'll kill him, too."

I looked closely at her face to see if she spoke in earnest or merely anger. I knew all too well that when Martha made such a threat I should take her seriously.

"If you did such a thing, you and Will would simply be hanged from the same gallows," I said. "We will find another way."

"What way?" Martha asked.

I could see the despair in her eyes, and I longed to take her in my arms as I would Elizabeth, and my daughter Birdy before her. I wanted to tell her that I would keep her safe from all harm. But while Elizabeth might still believe such lies, Martha had seen too much of the world to be so easily gulled.

Martha started up the stairs toward her chamber but stopped and turned to face me. "This is what I meant when I said you had too much faith in the law. Now that we cannot so easily manage Will's escape, you will spend the night finding some way to free him by proving his innocence in court. But the truth is that the law is a blind whore. She comes when powerful men call, and then lies back while they use her as they see fit. And if you cannot see this, Will is going to hang." With that, she turned and disappeared up the stairs.

I heard a soft cry behind me and found Elizabeth standing there, her eyes wide with fright.

"Will is going to hang?" she asked before breaking down entirely.

I rushed across the room and scooped her in to my arms. "No, no, he is not going to hang," I said. I felt tears on my cheeks as my fear for Will and hatred of Joseph overwhelmed me. "I will find a way to save him. I promise." It took me nearly an hour to regain myself and bring Elizabeth back from the edge of despair. Eventually she accepted my assurances, and thanked me for keeping Will safe. My heart broke as she wandered off in search of Hannah, and I feared that I had just told the most horrid lie of my life.

But try as I might—and I did not sleep that night—I could find no way to free Will from the snare that had been laid for him. Joseph had spread so many rumors, all indicating Will's guilt, that everyone in the city thought him a murderer twice over, culpable in George's death as well as his and Joseph's father's. It was not until an hour before sunrise that I remembered the pamphlet that Martha and I had penned a few days before and that the printer had said would be finished soon. If it were read by enough people, perhaps George's friends and allies on the City Council would rediscover their courage and act against Joseph. It seemed our only hope, and I resolved to go to the printer's as soon as the sun rose and take the pamphlets throughout the city myself.

At breakfast I told Martha of my plan. "Let us go to the printer's and see how many we can distribute today," I said. "I'm sure Peter Newcome will help us as well." She nodded sullenly, utterly unconvinced that it would make any difference. I could neither disagree with her sentiment nor propose another scheme.

Even before we had gathered our cloaks, someone began to pound on the front door. Martha peered out the window. When her face paled my heart began to race.

"It is Joseph," she said. "And Mark Preston with him."

"Ah, God's blood," I swore. What could he want? To this point Joseph and I had battled each other from afar. What did it mean that he now stood at my door?

He continued to knock. "Hollo! Aunt Bridget! I know you're in there! And I saw your maidservant looking through the window!"

"Let him in," I said. I did not see any other option.

Martha opened the door, and without awaiting an invitation Joseph and Mark bulled their way into my entry hall. Joseph smiled as soon as he saw me.

"There you are, Aunt Bridget!" He spoke as if we were the closest of friends. "I hope I haven't pulled you away from more pressing work."

"What do you want?" I demanded.

Joseph reached out and seized my hand before I could snatch it away. "I told you there'd be no ink, Mark," he said as he inspected my fingertips. "She is tip-toe nice, even when she stoops to scribbling."

"Perhaps she had her maid do the writing," Preston replied, and reached for Martha's hand.

With shocking speed, Martha pulled her left hand back and lashed out with her right, punching Preston squarely in the throat. He made a gugling sound as he fought for air, and his hands clawed at his neck. Martha followed her first blow with a second, this time striking him on the face. Preston toppled like a windblown tree and lay on the hall floor gasping for breath. Martha stood over him, fists clenched, daring him to continue the battle. It had been some time since I'd seen this side of her, and I thanked the Lord she'd not lost her skills in a fight.

I turned to Joseph, unsure how he would react to seeing his man humiliated, and found him on the verge of laughter.

"Very nice," he cried, hauling Preston to his feet. "Mark, I hope you will be more careful of this one in the future. She's of a different sort than her mistress."

Preston stared at Martha, his eyes blazing as he tried to recover himself. He dropped his good hand to the dagger he wore on his belt, and my stomach roiled. Joseph grasped Preston's arm and held it tight.

"None of that," Joseph said. "You cannot murder a maidservant in her mistress's hall simply for making a fool of you." Preston relaxed, but from the look on his face I knew he soon would return for his revenge.

"Now, Aunt Bridget, back to business," Joseph said. He

brushed me aside and strode into the parlor. Unsure what to do and bewildered by his mention of *business*, I followed him. He crossed to the hearth and warmed his hands on the fire before turning to me.

"Your printer friend nearly made a very poor decision," Joseph said. He produced a cheap pamphlet from his pocket and unfolded it. He read from the cover. "*The Murderous Son Turn'd Murderous Brother*. Aunt Bridget, I have to admit it's a brilliant title. The town would have snatched these up in mere hours, even with the witch-trials. There's no sating their appetite for scandal or blood, and this one has both."

My heart sank when I realized what must have happened.

Joseph turned to the fire and tossed the pamphlet in to the flames. "That was the last copy, of course. And the printer now knows better than to even consider printing such scurrilous words about one of the city's Aldermen." He turned to face me. "The question, of course, is what I am going to do about you. You set yourself against my witch trials, you pen a pamphlet accusing me of murder, and you allow your maidservant to assault my man. Obviously, I cannot allow this to continue."

"Will did not murder George Breary, and I'll not let him hang for it," I replied. "And you both should know that I'll not rest until I see George's true murderer dead and buried."

I'd hoped my reply would give Joseph pause, but he laughed out loud.

"I have no desire to hang Will," he replied. "At least not if he is innocent. But if it does come to pass, it *would* be just. I've neither forgotten nor forgiven his role in our father's death. My brother might not have murdered Mr. Breary, but he is far from guiltless."

"Whatever the case, you should not concern yourself with

Will," Mark Preston said. His voice rattled thanks to Martha's blow. "He is safe enough in Ouse Bridge gaol."

Joseph nodded in agreement. "Were I in your place, Aunt Bridget, I would look to my little ones. They are so vulnerable. Mrs. Hooke reminded you of that, but perhaps you forgot."

Fury roared within me and tore at my throat for release. I felt my hands fly up and watched my fingers, now claws, slash at Joseph's face. If my work as a midwife did not demand short fingernails, I might have had his eyes out. As it was, I did woefully little damage before he seized my wrists and forced my hands to my sides. Then he infuriated me all the more by laughing.

"Now *this* is a side of you I've never seen!" He squeezed my wrists and twisted my arms with such force that I had no choice but to sit. He leaned over me, and his smile vanished. "Because of your rank and your work as a midwife, the city's women look to you for guidance. I cannot have you working against me. If you continue to do so, I will take your family, I will take your work, and if that is not enough I will kill you myself. When my father was alive, you had his ear, and that made you a powerful woman. But he is dead, and I am in his place. His power is now mine."

Joseph released my wrists and stepped back. My body so trembled with fear and fury I did not dare rise.

"You will let the law run its course." Joseph spoke softly, but there could be no mistaking the steel edge to his words. "The witches will be tried, and the guilty will hang. Then my brother will face a jury. I will not interfere in their verdict, but if he is convicted, he too will hang. And you will do nothing about any of this, or you will feel my wrath."

Without waiting for a response, Joseph turned on his heel and strode from the room with Preston close behind. As if to show their contempt, or perhaps my vulnerability, they left the door wide open. They could return any time they chose, and there was nothing I could do to stop them.

After Martha locked the door we sat in silence. What action could we take that would not result in further mayhem? I asked the Lord for guidance. He kept His own council.

After a few minutes Hannah bustled in from the kitchen, and she immediately felt the dread that had filled the room. "What is it?" she asked. "What has happened?"

I shook my head. "I do not know."

The rest of the morning passed with torturing slowness. Martha and I attended our work only halfheartedly and with dread as our constant companion. We knew we had to find a way to save Will, but neither of us had the slightest idea of how we might do so. It was as if we awaited some awful and unavoidable news, and could not act until we knew the worst.

A knock at the door pulled us from our state. Hannah answered and called me downstairs where I found a girl of perhaps eleven years standing in the street. She had wrapped herself in a ragged wool cloak that billowed around her.

"Lady Hodgson?" she asked. "My mother sent me for you. She is in travail."

For a moment I considered sending her to another midwife, but I realized that I was doing no good to anyone by staying home. I sent Martha for my valise, and we followed the girl into the bitter cold of the day. The girl told me her name was Jane Potter, and that her family had only recently come to the city. She had one sister, and they lived above her father's tailor shop in Coney Street parish. Her mother had heard from her neighbors that I was a ready-handed midwife, and she sent for me when her travail started.

When we arrived at the tenement, Jane took us straight to the birthing room where we found her mother, Alice, and a half dozen of her gossips. I knew most of the women, and we fell to talking as Martha went to the kitchen to make the caudle to sustain Alice during her labor. Every midwife has her own recipe for caudle—some start with wine, others with ale, and there can be no agreement on how much sugar, ginger, or saffron to add—and Martha had begun to create her own. When Martha returned, I could see the strain of the day on her face, and I recognized how out of place it seemed in a room filled with joy and laughter. I wondered if the gossips could read my face as easily as I read Martha's.

I inspected Alice and found that the child was still some hours from being born. I told the women as much, and they immediately set to gossiping. I knew they would expect me to join in the merriment, but the chill that Joseph had brought to me that morning proved heartier than the combined warmth of the room, the company, and even the wine that Alice's husband brought. I could not help contrasting the gossips' lightsome chatter with the dangers that threatened my household: Will faced hanging, Elizabeth had been menaced by both Joseph Hodgson and Rebecca Hooke, and I had been threatened with murder. What escape could there be?

Throughout the day women came and went, bringing news, a bit of food to sustain the company, and good wishes for Alice in her travail. Nothing seemed amiss until the talk turned to the trials of witches.

"If we rid ourselves of such women, it's a job well done," one young mother said, gazing into the eyes of the infant at her breast.

She spoke softly and without the anger I had heard when Upper Poppleton's women turned against Mother Lee. I realized that she said those words, words that would send dozens of women to the gallows, not out of malice, but out of the love she bore for her child. It was common knowledge children were easily bewitched, and it stood to reason that if witches thrived, infants suffered. What mother would not want to protect her children from such a malign force?

In that moment I recognized for the first time the power behind Joseph's decision to bring the witch-hunt to York. At a time of war and death, when God in His wisdom had overthrown all that had seemed certain, people would do anything they could to protect themselves and their families. If a man would steal a loaf of bread to feed his hungry child, why wouldn't a kind and loving woman send a witch to the gallows to save hers? Joseph had not only taken power for himself, he had *given* power to the people of the city.

Looking back I realize that this was the moment when the seed of my terrible plan to overthrow Joseph was planted. But before I could think more on it, all was thrown into chaos when another of Alice's gossips arrived and announced that a child had been taken for witchcraft and carried to Ouse Bridge gaol.

My eyes flew to Martha's, and I could see the fear in her face as well. Could Joseph have acted so quickly? Would he have ordered Elizabeth's arrest? For the second time that day, terror banished all other thoughts and feelings from my mind. Alice's final travail had not yet begun, so I slipped from the room, scrawled a note, and found Jane, the girl who had summoned me earlier that day.

"Jane, I need you to take this to my home and give it to

my maidservant, Hannah," I said. I could not stay with Alice unless I knew that Elizabeth was safe. "Wait there for an answer. It should not take long."

"Yes, my lady," the girl replied. "What shall I do if nobody is there? Shall I put it by the door or give it to a neighbor?"

I paused. I knew that if Hannah were not home, it would only be because Elizabeth had been arrested.

"If nobody answers run back here pell-mell," I replied. "I must know that above all else."

The girl nodded and dashed off into the gloom of the evening. I do not know how long it took her to return, but it seemed like more than forever. When I wasn't looking out the window for Jane, I walked up and down the Potters' parlor alternately praying to the Lord and cursing Him for abandoning me to Joseph's wrath.

And I thanked Him when the girl appeared out of the darkness, walking rather than running.

"Your maidservant said all is well," she said as soon as she entered the parlor. I felt myself breathe for what felt like the first time in hours. As I climbed the stairs to Alice's chamber, I wondered what poor child had been taken and said a prayer for her deliverance.

If the gossips had missed my presence, they hid it well, for I found all the women still talking merrily while Martha walked Alice about the room. Martha looked at me when I entered and I smiled weakly. I could see the relief on Martha's face, and we were able to get back to the business of birthing.

The rest of the evening, and the rest of Alice's travail, were uneventful. I allowed Martha to bring the child into the world, and she acquitted herself perfectly. Custom said that she would remain my deputy for several years more, but I could not help marveling at how much she had learned in the time she'd been in my service.

It was a few hours after midnight when Martha and I donned our cloaks and started for home. As Jane had promised, Elizabeth was safe in her bed, breathing softly, deep beneath layers of blankets. I kissed her head and retired to my chamber in hope of a few hours of rest before the day would begin.

I was pulled from a deep and blessedly dreamless sleep by the distant sound of pounding on my door. I heard the front door slam before shouts of anger and terror pulled me fully awake. Still in my shift, I hurled myself from my bed and down the stairs to see what was the matter.

To my surprise, Samuel Short, the dwarf-jailor from the Castle, stood in the entry hall. Martha held him tightly, apparently trying to keep him from charging up the stairs toward me. Samuel looked up. The anguish in his face turned my blood cold. *Oh, God*, I thought. *The child they took for witchcraft was Tree.*

Chapter 18

My knees buckled, and I felt myself sinking to the floor. Samuel tore free from Martha's grasp and crossed the hall toward me. He looked into my eyes, his face awash in anger, grief, and despair.

"Tell me this isn't your doing," he begged. "They have taken Tree as a witch and your nephew signed the warrant. Tell me this is not because of you."

I felt my mouth working in vain to find a response adequate to his accusation. What could I say?

"I don't know," I croaked at last.

Samuel stared at me. He did not believe my words any more than I did.

"Yes," I said at last. "Joseph threatened me and all those around me. I feared for Elizabeth, since she is the closest to me. I never thought he would do such a thing to Tree."

Tears streamed from Samuel's eyes. "Then you must save him, my lady. You love him, and you must save him." Samuel did not need to say that if Tree died in prison or on the gallows, his blood would stain my hands forever. I knew that truth in my bones.

I nodded. "I will find a way." What else could I have said?

"Where did they take him?" Martha asked. "It was Ouse Bridge gaol wasn't it?" Her blue eyes flashed, and I glimpsed a mercilessness that reminded me of nobody so much as Rebecca Hooke. Here was a woman who would kill when justice demanded it, the law be damned. I took a breath and swore that she would not face the coming storm by herself.

"Yes, Ouse Bridge," Samuel replied miserably. "They said I could visit him there before the trial."

"That is where they have Will," Martha said.

"Aye," I said. "Arresting Tree and taking him to Ouse Bridge gaol is of a piece with moving Will there. Joseph is no fool. He suspects we tried to help Will escape and he is taking every precaution. No doubt he has his own men guarding the gaol. We'll have the devil's own time freeing them."

"But you will free them, won't you?" Samuel asked. "Perhaps if you put things right with Mr. Hodgson he'll relent and send Tree home to me."

"We will try," I replied. "You go to the Castle and gather food and blankets for Tree. If there is anything you lack, send a boy to me and I will supply it."

Samuel wiped his nose on his sleeve and nodded. He seemed grateful to have something to do that might help. I gave him a handful of coins for buying clothes and bribing guards, and he hurried off.

"Joseph is in no mood to make peace," Martha said.

"I know," I replied. "He would hang Tree even if we offered him ten thousand worlds. Tree's arrest is meant as a warning that he would do the same to Elizabeth. It is supposed to frighten me into submission."

"How are we going to get them out?"

This was the question that occupied us for the rest of the morning. It did not take us long to light upon the best solution, but I was reluctant to choose that path and insisted we consider other means. During dinner, I gazed at Elizabeth as she chattered on about a game of checkstones that she and Sugar had played earlier in the day. Even as I laughed I could not help thinking that if she told such a story to a witch-hunter he would see her hanged. After we'd eaten, Elizabeth nestled into my lap and we worked for a time on her letters. I sent her off to wash her hands and called for Martha.

"You've decided to go to Helen Wright, haven't you?" she asked.

"We have no other choice," I said. "We'll see her this afternoon."

The wind was blessedly calm as Martha and I made our way south through the city. We said nothing as we passed the Ouse Bridge gaol that now held both Will and Tree. Members of the Town Watch eyed us as we passed through Micklegate Bar but waved us along.

"Joseph has increased the guard," Martha murmured. "Even if we are successful in freeing them from prison, Will and Tree will be trapped in the city."

"Let us clear one bar at a time," I replied. "We will free them first and then sneak them out of the city."

When we arrived at Helen Wright's house I paused to gather myself. I had no illusions that the conversation would be an easy one. I'd insulted her too often to expect easy forgiveness. She would have me groveling before the afternoon had ended.

A maidservant I'd never met answered the door and summoned Stephen Daniels. Helen's man smiled when he saw us, for he knew we had come a-begging.

"Come in, come in," he urged. "You are nearly blue with cold." He led us into Helen's parlor, where a fire roared in the hearth. "I'll send for some wine. Mrs. Wright will be down in a bit. Can I tell her what brings you here?"

I paused before answering. "It is a delicate matter," I said. Daniels started to object, but I continued. "And one that does not lend itself to a short explanation."

He nodded, whispered a few words in the maidservant's ear, and sat in one of Helen's large and beautifully covered chairs. As was his habit, he removed a piece of wood and a folding knife from his pocket and began to carve the wood into the shape of a snake. An uneasy silence filled the room, broken briefly when the maidservant returned with three glasses of wine. Martha and I had nearly emptied our glasses when Helen strode into the parlor. Her maidservant followed close behind with a glass of wine for Helen and a pitcher to refill Martha's glass and mine.

"Lady Bridget, I hope the wine is to your liking," Helen said. I searched her face for a sign of insincerity but found none. Martha glanced in my direction, no less confused by Helen's hospitality than I was.

"It is marvelous," I replied. And it was.

"I trust you are here about the recent . . . developments in the city," she said. "If you continue to vex the city's rulers, you will become as much an outcast as I am."

I then understood her newfound charity: The world had finally put me in my place, just as it had her. For a moment pride reared up and urged me to deny her charge. But before I spoke I realized that she was not far from the mark. A witchcraft accusation against Elizabeth would mean her death, but it would also destroy my reputation within the city. I was as vulnerable as a bawd.

"We are here about my nephew, Will, and a boy named Tree," I said. "Will has been taken for murder, and Tree for witchcraft."

"And they are both innocent," Helen said. "But what would you have me do about it? I hold no sway with the courts, not on such serious matters."

I could not help feeling that she knew exactly why I had come and what I was about to ask of her. But she needed me to say the words aloud, to acknowledge my powerlessness. And in that moment all became clear. Since the day of my birth, I had done all that the world had asked of me. I married when I was told; I bore and buried my children without complaint. I hectored girls in the height of their travail until they told me who had gotten them with child. And then I delivered them for whipping. When the law saw fit to let a murderer go free, I meekly accepted the decision. I was the ideal wife, mother, and midwife.

And to what end? What had a lifetime of compliance done for me? My nephew and my son stood on the gallows, and an Alderman and his Searcher had threatened to send my daughter to join them. My rank, my name, my coat of arms—all were worth nothing. Had I been born a man, I would have towered over York, the greatest hero it had ever known. But because I was a woman, Joseph would soon destroy the life I had built, and there was nothing within the bounds of the law that I could do to stop him.

"I need your help to break them out of Ouse Bridge gaol," I said.

Helen nodded. She had learned these hard lessons years before and took no satisfaction that at long last I recognized the grim truth.

"It will cost you dearly," she replied. I did not know if she meant the money I would pay, or the effect that taking such a step would have on me.

"I have no choice," I said. "I shall also need help hiding them after they escape, and then sneaking them out of the city."

"You've thought this through," Helen replied. "Give me a moment." She motioned for Stephen Daniels, and the two of them withdrew from the parlor. Martha and I sat in nervous silence. After a few minutes Helen returned alone.

Without preamble she named the price of her help. It was high, but seemed appropriate given the magnitude of my request. I agreed.

"I will put some clothes and money for both Will and Tree in a bag in my stable," I said. "It will be enough to keep them comfortable until they can escape York."

"Good," she replied. "I will tell Stephen. For now it is best if you go home and stay there. Tonight you should invite friends to dine with you, the more powerful the better. No doubt Mr. Hodgson will accuse you in this, and you should have witnesses ready to deny your involvement. I will send word after it is done."

It was good advice, and as Martha and I walked home we assembled a list of supper guests. I did not know how I would remain calm while Will's and Tree's lives were at stake, but what choice did I have? In one of the strangest moments of a strange day, Martha and I stopped at several stores and purchased the meats, breads, and cheeses that we would need for the evening. What a world we lived in, thinking of dinner with so many lives hanging in the balance! When we arrived home, I filled a canvas bag with clothes, blankets, and money for Tree and Will and put it next to the feed bin in my stable.

If you had asked me the next morning who had come to supper, I could not have told you. I imagine I invited some of George Breary's friends, along with their wives. I probably sent for one or two of the women I'd delivered, but I could not say for sure. Nor could I tell you what we talked about or even what I served. Once the guests had gone, I lay awake for hours, sometimes praying, sometimes listening to the wind whistling outside my window. A few times, hours apart, I was sure I heard gunshots, but I knew that even if something had gone wrong, I was too far from Ouse Bridge to hear anything. News of Will's death, or Tree's, would come in the morning with a knock on my door, not a gunshot in the night.

I abandoned my chamber well before sunrise and made my way to the kitchen where I found Martha kneading dough and shaping it into loaves. I did not think she had slept either. Without a word, I joined her in the work, and together we baked enough bread to feed the parish poor for a week. I did not know if Martha prayed—I doubted it—but if ever there were a time when she would appeal to a loving and generous God, or at least hope for His existence, this was it.

The rising sun found Martha and me sitting in the dining hall, nervous and completely exhausted. I felt like nothing so much as an anxious father awaiting the outcome of a difficult birth. Soon a door would open, and someone would give me news of life or death. When the knock I'd both feared and hoped for came, Martha and I raced to the door, but Elizabeth bounced down the stairs and arrived before we did. She pulled open the door and let out a small cry at the sight before her.

Stephen Daniels stood before us, leaning heavily against the doorpost. Though he was wrapped in a heavy wool cloak his deathly pallor made it clear he'd been grievously wounded. Martha and I stepped past Elizabeth and threw Stephen's arms over our shoulders. We dragged him to the parlor before Martha dashed back to close the door behind us.

"Was anyone following me?" Stephen asked. His voice barely rose above a whisper, and in his weakness he seemed an entirely different creature than the one we'd seen the day before.

"Nobody was in the street," Martha replied. "You're safe for now."

Stephen closed his eyes, and his body relaxed. Whether he slept or fainted I did not know, but it was clear that he had drifted away and would not return for some time. I could only hope that when he came back he would explain what had happened.

"We cannot keep him down here," I said. "Call for Hannah and help me take him upstairs."

My mind raced as the three of us wrestled Stephen's lifeless body up the stairs. I worried for Will and Tree, and I wondered if we could expect a visit from the Town Watch. If the constables came, how would I explain the wounded man—or corpse, if it came to that—in one of my bedchambers?

We half carried, half dragged Stephen into the room where Tree usually slept, and lay him on the bed. I opened Stephen's coat to find his doublet soaked with blood. Martha ran from the room, returning a moment later with a pair of scissors. As she cut away Stephen's clothing, I turned to Hannah.

"Lock the doors and close the curtains," I said. "If anyone knocks, do not answer. Nobody is here."

Hannah nodded. Her expression was no different than if I had asked her to dress a capon for dinner.

"Heat some water, and take Elizabeth up to the garret," I called after her. "You'll have to mind her while Martha and I tend to—our guest."

I turned back to Stephen. Martha had stripped away all his clothes, which lay in a bloody pile on the floor. Martha was inspecting his torso, and I gasped at the sight, for he seemed to be more blood than skin. I joined in the examination, and while most of the wounds were of little consequence, several would require sewing. Without a word, Martha dashed from the room and returned with my sewing basket and an armful of linen.

"We must vinegar the bandages before we apply them," I said.

"Aye. I bound more than a few of my brother's wounds in our time together," she replied. "If we add saffron, they heal all the quicker." Saffron was indescribably dear, but I nodded in agreement.

For the next hour or so, Martha and I worked our way from wound to wound, washing, sewing, and binding. In the distance I heard a knock on my door, but paid it no mind. By this time Martha and I were both covered in Stephen's blood and in no position to explain ourselves, regardless of who had come. By the time we finished, we'd wrapped Stephen in linen nearly from his waist to his neck. Martha pulled a blanket up to his chin, and we took a step back.

"Viewed from here, he could just be suffering from the ague," she offered.

"And that's what we'll tell the Town Watch if they should ask to search the house," I replied. "They'd want to come this close but no closer. When he wakes, try giving him some caudle. If it's good for a woman who's bled overmuch, why not a man?"

"I'll make some now." She paused. "What about Will and Tree? We should go to Helen Wright's."

"That will have to wait," I said. "I must stay here until the constables come, and I cannot let you wander the city alone, not until we know what has happened."

"You know I would be safe," Martha replied.

"You cannot hold off a squad of the Town Watch. And there has been enough blood spilt already." I could only pray that none of the blood was Will's or Tree's. "Come, let us change our clothes. If we are going to say that Stephen suffers from the ague, we cannot answer the door covered in his blood."

We did not have long to wait for the constables. This time they did not knock, but pounded hard enough to shake the door in its frame. I looked at Martha and raised an eyebrow. She nodded in response. We were ready.

I descended the stairs and threw open the front door. "What is the meaning of this?" I bellowed. The constable stood on my doorstep, his hand still raised for the knocking. His mouth hung open in surprise. "What is it?" I demanded. "If you are going to crash through my front door, you should have a reason."

After a few moments gibbering, the constable found his voice. "My lady, we are here for your nephew," he said at last. Two beadles stood behind him, their eyes as wide as the constable's.

"I have two nephews," I replied. "And neither is here."

I started to close the door, but he would not be so easily dissuaded.

"I have been ordered to search your house, my lady. By the Lord Mayor."

I considered my choices. If I refused, it would simply draw more attention to my house, and he would surely return with more men to force the issue.

"Very well," I said. "But you must tell me why."

A look of relief crossed the constable's face. "I do not know," he replied. "I was sent to find your nephew William Hodgson. The town's constables and beadles all have been called in to search for him."

"He is not in Ouse Bridge gaol?" I asked. At that moment I wished for nothing so much as Martha's skill in dissembling, for I felt as false as new-clipped coin, my edges shiny, sharp, and impossible to miss.

"Apparently not, or they wouldn't have sent me here to find him, would they? I'm to look for him and a boy. I didn't ask questions beyond that, and the Lord Mayor didn't invite any." My heart raced at the news, for it meant that both Will and Tree had escaped. I tried to hide my pleasure.

"Then you must come in from the cold," I said. "He is not here, but I'll not keep you from your duty. Perhaps you should start with the stable." The words died on my lips even as I spoke them. With all the morning's trouble I'd entirely forgotten about the bag of clothes and money I'd left for Will. Was it still there? I'd find out soon enough.

Keeping my face as still as possible, I led the constable and his men to the kitchen and let them into the courtyard behind my house. They crossed to the stable and went inside. I held my breath for an age before they emerged. My guts roiled and I swore to myself when I saw that the constable held the bag of clothes.

"I have a question, my lady," he called out as he crossed the courtyard.

Chapter 19

My head spun as I sought an explanation for the clothes that would satisfy the constable.

"What is it?" Martha asked as she came into the kitchen. I nodded toward the constable, and she swore when she saw the bag in his hand.

"I forgot we'd put that there," she said. "What do we tell him?"

"I have no idea," I replied. I could see her mind working as the constable climbed the steps to the door and came into the kitchen. I prayed that she would think of something, because I still had not.

"My lady," he said. "I found this bag in your stable. It contains clothes for a man and a boy, as well as fifty shillings. What is going on?"

"Sir, I put them there," Martha announced. "Before he was arrested, Mr. Hodgson—the one you are seeking, not the Alderman—gave me the money and told me to pack it in a bag with the clothes."

"Martha!" My surprise was genuine, though not for the reason the constable thought.

"Do not worry, my lady," the constable said. "I cannot imagine you had any role in this. It is your maidservant who must explain herself."

"Yes, I should like to hear this as well," I said. I thanked the Lord that the constable did not hear the smile that had crept into my voice.

"When did he ask you to put the bag in the stable?" the constable demanded.

"The day before he was arrested, sir." Martha was the very picture of servile deference.

"You must have known what he intended to do." The constable's voice had a new edge to it. "Why did you agree to it?"

"Sir, I did not dare disobey. The Hodgsons are powerful men. You know what his brother is like. What else could I have done?"

The constable's eyes narrowed as he considered Martha's story. "And when he was sent to gaol, you just left the bag out there? With over two pounds in silver coin?"

"I did what he told me," she replied, lowering her eyes. Who could fault a servant for unquestioning obedience?

"Why did he want you to include the boy's clothes?" the constable asked.

"Sir, I do not know and I did not ask. Perhaps he planned on taking the boy with him. I did not think to question his will."

The constable grunted in response and handed me the purse of coins he'd found in the bag. "You should have these, my lady. I'll have to tell Mr. Hodgson and the Lord Mayor what I found."

"I understand," I replied. I took a deep breath before beginning the second and more dangerous act of our little play.

"Would you like to see the rest of the house? Despite what you have found, I have nothing to hide." I knew that he would want to search the entire house, and thought it better to offer before he asked.

"Thank you, my lady," he replied, and I led him upstairs. As we went from room to room, he glanced briefly into my chamber and Elizabeth's before we came to the door of Stephen Daniels's room. I paused.

"The man in here is very sick," I said.

"You said nothing about having a man here. Who is it?" the constable demanded. The tone he'd used with Martha had returned, and I knew that I'd aroused his suspicions.

"You did not ask if anyone was here. You asked about Will, and this is not him," I said. "He is my cousin from Hereford come of late to the city. The journey was a hard one, and he is suffering from the ague. I do not know how dangerous it might be, but you are welcome to enter." I paused for a moment. "I do not *think* he is infectious."

The alarm on the constable's face told me my words had the intended effect. I opened the door and gestured for him to enter. The constable peered into the room without crossing the threshold.

"Your cousin, my lady?" he asked.

"Aye," I replied. "As you can see he looks nothing like my nephew."

The constable nodded and stepped back. "There are more rooms?" he asked.

I took the constable through the rest of my house, including Martha and Hannah's room in the garret. The constable found nothing else to raise his suspicions, of course, and I soon sent him on his way.

"My God," Martha breathed as the door closed behind him.

"Aye," I replied. "That was too close by half."

"Do you think our stories will hold?"

"Not if anyone cares to study them too closely. I'm not sure how I'd explain my 'cousin's' bandages. The ague does not usually cause such bleeding."

"Now we must find Will and Tree," she said, "and get them out of the city."

The problem, of course, was that we had no idea where to look for them. While Stephen Daniels was able to take some of Martha's caudle and did not seem to be in any danger, neither did he wake long enough to tell us anything of use. Our best—and perhaps only—hope of finding Will and Tree lay with Helen Wright. Martha and I were preparing to depart when Hannah called to us from upstairs. I found her in Elizabeth's chamber, which looked out over the street. Hannah stood at the window, peering toward Stonegate.

"What is it?" I asked.

"I noticed a man standing in that alley about an hour ago."

I looked in the direction she indicated, but all I saw was an empty street.

"Just wait," she said. "Every few minutes he'll poke his head around the corner and look toward us. He's not selling anything, not doing anything, just standing there watching."

I waited for a time, and just as Hannah had promised a figure appeared around the corner before withdrawing into the alley. I could not be sure, but for a moment I thought it might be Mark Preston. I went in search of Martha.

"We're being watched," I said, and described the man in the alley. "If we leave, we'll surely be followed."

"And we cannot be seen going to Helen Wright's," Martha said. "Is there anyone watching the alley behind the house?"

"I don't know, but we'd be foolish to assume that we can just leave by a different door."

I considered the problem before us. When the solution came to me, a smile spread across my face.

"Dig through the closets and find two ragged coats," I said. "The worse the better. Tear the seams if you must, but make sure we look like beggars. I'll explain while we change."

Martha and I slipped out the back door into the courtyard that lay between the house and the stable. The wall separating my yard from the neighbor's stood about eight feet high, so together we rolled an empty barrel across the yard and Martha climbed on top. Without a moment's hesitation, she scaled the wall and pulled me up after her. I heard fabric rip as I dropped into my neighbor George Chapman's courtyard, but I paid it no mind for it only improved my disguise.

We walked to the back door and I began to pound on it with all my might. Within moments Chapman appeared, his face already bright red with apoplexy. He'd been my neighbor, and thorn in my side, since my arrival in York. Even the most charitable soul would describe him as God's own ape; I lacked such charity and instead called him the most base-witted man in all of York. He peered through the window at us, trying to figure out how two beggar-women had gotten into his garden.

"Mr. Chapman, it is me, Lady Hodgson," I called out. "Open the door!"

He squinted at my face, utterly confused by this turn of events.

"Oh, for God's sake," Martha sighed. She reached out and

tried the doorknob. To Chapman's surprise and consternation, the door swung open, and Martha and I slipped past him into his kitchen. Chapman sputtered and spat but found no words appropriate to the situation. One of his maidservants, a pale, thin-faced girl, stared at us in astonishment.

"Good day, Betty," Martha cried. "We must be going!"

With Chapman close behind and still choking on his rage, Martha and I passed through the house toward his front door. We paused for a moment to wrap ourselves in our scarfs and then stepped into the street. From the corner of my eye I saw a figure emerge from the alley and stare at us intently. I turned to Chapman, who now stood in the doorway, utterly fuddled by our sudden appearance and immanent departure.

"Thank you, sir," I cried out. "The poor widows of St. Helen's will be eternally grateful for your generosity!" Martha and I curtsied deeply and turned toward Stonegate. I affected a limp, dragging one leg behind me and Martha hunched over as if the entire world lay on her shoulders. Together we made an ancient and decrepit pair; at least that was our hope.

Martha and I passed the alleyway, not daring to look anywhere except straight ahead. When we reached Stonegate, we turned left and slipped into a grocery. Now we would find out if the spy had recognized us. We peered through the window toward my street and after a moment breathed a sigh of relief; nobody had followed us.

"Well done," Martha said approvingly. "I wouldn't have expected such sneakingness from a gentlewoman."

"I have a fine teacher in such things," I responded. "Now let us go to Helen Wright's."

The rest of the trip south was uneventful, at least until we reached Micklegate Bar. Even before the gate was in sight, we knew that something was amiss, as carts trying to leave the city were lined up for over fifty yards. We bypassed the carts and discovered the problem. Members of the Town Watch were searching every cart and questioning all the men as they tried to leave the city. Any doubt as to the reason disappeared when we saw a man and a young boy pulled down from their cart.

"My name is John Harris," the man insisted as we passed by. "And this is my son!"

The watchman waved for his sergeant, who was closer to the gate. The sergeant peered at the man and shook his head. "Not him!" he shouted. "Let 'em go."

Martha and I wove through the jumble of carts, horses, and people, and out the gate with barely a second look from the guards. They were looking for Will and Tree not two ancient widows.

As soon as we were past the gate, we hurried to Helen's door. I knocked softly, not wanting to call attention from her prying neighbors or some meddlesome passerby. Helen's maidservant answered.

"What d'you want?" she asked. "If it's bread, go around the back."

I pulled down my scarf to reveal my face. "I am Lady Bridget Hodgson. I am here to see Mrs. Wright."

The maidservant looked at me in shock before ushering us in. "I'm sorry, my lady," she stammered. "It's just that the clothes . . ."

"Do not worry," I replied with as much of a smile as I could manage. "I wore them so none would know me, so I cannot fault you."

When Helen joined us in the parlor, I could tell that she

was no less worried than we were. "What has happened?" she asked. "Stephen never returned last night."

"He is safe at my house for now," I replied. "He was wounded, but if he can avoid infection, he will be fine."

Helen's entire body relaxed at the news, and I wondered if Stephen might be more to her than an ordinary manservant. If so, the risk she took by sending him after Will was far greater than I had realized, and I found myself filled with gratitude for her generosity.

"Do you know what has happened to Will and Tree?" I asked. "The constables are searching for them, so we know they have not been captured, but beyond that—"

"Both are safe and well," Helen replied. "They are still in the city, but I have them hidden."

A sob escaped Martha's lips, and I said a prayer of thanks. Why God had chosen that day to change His killing ways, I did not know. But I also would not believe that He had truly stayed His hand until Will and Tree were safely out of York.

"How do you know they are safe?" I asked. "If Stephen is with me—"

"Stephen took my man Ezra with him," Helen said. "He came back last night without Stephen."

"What happened?" I asked.

"Things did not go as planned," Helen said. "Stephen and Ezra went well armed, with pistols and knives. They thought the guards would recognize they were overmatched and surrender."

"And they didn't," Martha said.

"No, and there were more of them than we expected. One drew his sword, and then the shooting began. After that all was chaos."

"At what price?" I asked. I knew did not want to hear the answer.

"Two guards are dead. Two wounded. When the shooting stopped, Stephen told Ezra to take Will and the boy to my tenement as we had originally planned. Then they parted ways. Ezra hid Will and the boy, while Stephen found his way to you. Thank you for helping him."

I let the news wash over me, and my feeling of relief that Will and Tree were safe grappled with my horror at the price of their freedom. I realized I was going to be sick and dashed to the kitchen. I found a waste bucket and cast up all that I had eaten that day. When I had purged myself, I felt someone helping me to my feet. I turned to find Martha looking into my eyes with compassion so complete it overwhelmed me. I collapsed into her arms and began to sob.

"Two men are dead," I said, once I regained my breath. "Because of me, because of my decision, because of money I paid, two men are dead. They did nothing wrong, and I killed them."

"And two others—also innocent, mind you—now have a chance to live," she replied calmly. "There was no other way to save Will and Tree, or else we would have chosen it. Two people were going to die, either Tree and Will or two guards you've never known. Tree and Will are yours, and you owed them your protection. You had to do this."

Martha returned to Helen, while I stayed in the kitchen considering what she'd said. I thought of the guards who had died so that Will and Tree might live. They had committed no sin. They were not Joseph's comrades, nor were they party to his schemes. For all I knew, I had delivered their wives. I fell into prayers for the dead, the wounded, and their families, but soon enough my mind turned to Will and Tree, and my prayers for forgiveness became prayers of thanks. After a few minutes—or so it seemed—peace welled up within me. God was inscrutable, but He had decided that Will and Tree should not hang, and for that I was grateful.

I do not know how long I remained in Helen's kitchen, or what she made of my sudden collapse. When I returned to her parlor, Helen and Martha were waiting for me as if nothing untoward had happened. Helen called for her maidservant, who returned a few minutes later with cups of wine. I dared not meet her eyes as I drank.

"I understand how you are feeling, Lady Bridget," Helen said after a time. "But right now we should concern ourselves more with the future than with what is past. If we do not, Will and Tree will be caught up again."

I glanced at her for a moment and nodded. "What do we need to do?"

"First we must secure ourselves," she replied. "Under the best of circumstances, the constables would be desperate to find Will and Tree. With two guards dead, they will be rabid. And when Joseph Hodgson finds out his brother has escaped . . ." Her voice trailed off.

I finished her thought. "I can only imagine his fury."

"Have the constables come to your house yet?" she asked.

"Aye. They saw your man Stephen. I said he was my cousin fallen ill with a fever. They seemed satisfied, but—"

"There is no telling how long the illusion will last," Helen said. "If they realize someone was wounded, they will return all too soon. We will have to hide him as soon as possible."

"I should like to hide Elizabeth as well," I said.

Martha looked at me in surprise.

"I don't want her out of my sight, but we have no choice,"

I explained. "Joseph will have his revenge, and if he is willing to hang Tree as a witch, he would not hesitate to do the same to Elizabeth."

"We can send both Stephen and Elizabeth to the tenement where I've hidden Will and Tree," Helen said. "It will be crowded, but they will live."

"It will not be so easy," said Martha. "Joseph's men are watching the house, and Stephen is weak."

"And none but a blind man would miss Elizabeth," I added. "Not with that hair."

We sat in silence puzzling over the challenge before us. A solution came to me without warning.

"Elizabeth will not be pleased," I said, "but if we can get Stephen back on his feet, I know how we can get them to safety." I explained my plan, and Helen nodded in satisfaction.

"Stephen is stronger than you can imagine," Helen said. "He will be walking before you would expect."

"We can only hope that it's soon enough," I said.

"I'll not tell you where Will and the boy are hidden," Helen said. "It is safer that way. Stephen knows, and he can get there from your house."

Martha and I wrapped ourselves in our threadbare cloaks and prepared to depart.

"Send word when they are safely away," Helen said. "The next step will be to spirit them out of the city."

"Thank you, Helen," I said. "For everything you've done for me and mine." I did not apologize for the hard words I'd spoken in the past, but I did not think I needed to.

She nodded and closed the door behind us.

"Hiding Elizabeth and Stephen Daniels will not bring peace," Martha pointed out as we made our way toward Micklegate Bar. "It will simply give Joseph fewer options for revenge. If he cannot hang Tree or Will, and can no longer threaten Elizabeth, he will come for you."

"For both of us," I said. I thought for a moment. There seemed only one solution. "Once Elizabeth is safe, Hannah, you, and I will quit York for my estates in the south."

It would be a hurried and ignominious departure, to be sure, and I hated the thought of abandoning the city I'd come to call my home. But we would be safe in Hereford, and for now that was my only concern.

Martha and I hurried north through the gate and into the city. The Town Watch were still searching carts and questioning all men and boys trying to leave, and I said a prayer that the Lord would keep Will and Tree safe when the time came for them to flee.

When we turned from Stonegate onto my street, Martha and I pulled our hoods low over our heads to hide our faces. From the corner of my eye, I caught sight of the man who had been set to watch my house. He paid us no mind as we passed.

When we arrived at my door, I reached for the handle, but Martha stayed my hand. "Beggars would knock," she pointed out.

Despite all that had happened that day, the look of surprise on Hannah's face when she answered our knock brought a smile to my lips. Martha and I hurried into the house, and when I looked back at our sentry's alleyway it remained empty.

"It seems that we escaped the guard's notice," I said. "Now let us see how Stephen fares, and make plans for his escape."

Chapter 20

"He awoke not long ago," Hannah said as we climbed the stairs to Stephen Daniels's room. "He ate nearly half a capon, drank a full pot of ale, and went back to sleep. I checked and changed his bandages. Considering all he's been through he's healthy enough."

I found Stephen as Hannah described him: asleep, but far less pale than when we'd left. I slipped out without waking him.

"With luck he'll be able to walk in the morning," I said. "We should see to Elizabeth. I'll bring her to the kitchen."

I found Elizabeth in her chamber playing with a little family of poppets, calling one Martha, one Hannah, and one Ma. They were joined by a smaller one I'd had made using a lock of Elizabeth's own hair. A lone figure wearing men's clothes—Will, I supposed—sat by himself off to the side. I entered the room and sat on the edge of her bed.

"Elizabeth, I must speak to you," I said.

She looked up from her game and smiled with such warmth

I thought it could banish the winter from all of England. She rose from the floor and crawled into my lap.

"Did Martha tell you why the man is sleeping in the other chamber?" I asked.

"Hannah told me he was your cousin, suffering from a fever," she said. "But I went in and kissed his forehead, he seemed cool not hot. Is he better?" The image of this beautiful girl kissing a man like Stephen Daniels to check for fever— just as I did with her—brought a smile to my face, and I held her tight.

"His name is Mr. Daniels, and he is getting better," I said. "But there are some things we did not tell you."

Elizabeth furrowed her brow but let me continue.

"Mr. Daniels led Will out of the gaol," I said.

"Like Moses and the Israelites," Elizabeth cried. She leaped from my arms, unable to remain still in the face of such good news. I'd been telling her of Israelites and Egyptians, and she sought parallels in the world around her.

"Aye," I said. "And now he is hiding. Tree is with him."

"Will they be home soon, then?" she asked. "I should like to see them both. I miss them."

"It is not quite so easy," I replied, and took her back into my arms. "Tomorrow, if he is well enough, Mr. Daniels is going to take you to them."

"What about you and Martha?" she asked. Concern darkened her delicate features. She had already lost one mother, and she would be a fool not to worry about losing another.

"We are going to stay here for a time," I replied. "In a few days, though, we will all go for a journey."

"All of us?" Elizabeth asked, smiling brightly.

"All of us," I said. "But first, Martha needs you in the kitchen. There are some things we must do before you go. First we must put you in your shift."

"Why?" she asked.

"If we are going to send you to Will and Tree, you are going to need a disguise," I explained.

"What disguise?" she asked. "My shift is no disguise."

"No," I agreed. "We are going to cut your hair and dress you as a boy."

Elizabeth's mouth dropped open. "What? My hair? A boy! No, never!" She struggled to escape my embrace, but I would not let her go.

"You must," I said. "It is the only way for everyone to be safe. Think of it: You will be like a spy."

Dressing as a spy pleased Elizabeth far more than dressing as a boy. "A spy? For the King?" Her face had become serious, and I could see she considered the task of the utmost importance.

"Aye, for the King," I replied.

Elizabeth nodded, and we went to the kitchen where Martha waited with the scissors. It took over an hour, but by the time she had finished, Elizabeth seemed an entirely different child. She was no less beautiful, of course, but if we put her in Tree's clothes and a heavy cloak she easily would pass as a boy.

At least that was my prayer.

The next morning I woke early and looked in on Stephen. He still slept, but his breathing was strong and even. Helen had been right—he would be a hard man to kill. Martha and I were in the dining hall when we heard heavy footsteps above and knew that Stephen was up and about. We found him standing in his chamber, a blanket wrapped around him.

"My clothes," he said when we entered.

"Burned to ashes." Martha laughed. "They were so bloody, there was no saving them. And if the constables had found them when they came, all would have been lost."

"The constables were here? What happened to Ezra, Will, and the boy?"

"They are safe," I said, "and so are you. We told the constables you had a fever, and they kept their distance."

"Did they?" he asked with a smile. "Well done, then. I thought I heard voices, but I didn't know if it was a dream."

"But now we must see you all out of the city," I said. "And the first step is hiding you and Elizabeth."

"Then I'll need some clothes," Stephen said.

Of course the only men's clothes we had were Will's, and while Will was hardly a small man, fitting them on Stephen was no easy task. I had to slit a doublet in the back in order to button it in the front—a cloak would have to cover my work—and we stretched Will's hose to the tearing point. If he were stopped and searched, all but the dullest beadle would know something was amiss, but absent a close look he would be safe. Dressing Elizabeth was a far easier task, for I had a chest full of clothes I'd bought for Tree. Indeed, since he refused to wear the silks I'd bought for him—*too fine for a boy*, he'd insisted—Elizabeth looked like a proper gentleman by the time we finished.

My entire household joined in a dinner of ham, cheese, and bread, and then it was time for Elizabeth and Stephen to test their luck. My heart lurched and I fought back tears as I wrapped

Elizabeth in a cloak and pulled one of Tree's hats down over her ears. She was mercifully unaware of my state, having spent the afternoon peering out the windows in preparation for her work as a spy.

I hugged her tightly and prayed for her safety before letting her and Stephen out the door. I watched the two of them walk toward Stonegate, and I nearly cried out in horror as the sentry dashed from the alley, his sword drawn.

Stephen stopped and held up his hands in a gesture of supplication. The sentry shouted over his shoulder, and two more men—these in the uniform of the Town Watch—approached. The three men gathered around Stephen and looked him over. I could see him trying to explain himself, and I said a prayer that they would listen. One of the watchmen peered at Elizabeth and then looked up at Stephen.

"If they don't know Will, or have a poor description of him, they might take Stephen by accident," Martha murmured. "They are looking for a man and a boy, and we've provided them with both. Never mind that it's the wrong man and a girl."

"Aye," I said. "I never thought I'd pray that Will's pursuers would know their quarry, but I do now." I could tell from the look on Stephen's face and the increasingly violent gestures of the watchmen that things were not going well. When one of the watchmen poked Stephen in the chest, and Stephen nearly fell to the ground from the pain, I darted out the door and into the street. By the time I reached Stephen's side, my skin had turned numb from the cold.

"What are you doing?" I demanded. I saw that one of the watchmen wore a sergeant's stripes, and I turned my attention to him. "Explain yourself!"

The sergeant could not have been more surprised if the

Queen herself had charged down the street and challenged him. It took him a moment, but he eventually found his voice.

"We are in search of an escaped prisoner," he said. His eyes narrowed, and I knew that he recognized me. "But you know this, for it is your nephew. This man came out of your house."

"Were you told how tall my nephew is?" I asked.

The sergeant nodded. "A bit under six foot."

"And how tall is this man?" I demanded.

The sergeant looked up at Stephen. He frowned, and I knew that I had won the day.

"Any fool could see he is not my nephew," I concluded. "Let him pass."

The sergeant looked down at Elizabeth, and his brow furrowed. Before he could speak, I whipped off her hat, showing her newly shorn hair.

"And this is not the boy you seek, either. No doubt you were told he had brown hair, and as you can see, this boy's is red."

Elizabeth looked up at me and opened her mouth to object to my calling her a boy. I popped her hat back on before she could.

"Well and fine," the sergeant growled at last. "Let them go."

I held my breath until Stephen and Elizabeth were safely out of sight. To my relief, none of the guards followed them. It seemed that our plan had worked. I nodded to the sergeant and returned to my house, desperate for the warmth within. As soon I entered, Hannah wrapped me in a blanket and hurried me to the kitchen. It took nearly half an hour before the cold began to seep from my bones. As evening fell, I sat in my parlor and looked into the darkening street, wondering how we could escape the city. Martha joined me with the same question.

"I don't know," I said. "The Town Watch is minding the gates so closely, I don't want to try sneaking Will, Tree, and Elizabeth out just yet. If they are caught, all will be lost."

"So we wait while Joseph and his men search the city room by room? They cannot stay hidden forever."

"There is nothing we can do tonight, but tomorrow we will speak to Helen Wright," I said. "If she can see them out of gaol, perhaps she can ease them through the city gates as well. I should be surprised if she hasn't already begun to plan for their escape."

I don't know whether Martha or Hannah slept that night, but I lay awake for hours puzzling at the dangers we faced. After a time my mind returned to the murder of George Breary, so easily forgotten in the fire and smoke of my battle against Joseph. I remembered that if I could somehow prove Joseph's role in the murder, our problems would fall away in a matter of days. However I tried, though, I could not imagine a way to do this.

I had just drifted to sleep when a knock roused me once again. My first fear was that the Town Watch had found Will, Tree, and Elizabeth, but the knock was far too gentle for that. Instead of a constable, Hannah admitted one of Matthew Thompson's lads calling me to Grace Thompson's travail.

"With all our running about I'd near forgotten I was a midwife," I said to Martha as we wrapped ourselves against the cold. I was pleased to have the Thompsons' man with us as we wound our way toward Micklegate. Joseph's rage when he learned of Will's escape would know no bounds, and I did not know how he would react. If he had seen fit to crush George Breary's skull, I did not know why mine would be sacrosanct. The moon hung cold and bright in the night sky; sometimes it lit our path, but it also made the shadows seem that much more threatening. We kept to the light as best we could, but the darkness seemed to reach out, intent on catching us up. Relief flooded my body when we climbed the steps to the Thompsons' home.

As befitted his place in the city, Matthew's home was among York's largest and most impressive. The Thompsons had filled every room with the finest furniture and wall coverings. Grace's chamber was twice the size of my own, and I could not avoid a twinge of envy when I saw the exquisite quality of her quilts. Such uncharitable feelings dropped away when I felt the warmth of the women's welcome. They waved Martha and me into the room, thrust glasses of wine into our hands, and peppered us with questions about Will and Tree's escape from Ouse Bridge gaol. Martha and I pretended amazement, of course, and joined them in their wonder of how such a thing had come to pass. If the women worried about the men who had died that night, they hid it well, but I could not avoid thinking about them.

It took some doing, but after a time I convinced Grace to leave off gossiping and let me examine her. I found that she was still many hours from her final travail, so we returned to the other women and their merry conversation. It did not take long, though, before the days and nights I'd spent worrying about Will, Tree, and Elizabeth began to drag me down. I told Martha I required some sleep, slipped into a neighboring chamber, and fell into a large and exceedingly comfortable bed.

It was full daylight when I awoke to a burst of laughter from Grace's room. I called for a basin of water, splashed some on my face, and returned to the gossips. Martha was clearly exhausted, so I sent her to the bed I'd just left. Gossips came and went in a steady stream as Grace's labor pains became more frequent.

Grace tried to rest as well, and her gossips began to talk in hushed tones. To my surprise I heard Rebecca Hooke's name. I joined the conversation, eager to hear whatever news they might have.

"He was standing below her window," Susan Baird said. Her husband was one of York's wealthier merchants and had built a home not far from the Thompsons. "I saw him myself. It was cold as could be, but he stood there, gazing up at the window. Then he hurried off."

"What is this?" I asked. "Someone is wooing Rebecca Hooke?"

Laughter greeted my question. "Not Rebecca," said Susan. "Though that would be a man to meet. No, I saw James Hooke. He was gazing at the Lord Mayor's house. We live just across the street from the Lord Mayor, you know. My husband speaks to him all the time." Susan's nearness to the Lord Mayor was not something she'd let anyone forget.

"And James Hooke was staring at the Lord Mayor?" I asked. My head was still fuddled with sleep, and I could not puzzle out what she was saying.

Once again the women laughed long and loud.

"If he was looking for the Lord Mayor," one woman replied, "it was only to cast an evil eye and hurry that old pantaloon into his grave."

"Then what was he doing?" I asked.

The women laughed again, and I felt frustration rising within me. Susan saw this and took my arm. "It's the Lord Mayor's wife," she whispered in my ear. "Like every other young man in the city, he's besotted with Agnes Greenbury. The only difference is that he's too doltish to hide it."

I could not help feeling disappointed in the news. The fact

that James had, yet again, fallen in love with the wrong woman would hardly help Will and Tree escape the city. I withdrew from the company and called for a glass of barley water. Grace's final travail would begin soon, and I wanted to be ready. When Grace's labor pangs became more frequent and regular, I summoned Martha, and soon after the child came bellowing into the world without any hindrance.

That was when the problems began.

Martha received the child—a baby girl—and the gossips started to help Grace from the stool to her bed, but Martha cried out in alarm.

"Put her back down," she ordered. "Lady Bridget, come here!"

In an instant the room went silent save the cries of the child. The women lowered Grace back onto the birthing stool. Good cheer fled the room, and fear took its place.

"What is it?" I rushed to Martha's side.

"The navel string is too short," she replied. I took the child and found that Martha was right. She was so closely tethered to her mother that Grace could hardly move.

"We must cut it now," I said. "If the cord pulls itself from the after-burthen—" I did not finish the sentence, nor did I need to.

"But what would happen if the string falls back inside?" Martha asked.

I shook my head. I had never seen a case such as this, and I had no ready answers.

Grace peered down at us, her eyes bright with fear, but she did not speak. After a moment, the answer came to me.

"Get a ribbon," I said to the women behind me. "A fine one if you have it." Within moments, one of Grace's gossips had whipped one from her dress and handed it to me. I took my small knife from my apron.

"Grace," I said. "The navel string is so short that it may fall back inside you when I cut it. I do not want to lose it, so I am tying this ribbon to it. Do you understand?"

Grace nodded, and as quickly as I could, I tied the ribbon and cut the string. One of the gossips took the child for washing and swaddling while Martha and I saw to Grace.

"Bring some hellebore," I said to Martha. "I want to bring the after-burthen out as soon as we can."

"I already have it," she replied, handing me a small bag. Were the situation not so strange and dangerous, I might have commended her for her ready-handedness.

"Grace, I want you to cough. If that doesn't work, I'll have you breathe in this powder. It will hurt, but it also will help you bring forth the secundine."

Grace coughed and coughed, but to no avail. When she took in the hellebore, her body twitched and flew, and I watched as the navel string drew back into her body. I gave thanks to God that I'd tied the ribbon, but I knew that Grace had not yet reached a safe harbor. I anointed my hands with oil of lilies, and as gently as I could I reached inside Grace. I knew that if I didn't discover the problem, she could die before she'd even nursed her child.

To my dismay, I found the afterbirth still entirely attached to the side of Grace's matrix. Not daring to remove it myself, I withdrew my hand and gestured for the gossips to lay Grace in her bed and give her the child. Grace looked up at me, the strain and fear of the day etched upon her face. She did not speak, but I knew her question.

"The after-burthen has not yet come," I said. "It is best if we wait and allow it to be born on its own." I did not tell her it held so fast to her matrix that we had little choice in the matter. If I tried to draw it forth myself, her matrix would flood, and she would bleed to death in mere minutes.

"For now, you should rest, and feed both the child and your-self," I said. "If her cries are any sign, you will need all your strength to care for her."

To my relief Grace laughed, and I smiled when she put the child to her breast. When the gossips had gathered around Grace, I took Martha by the arm and pulled her aside. She alone recognized the concern on my face.

"What is it?" she asked.

"I don't know. In all my years, I've never seen anything like it. It is possible that she will deliver the afterbirth and all will be well, but it is quite unnatural."

"What can we do?"

I ran through our choices in my head. I could try to de-liver the afterbirth by hand or with a crotchet hook, but I was loath to be too rough with it. We could summon a surgeon, but with the child safely born there was nothing he could do that I could not.

"Get some masterwort from my valise and boil it in wine," I said. "I've heard it sometimes works in difficult cases."

Martha nodded, but before she had even left for the kitchen, a scream like none I'd ever heard tore through the room.

Chapter 21

Martha and I dashed to Grace's bed. She lay on her side, knees clutched to her chest. When we turned her to her back, I felt that her skin had become as hot as a blacksmith's forge.

I turned to one of the gossips. "Get some wine and a clean cloth," I told her. "And hurry."

Martha and I comforted Grace as best we could. Fearful of what I might find, I glanced under her blanket. I thanked the Lord that she'd not flooded. When Grace's gossip returned with the wine and cloth, Martha and I bathed her in it, hoping to cool her fever. Grace lay back, her eyes closed, and mumbled to herself. Then she slept. I watched as her chest rose and fell in a slow, steady rhythm. The gossips seemed relieved, but I knew that Grace would remain in desperate danger until she delivered the afterbirth.

"I must talk to her husband," I said.

"What will you say?" Martha asked.

"I'll bring him the child and tell him the truth about Grace," I replied. "If the mother's life is in peril, you must tell her husband. If you promise that she will survive, and she does not, he will fault you for it."

"I don't envy you this task," Martha said.

"It will be yours soon enough."

I took the child in my arms and went in search of Matthew Thompson. I found him in the parlor, surrounded by his friends. His face was pale and drawn—he clearly realized that Grace's labor was not going smoothly. He smiled when he saw the child in my arms, and took her from me.

"The child is well?" he asked.

"She is as healthy as any bairn I've delivered," I replied.

"And Grace?" His voice cracked as he asked the question.

"There is danger," I replied. "She has not delivered the afterburthen, and if she does not, she will die."

Matthew nodded. Though death in travail was not common, we all had a friend, a neighbor, or a relative who had died while giving birth. "What can you do?"

"She is sleeping now, but there are medicines I will give her when she awakes. They may help."

"Should I call for a wet nurse?" he asked. A tear ran down his cheek. "In case she . . ." His voice trailed off.

"It is probably for the best," I said. "Even if I deliver the afterbirth, Grace will be weak, and the child will have to suck." I gave him the names of a few women in Micklegate who might help and returned to Grace.

After she had slept for perhaps two hours, Grace's eyes fluttered open and she looked about the room as if surprised to find herself there. I took her hand and was relived to find it cool. The fever had broken.

"How am I?" she asked. "I had such a grief, but I feel like it has passed."

I watched her face as I placed my hand on her belly and pressed. She showed no hint of pain. "You may have delivered the after-burthen on your own," I said. "Let me see."

Sorrow welled up in my breast as soon as I lifted Grace's blanket. She had delivered the afterbirth, but at the cost of her life. The bed was soaked with her blood. I lowered the blanket, thankful that nobody else had seen the harbinger of Grace's death. There was nothing I or any man alive could have done to stop such a flux of blood. I took her hand again. It remained cool to the touch, but now the coolness bespoke not life, but death.

"Might I have another blanket?" Grace asked. "I am very cold."

Perhaps it was that question that alerted the gossips to her condition, for with a fire blazing in the hearth, the room was more than warm enough. They laid another blanket on the bed and gathered around her. Susan Baird took her other hand.

I caught Martha's eye. She nodded and slipped from the room. A few moments later, Matthew joined us and took my place by Grace's side. Grace smiled up at him and caressed his face. The gesture was too much, and he began to sob. The women—all crying now—stepped away from the bed so Grace and Matthew could talk. They whispered to each other, sometimes laughing, sometimes crying. After a time, Grace slept. And then she died.

Matthew sent for the minister, and we prepared Grace's body for burial. Thankfully, she would be buried in the church itself, for the frozen ground was so hard that it would have taken days to dig a grave in the churchyard.

The sun had set by the time Martha and I left the Thompsons' house and began the journey home. To my dismay, the lantern Matthew had loaned us blew out in a gust of wind before we reached the end of the street. The moon passed in and out of sight as clouds whisked across the night sky. Every few steps we were plunged into darkness or bathed in a cold, lunar light. Martha and I leaned on each other, utterly exhausted in our minds and bodies. Perhaps it was our weariness, perhaps it was the wind, but neither of us heard the footsteps approaching from behind.

Martha sensed a presence before I did. She started to turn and raise her arm, but it was too late. She cried out, but the blow silenced her, and she fell to the ground in a heap. I swung the lantern in an agonizingly slow arc at our attacker's head. To my surprise it reached its target, and the glass shattered into dust, but I knew that it would not shake our attacker.

At that moment the moon broke from the clouds and illuminated the scene before me in terrifying detail. Mark Preston stood over Martha's body like some hulking beast, a small, ugly cudgel in his hand. When he turned to me I saw a thin line of blood sliding down his temple, but that was all the damage my blow had done.

"Your nephew has had enough of both of you," Mark hissed. He smiled and took a step toward me. I had a terrible decision before me, and I made it in an instant. If I stayed and fought I would surely die, and then Martha would, too. But if I led Mark away from her, she might recover herself and escape. That was my hope, at least. I hurled what was left of the lantern at Mark's head, turned, and ran.

After a few steps I looked over my shoulder and saw that Mark had slipped on the slick cobblestones and fallen. He regained his feet all too quickly, but it gave me the time I needed. I looked back again when I reached the south end of the Ouse

Bridge, and I cried out in dismay. Mark had very nearly caught me. If I tried to cross the bridge, he would have me long before I reached the far side.

I dashed down the stairs to the staith that ran along the water's edge. Until the river froze, sailors from around Europe had docked their boats there, but now it was naught but a broad and deserted avenue, with warehouses on the right and the river on the left. I heard Mark clattering down the steps behind me. I ran to the edge of the staith and dropped onto the ice. Though I knew the risk, I ran straight toward the middle of the river. The ice was rough beneath my feet, and more than once I caught a toe and nearly fell. When I heard the ice creaking below me, I slowed my pace and turned to face my pursuer. Mark stood ten feet away, breathing hard, the cudgel still in his hand. I shifted my weight, and the ice creaked ominously.

When he was near enough for my purposes, I dashed away once again and threw myself forward onto my stomach. I'd hoped to slide even further away, but ice was far too rough. Rather than gliding to safety, I crashed forward and bloodied my nose before rolling onto my back.

I looked up to find Mark approaching me. I tried to sit up, but my left hand broke through the ice and plunged into the frigid waters of the Ouse. Pain shot up my arm, and I pulled my hand out. My entire arm was numb. I heard the ice crack below me and lay back as far as I could.

"Come now, Lady Bridget," he said. "It is over. One knock on the head, and we'll be done here. At least *you* will be." I lashed out at him with my feet. He danced back a step and smiled before beginning his approach anew, circling closer and closer until he could deliver the final clout. I turned in place, trying to keep my feet between us and force him toward the middle of the river. As we turned, the moon illuminated his face, and I knew that if my plan failed, his vicious smile would be the last thing I saw.

I think he recognized my trap an instant too late. A look of surprise flashed across his face as he broke through the ice and dropped into the river. I pushed myself back toward shore before I dared sit up. Preston's head and arms were still visible as he clawed desperately at the ice, hoping to haul himself out. I did not know what I would do if he succeeded. But on that night the Lord had mercy on me. Preston's cries grew feebler as the cold choked the life out of him. I looked into his eyes, watching in fascination as the river overcame him, and he slowly slipped out of sight.

I rolled onto my stomach and, dragging my numbed left arm behind me, pulled myself toward the staith. I clambered off the ice and back onto the cobbled street. Without a look back, I hurried up the stairs to where I'd left Martha. I found her sitting in the middle of the street with her head between her knees. I took her by the arm, and she staggered to her feet.

"How are you? Are you hurt?" I asked.

"I'm fine," she said. I released her arm, and she took a few wobbly steps.

"Who was it?" she asked. "What happened?"

"Mark Preston came for us at last," I said. "Come, we must get home." I led her across the bridge, casting a glance at the ice below. I could see the hole through which Mark had fallen, but that was the only sign of our struggle.

"Where is he?" Martha asked.

"Dead," I replied. Only then did I realize that my hands had been stained by yet another man's blood. "I led him out onto the ice and when I lay flat, he fell through."

"You remembered what the Hollander boy told you," she said.

"Aye, and now he's saved my life twice," I replied. "But enough talk, let us hurry home before the cold takes us as well."

I pounded on the door for Hannah to let us in. Her eyes widened when Martha and I tumbled into the hall. Rather than asking what had happened, she dashed off for towels, water, and blankets. Though it was not in either of our natures, Martha and I let Hannah care for us as we told her all that had happened. Her horror at Grace Thompson's death and Mark Preston's subsequent attack was something to behold. I'm sure she wondered how my world—and as a consequence, *her* world— had become so bloody, but what else could I have done? By the time the sun rose, the feeling had returned to my arm and, except for a bump on her head, Martha seemed a picture of health. We both knew she'd been very lucky. As Hannah busied herself about the house, Martha and I dragged ourselves to our beds.

I awoke that afternoon utterly famished, and I realized that I'd not eaten since before Grace Thompson's final travail. I found Martha and Hannah in the kitchen finishing dinner preparations, and the three of us sat together to eat. We all gazed at the empty chairs around us, and I said a prayer for the safety of our missing family. After we ate, I retired to my chamber and tried to busy myself with the accounts from my estates. I trusted my stewards, of course, but I liked to keep my eye on the rents as they came in. As much as I tried to prevent it, my mind kept returning to the new danger Martha and I faced. It would take Joseph some hours to realize that we had survived his murder attempt, but when he did, hell itself would be loosed on the city. Will, Tree, and Elizabeth were safe for now, but how would Martha and I weather the coming storm? As I gazed at the papers before me, I realized we had only one choice if we were going to survive: Martha and I had to flee the city even before Will, Tree and Elizabeth did. I began to write the necessary letters.

Hannah called me for supper, but I was too busy writing. She brought me bread and cheese, which I ravened up without tasting it. My letters were nearly done when fatigue once again threatened to overcome me. Martha appeared at my chamber door and, without knocking, entered and sat on the edge of my bed.

"What now?" she asked.

"We must leave York as soon as we can," I replied.

Martha nodded. She had come to the same conclusion. "It will not be easy," she said. "It is your home."

"What choice do we have? Joseph intends to hang Will and Tree. And when he discovers Mark Preston's death, he will find a way to have his revenge on you and me. I do not see how we can defeat him." I held up the letters I'd written. "We will hire a carriage tomorrow morning, and we'll be gone before sunset. By the time we reach Hereford, my house will be ready for us. Once there, we will be safe."

"What about Will and the children?"

"We will have to leave them in Helen Wright's hands," I replied. "If she can get them out of the city, Will can keep them safe during the journey south."

"And then? You can hardly keep up your midwifery in such a place." Pontrilas was barely a village, and Martha knew it.

I shrugged. "There are villages nearby. There will be fewer mothers, that is sure. But we have few choices."

"There is London," Martha ventured.

I laughed out loud. "A few years in York and you've become a city girl, have you? That is fair. Once we are settled, we will consider our options."

Martha helped me to bed and disappeared upstairs to her chamber. As I lay there, I considered her suggestion that we settle in London. I'd never been to the city before, and I could not help wondering if my family's future might lie in that direction.

At sunrise I sent Hannah to post my letters to Hereford and find a carriage to take us south. Martha and I then began gathering everything we would need for the coming journey. I sent letters to friends in the city, calling in the debts they owed me. I knew few would have enough ready money to pay me in full, but if each sent a portion we would have enough. With Will, Tree, and Elizabeth safely hidden, and a carriage coming soon for Martha, Hannah, and me, I felt for the first time in weeks as if all might be well. Indeed, I had become so hopeful that when I heard a knock at the door, I opened it without a moment's hesitation.

My knees buckled when I found Joseph standing in the doorstead.

I steeled myself for his rage, but what he offered instead was far worse. He smiled.

"Aunt Bridget, might I come in?" Without waiting for a response, he strode past me. I followed him to the parlor, suddenly feeling like a stranger in my own home. Somehow his careless manner frightened me more than his wrath. He reached the parlor and turned to face me.

"What do you want?" I demanded. "I had nothing to do with Will's escape, and I don't know where he is."

"You are lying about his escape," Joseph replied brightly. "But I have no doubt you are ignorant of his whereabouts."

I tried to imagine what he meant by this, and in a terrible moment I realized what had happened. I stood in silence as I waited for the grim news.

"Last night, mother hen," Joseph said, "the Town Watch found your entire brood. They all are mine now."

Though his message was plain, I stared at Joseph trying to make sense of his words. I wanted them to have some other meaning; I wanted to find a reason for him to lie about this. But the truth was there before me and could not be denied. He had taken them all: Will, Tree, Elizabeth, and Stephen. My entire body felt as numb as my river-dipped arm had the night before. Sorrow, horror, and fury vied for expression, but none could win the day so I stood mute.

"What, nothing to say?" he asked. I had never seen a man so pleased with himself. "You are usually more talkative than this. Very well, I shall continue. They are taken, and they will hang, most of them anyway: Will for murdering George Breary, the ruffian Stephen Daniels for killing Will's guards. We'll try the boy as a witch, and I imagine he will hang as well." A smile flitted across his lips at the thought.

"Oh, and the girl," he said, as if Elizabeth were an afterthought. "You'll not have her back, for you've no claim to her at all. You can't just take an orphan off the street and into your home. There are laws. The city will see to her. *I* will see to her."

I felt a presence behind me, and I recognized Martha's touch as she put her hand on my shoulder. I glanced at her face and could tell she'd heard everything.

"They are innocent," was all I could say. "*You* killed Mr.

Breary, and now you'll see your brother hanged for it. A thousand times worse than Cain, you are."

For a moment Joseph seemed as puzzled as if I'd accused him of popery.

"You know full well that Tree is no witch," I continued, my voice rising with every word. "And you cannot take Elizabeth. She is my charge, not yours."

For the barest of moments I thought that my words might make an impression on Joseph, that he might relent and let his brother live, for surely he could not be such a monster. Then he smiled. It was a smile as sharp and cold as the north wind, and I knew that there would be no changing his mind.

"I cannot fathom your insistence that I murdered Mr. Breary," he said. "But whatever the case, you and yours are over and done."

His voice was a knife, and I could feel it between my ribs slicing through my flesh in its inexorable journey to my heart.

"If I could hang you for the murder of the guards, I would," he continued. "And I don't know what you did with Mark Preston, but he was my friend, and you can be sure I will have my revenge for his death. Not today, perhaps, or even tomorrow, for the law moves slowly. But from this day forward, you will go to sleep knowing that someday I will hang the both of you in the market square. And I will pay the executioner to botch up the knot so you strangle slowly. It will be a terrible sight to behold, and a worse one to suffer."

Joseph smiled again as if his promise of a slow death were meant to reassure us. Then he strode from the room and out the door.

Chapter 22

Martha and I sat next to each other in numb silence, neither of us daring to give voice to our despair. It seemed our battle was over. The moment Joseph had taken Will, Tree, and Elizabeth, he had won. There would be no escape, no mercy from a judge. Will and Tree would hang, and God only knew what fate awaited Elizabeth. I felt panic roiling within me at the thought of losing my family again. I had buried the children born of my body, and their deaths had brought me to the edge of hopelessness and nearly murdered my faith in God. If I lost Will, Tree, and Elizabeth, Joseph would not need a hangman to see me dead. Sorrow would do that work for him.

I looked at Martha, who seemed no less stunned than I. I waited for her to speak, hoping that she would find a solution to this, that she would concoct a plan to set all our loved ones free. Instead she buried her face in her hands and began to sob. I put my arm around her shoulders and pulled her to my side.

I heard a timid knock from the front door but ignored it.

What visitor could I want to see now? When I heard the front door open, I assumed it was Hannah returned from the market.

"Hello? Lady Hodgson! Please, are you here?" A girl's voice echoed through the hall. I did not recognize her, but there was no mistaking the panic in her voice. Martha and I hurried to the entry hall. There we found a young serving maid, perhaps sixteen years old, looking wildly about, desperate for help. From her clothes I could tell she was one of the poorer sort, and her cloak was entirely insufficient for the winter's cold. Her teeth chattered as she tried to speak.

"Thank God you are here," she cried out before falling to her knees and clutching the edge of my skirts. "Lady Hodgson, you must come! It is my younger sister. She is in travail, and the child will not come. She is all alone."

My first instinct was to send her to another midwife, but after a moment I grasped the meaning of her words. "Your *younger* sister?" I asked. "How old is she?"

The girl's face fell. "She is fourteen," she said. "Our stepfather ..." Her voice failed but the meaning was clear enough. I felt fury welling within me at the violation the girl had suffered, and in that moment her stepfather became the author of every abuse that the weak suffered at the hands of the strong. I knew that I could not ignore the opportunity to mete out a measure of justice: The stepfather would hang for ravishing so young a child. I looked at Martha and saw that she felt the same.

"I'll get my bag," I replied. "I'll see your sister delivered and your stepfather punished."

Martha and I followed the girl toward St. John-del-Pyke, one of the poorest neighborhoods in York. We wound our way through an ever-shrinking series of streets until the road was so narrow that the sky was nearly blotted out.

We reached the end of an alley and stopped in front of a tenement that seemed on the verge of collapse. The girl peered behind us as if worried we might be followed.

"It is here," she said. "You must follow me."

I glanced at Martha and could tell that she too sensed something was amiss. I reached into my apron and grasped the small knife I kept there. I used it for cutting navel strings, so it was sharp enough for ordinary flesh.

"Be at the ready," I said.

We followed the girl up two sets of rough wooden stairs. As we climbed, my concerns abated somewhat, for the building was full of life. Children played on the stairs, and we could hear their parents talking behind ill-hung doors. If someone intended to ambush us, he'd have plenty of witnesses.

The girl paused when we arrived at the top of yet another staircase. The voices from below suddenly seemed far away, and I gripped my knife once again.

"She is in here," the girl said. "My sister." She took a step back and gestured for us to enter. "Go on in."

There was no question that the girl was lying about something, but Martha and I were in no mood to run.

I glanced at Martha, and she nodded. We were ready. Martha reared back and kicked the door with all her strength. The door flew open and with a screech pulled loose from one of its hinges.

A woman stood just inside—the door must have nearly struck her in the face—and she stared at us in astonishment. Martha and I returned her gaze, no less thunderstruck. Of all the people in York, the last I'd expected to find behind the door was Rebecca Hooke.

* * *

"You know how to enter a room, I'll admit that," she said with a cold smile.

I turned to face the girl who'd summoned me, but she'd already fled down the stairs.

"You might as well come in," Rebecca said. "Neither of us wants this meeting to become common knowledge."

I peered through the doorway and saw that Rebecca was alone. I stepped inside with Martha close behind. Martha wrestled the door closed as best she could while I looked around the small room. The only piece of furniture was a rough wooden bed, and the small horn window provided scant light. If Rebecca had not brought her own lamp, I might not have recognized her at all.

"What is it?" I asked. I did not bother trying to conceal the hatred or fury in my voice. "You've gone to a great deal of trouble, so you must want something of significance."

"I want nothing," she responded. "Rather, I have an offer. And after the news you received this morning, you'll want to hear what I have to say." She paused. "I can save your nephew and the children."

For a moment, hope leaped in my breast, but I choked it down. Rebecca Hooke would sooner see me hanged than do me a favor.

"And why would you do such a thing?" Martha demanded, giving voice to my own suspicions. "Because it is for the good?"

Rebecca laughed, high and cruel. "Of course not," she replied. "Let's just say I have my own reasons. Do you want to hear my offer or not? There are other ways to achieve my ends, but this is the easiest for me, and it is the only one that will save your litter of pups."

"What do you propose?" I asked at last.

"I should like to see Joseph Hodgson hanged before the week is out," she said. "But I need your help to for it to happen."

How long did I stare at her trying to make sense of her words? Seconds? Minutes? Hours?

Martha broke the silence. "Why would you do that?"

"I'll not tell you that," Rebecca replied. "Obviously I would not undertake such a task lightly, so you may rest assured that my reasons are good ones. The problem is that I cannot hang him myself. As much as it galls me, I need your help."

"I would never." I forced my words through clenched teeth.

Rebecca laughed. "Well, I know in *ordinary* times you'd sooner hang me than help me, but we hardly live in ordinary times, do we? Hear my offer and then consider your options. If you'd rather see your family hang than accept my bargain, I'll send you on your way."

"Never," I repeated.

"No?" she asked. "Lady Bridget, you cannot be insensible to how desperate your position has become. You have made an enemy of York's most feared man, and tell me, what friends do you have left? And I don't mean the women—they will stand by you come Judgment Day. But it is the men who matter, and what man will hazard all for your sake?"

She paused for a moment, knowing full well I could not refute her claim.

"All your friends are fled or dead," Rebecca continued. "The very best you can hope is that Joseph Hodgson will only drive you from the city. But even that may be a fond hope. His fury at Mark Preston's disappearance was something to behold. He will have his revenge. If you do not join me, he will hang the both of you for murder."

She paused for a moment and let her words sink in. I still could find no answer that would not choke me.

"While you consider my offer, I must ask you one more thing." By now Rebecca's smile seemed to cover her entire face. I'd never seen her so satisfied. "What did you do with Preston's body? It is an impressive feat to kill such a man, but to dispose of his corpse as well? It is not as if you could simply cast him into a privy."

In an instant I knew that she was jesting about the murder of her infant grandson, who had been thrown into a public jakes and left to die in a pile of shit. A roar fit for a beast tore from by throat as I gave voice to the fury I'd held inside ever since that killing. I flew at Rebecca, my arms flailing wildly, bent on exacting justice for the lost child. Blood cried out for blood, and I would have hers. My hands found Rebecca's throat, and my muscles sang with joy as they tightened on her neck. It was not the hangman's noose, but it would do.

Rebecca fell backward onto the bedframe behind her, and I threw myself on top. I felt her hands battering my face, but for all the effect they had, they might as well have been striking someone else. I was dimly aware of a voice shouting my name, and through the fog of my anger I wondered how Rebecca could speak with my hands clamped on her gullet. I redoubled my effort to choke the life from her body, thankful that the years of delivering children had strengthened my hands for this task.

I could feel Rebecca's strength beginning to fade when I was knocked from on top of her. I screamed in rage as I lost my hold of her neck and tumbled to the floor. I fought to regain my feet so I could resume my murderous work, and only then realized that Martha sat on top of me, holding my wrists.

I twisted my arms in desperate hope of freeing them and lashed out like an unbroken colt, but she would not be thrown.

"Bridget, you must stop." I do not know how many times she said the words before I heard them. Eventually I ceased my struggles and peered past Martha to see if I'd accomplished my goal. To my dismay, Rebecca had pulled herself upright and sat on the edge of the bed, her head between her knees. Her shoulders heaved as she tried to regain her breath. I tried once again to free myself from Martha's grip but could not.

"You must stop," she repeated. "Your revenge can wait. For Will's sake, and Tree's, we must hear her out."

I breathed deeply and nodded.

Martha looked at me distrustfully and did not release my wrists.

"I'm done," I said at last. "I won't hurt her."

Martha helped me to my feet, and we turned to face Rebecca. My assault had knocked her hat askew, and a thin trickle of blood ran from one nostril to the corner of her mouth. Even in the dim light of the room I could see the marks my hands had left on her neck—by morning she would have terrible bruising. Her breathing was quick and ragged; every few breaths she would cough and then spit blood onto the floor. After a moment she looked up at me with hooded eyes. In my time as a midwife I had made more than a few women into my enemies, but none had ever stared at me with the pure hatred I saw in Rebecca Hooke's face.

She tried to speak, but only a weak mewling sound escaped her throat. She paused and tried again. "Now, if we are to hang Joseph Hodgson we must be wise as serpents," she croaked.

After Rebecca explained her plan, she went downstairs to give Martha and me time to consider her proposal.

"It would work," Martha said.

"It might," I admitted. "But what is her game? Why would she help us?" I was loath to say so aloud, but I could not help admiring the cold brilliance behind Rebecca's scheme. She seemed to have considered every possibility. God, what a dangerous man she would have been!

"That's what worries me as well," Martha replied. "Could she intend to turn the proceedings against you?"

"It is possible, but why discuss it with us ahead of time? If she intended to hang the two of us as witches, she'd have conspired with Joseph. It would have been much easier than this." I paused. "I wish I knew why she has turned against Joseph."

"So you will accept her offer?"

"If we are going to save Will and the children, I don't know what choice we have. I presume that if you had a better scheme you'd have mentioned it already."

Martha smiled wanly. "No. This is the best chance we have."

We descended the stairs and found Rebecca waiting just inside the front door. She had recomposed herself, and her scarf covered most of the wounds from our battle.

I nodded as we approached. "We will do it," I said.

"Good." Rebecca nodded and opened the door. "You should leave here first. I do not think that Joseph suspects me, but this is not the time to be careless."

Martha and I stepped past her and into the cold winter wind. The door slammed behind us as we wended our way back toward St. Andrewgate.

We had far too many hours to wait until Rebecca's scheme would begin in earnest. Martha and I busied ourselves about the house as best we could, but it was impossible to focus on any one task for more than a few minutes. I could sense Hannah's growing annoyance, and thanked God for sending such a patient servant to me.

Eventually the appointed hour arrived. Martha helped me into my most luxurious gown, and the two of us walked to the Council Hall. Before we entered I peered over the river and saw that ice now covered the hole through which Mark Preston had fallen. For a moment I wondered where his body might be, whether it would surface in the spring or be washed out to sea, but I pushed that a thought away. It would take months for me to wash the blood from my hands—if such a thing were possible—but now was not the time to start. I gathered myself for the task ahead, and Martha and I stepped into the Council chamber.

Chapter 23

When we entered the Council Hall, we found Joseph standing at the end of the table opposite the Lord Mayor. He had his back to us and was in the midst of a speech about God's will. It galled me that such sentiments came from so heartless a man, and I took comfort in the fact that—if all went well—these would be the last words he spoke to the Council. I said a prayer of thanks that none of the Aldermen noticed our arrival. Martha and I remained quiet as Joseph spoke, keeping to the shadows behind him so that he would not notice us. The less warning he had, the better our chances of success.

Eventually Joseph ended his sermonizing and took his seat. Lord Mayor Greenbury asked if anyone else had business for the Council. For a moment I thought he glanced past Joseph in our direction, but I dismissed the idea. How could he know what we had planned? I took a breath to gather myself and stepped out of the shadows.

"Yes, my Lord Mayor," I called out. "I do, and I must address the Council." My voice echoed through the Council Hall with more authority and confidence than I felt. I counted it as a blessing.

Nearly every head turned in my direction, perhaps surprised that a woman would take such liberties. Joseph merely cocked his head to one side, but it was clear he recognized my voice.

The Lord Mayor peered at me, his eyes glittering in the torchlight. "This is unusual, to say the least. What business do you have?"

"It is a matter of greatest and gravest importance to York, the city which I love beyond measure," I replied. I kept behind Joseph as I approached the table. If Joseph wanted to see me, he would have to turn his back on the rest of the Council. "It concerns the plague of witches that has so recently descended upon the city." My mind went back to the night when Rebecca Hooke had spoken similar words to the same men, and I hoped I could speak half so effectively.

"We were told by ministers and magistrates alike that we must cut the cancer of witchcraft out of the city before the Lord God will bring this endless winter to a close. Since then the city has arrested dozens of witches. Some we have hanged, and the rest sit in prison, laid in double irons. We have done all that the Lord asked of us, yet the killing cold endures."

Joseph rose to defend his actions. "To question the will of God in this way is blasphemy," he cried out. "The cold continues because the Lord still finds fault with the city. It means that we must continue to labor in His vineyards."

"I am not questioning the will of God, but the actions of men," I replied. "The horrible truth, the truth that holds us in these frozen fetters, is that even as we have sent some witches to the gallows—and praise be to God for that—we have missed Satan's Adam, his very first witch, the one who lured all others into that damnable art."

"Speak plainly, Lady Bridget." The Lord Mayor's voice seemed curiously strong coming from such an aged body. "Who is Satan's Adam? Who is this witch?"

"He is here in this room," I replied.

Complete silence greeted my words. While most on the Council looked around the room wondering whom I meant, Joseph sat still as a stone. I could not imagine that he understood my plan—or, to be fair, Rebecca's plan—but it seemed clear that my words had taken him unawares.

"You might wonder how your colleague, Mr. Joseph Hodgson, has become so skilled in finding witches," I continued. "And it might seem strange that he is so adept in gaining their confidence and confessions. After all, what instruction has he had in that work? There were no witches in Parliament's armies, and there were none in his household. He has never been to university, nor did he study demonology under some master. How then does he know so much of witches and witchcraft?"

The Council sat in silence, every one of them now looking past Joseph at me. For a moment I wished I could see Joseph's face to better judge his reaction, but I kept my place behind him. All in the room must have known, or at least guessed, what I was about to say, but nevertheless they waited for the words.

"The truth is that the devil counts Joseph Hodgson among his most loyal agents."

Joseph leaped to his feet shouting his objections, and most on the Council began to shout along with him, drowning out his protests. The Lord Mayor pounded on the table, hoping to restore some semblance of order, but it only added to the din. Joseph turned to face me, his eyes alight with fury. He started to speak, but I could not hear him for all the noise. After a moment he realized he'd turned his back to the Council and risked losing them. He cursed, turned around, and resumed crying up his innocence.

"You may wonder how I know this," I cried.

A few of the Aldermen closest to me heard my words and stopped their chattering. Others soon followed suit.

"You may wonder if this is not some fantasy born of overheated dreams," I said. "But I have a witness, one who can attest to the truth of my words. And she is here now."

Rebecca Hooke's footsteps echoed through the chamber as she stepped out of the shadows. I had left the hall's door ajar so that she could enter silently. She continued past me until she reached the Lord Mayor's side. Now we stood at either end of the table, the City Council between us, owned by us.

"Members of the Council," she said, her voice still weak from the throttling I'd given her. "For these last weeks, I have been Mr. Hodgson's helpmeet in his search for witches. During that time I believed that he had an especial talent for finding those who had joined Satan's ranks. And I was happy to be a solider in the army of the Lord."

I could not help admiring how skillfully she had reduced her role in the hangings from war-captain to mere foot soldier.

"But I have recently discovered that I have been an unwitting aid to the devil himself, and that Mr. Hodgson owes his success in finding witches not to the Lord our God but to that fallen angel, Satan himself. Not ten days ago I found in his possession a bead-roll of all York's witches, a list of every last one. And each name had been written in the same infernal and unnatural hand. Joseph Hodgson has been able to find witches because he is among their number and because the devil has *told* him who they were!"

The Aldermen leaped to their feet, and once again chaos reigned. Some demanded to see this book, some shouted for Joseph's arrest, while Joseph insisted over the din that there was no such book. It took some doing, but at last the Lord Mayor imposed order on the crowd. The Aldermen turned to face Rebecca.

"You must wonder why I did not expose Mr. Hodgson as soon as I saw his book." Some on the Council nodded in agreement. "The truth is that I feared for my life. And it was not until I learned that Lady Hodgson shared similar suspicions that I could muster the courage to confront Mr. Hodgson."

The Aldermen looked between Rebecca and me before their eyes settled on Joseph. He remained still, but I had no doubt he was considering how best to defend himself. The answer seemed obvious: He would cast both Rebecca and me as witches and see us hanged. The question was whether he could accomplish this end.

"And my fears were well founded," Rebecca continued, her voice rising as she spoke. The Aldermen's eyes returned to her. "For today, mere moments after I determined to tell the truth about Mr. Hodgson, one of his devils—perhaps it was his familiar—burst into my chamber and did this!" Rebecca violently pulled down her scarf to reveal the bruises, by now a bright and angry purple, that *I* had given her just a few hours before.

The Aldermen gasped as one, and I choked back a cry of amazement at her audacity. Joseph started to speak, but Rebecca would not give him space.

"Even as I was at prayer this creature burst into my chamber and laid violent hands on me. Oh men, his black-scaled hands were hard as glass and cold as ice. I have no doubt that he had come to murder me, and I can only thank the good Lord that I did not perish at that demon's hands."

Rebecca glanced in my direction, and I thought a smile dashed across her face. I was the demon, of course.

"But it was not the Lord's will that I should die," she continued. "Nor was it His will that Mr. Hodgson should triumph, for neither Satan nor his agents ever will. But if the Council wishes to cleanse York of the stain of witchcraft, you should turn your attention to one of your own. The chief witch in all York is Joseph Hodgson."

The Aldermen looked at Joseph with a mix of fear and uncertainty. They had followed him for so long and were reluctant to turn against him. This was the moment when the battle would be decided, either for good or for ill.

Joseph stood to speak. "My Lord Mayor, these accusations are baseless, slanderous, and a crime against God's truth. It is well known that, through no fault of my own, Lady Hodgson has become my avowed enemy. And I need not remind you that her nephew has been taken for the murder of George Breary. Nor do I need to say that a boy from her household has been accused of witchcraft. I bear no malice toward her for her wanton words. She is merely a woman, a widow without a master to govern her, who will say anything in order to save her murderous family. She does not care that they have committed the most hateful of sins, she thinks only of her private interests. Let us drive this woman from the Council chamber and return to business."

It was a weak reply at best, and for that I had to give credit to Rebecca. How could Joseph argue with the bruises she had displayed? She had shaken him to his bones.

"And what of Mrs. Hooke?" The Lord Mayor's voice echoed through the hall, cold as stone and steel. "The meanest beggar in York knows that she hates Lady Hodgson above all others in the city. Why would she turn against you and run into the arms of her enemy?"

Joseph stared at the Lord Mayor and Rebecca, trying to find an answer to this question. Why *had* Rebecca betrayed him? His answer did not come soon enough. The Lord Mayor inclined his head to the side, and two bailiffs stepped forward to seize Joseph by his arms. As they did, Joseph began to berate all who were present in the most horrible terms. He called Rebecca and me lying whores, and he accused the Lord Mayor and the rest of the Aldermen of being bewitched by the two of us. The Alderman shouted back at him, and confusion ruled the day.

I watched Joseph's face as the bailiffs bound his hands and saw him come to some sort of realization. He straightened himself and set his shoulders. "My Lord Mayor," he cried. "You must hear me! It was James Hooke! He—"

Before Joseph could say any more, Rebecca took a candlestick from the table and struck him a vicious clout to the mouth. Joseph tried to continue, but Rebecca's blow left him spitting blood and teeth onto the floor. The bailiffs dragged him from the hall before he could say another word. I found Martha in a corner of the room, where she had hidden. She stood there, wide eyed and open mouthed.

"She did it," Martha breathed when I reached her side. "She brought him down."

"That is not all," I said. "I know who killed George Breary."

Martha looked at me in confusion. "Not Mark Preston? Or Joseph Hodgson?"

I shook my head and gestured for the door. It would not do to have this conversation in public. We slipped outside, and I guided her to the shelter of a doorway where we could speak without fear of being overheard.

"When we were at Grace Thompson's travail, the gossips were talking of the Lord Mayor's wife," I said.

"It *was* Agnes Greenbury!" Martha cried. "*She* had Mr. Breary killed!"

"It was not so simple," I replied. "They said that James Hooke was pining for Agnes Greenbury. They had seen him waiting outside her window, just hoping to catch a glimpse of her face. He was in love with her."

"It was James?" Martha considered the idea. Her face lit up when the pieces fell into place. "As soon as Joseph mentioned his name, Rebecca clouted him with the candlestick."

"Aye," I said. "That was when I solved the puzzle. Perhaps James saw George as his rival and killed him for it. Perhaps Agnes demanded it of him. We may never know, but it explains everything."

"Could Rebecca have demanded he do it?" Martha asked. "Mr. Breary was her enemy as well. He intended to remove her as the city's Searcher and put you in that position. She could never allow that."

"She is certainly capable of doing such a thing," I said.

"Joseph must have recognized James's guilt," Martha continued. "And that is why Rebecca turned against him. To save her son."

Martha and I stood in the doorway and watched as the Aldermen and their followers drifted out. Soon enough Rebecca and her footman stepped through the door and started walking toward her home in St. Michael's parish. Martha and I fell in behind her. When we were safely away from the Council Hall I called her name. Rebecca and her man stopped and waited for us to approach.

"We must speak," I said.

Rebecca understood the tone in my voice. "Wait at the corner," she told her man. He bowed and disappeared into the shadows. "What is it?"

I saw no reason to mince my words. "Your son murdered George Breary."

"*Another* murder accusation?" Rebecca asked. "You have done this before, and it did you no good. Must we put on the same old play?"

"George was my friend," I said. "Your son killed him, and I must know why."

"Why?" A harsh laugh escaped Rebecca's throat. "Who knows with such a blockish boy? Sometimes, Bridget, I think you were lucky to lose your children so young. They never reached an age when they could disappoint you."

"You pushed him to do it," Martha said. "Mr. Breary was going to rob you of your power, and you would not have it."

Rebecca laughed again. "And you think I would send James on such a mission? Have you met him? I cannot send him for a loaf of bread without something going wrong, let alone to murder a grown man. No, it was his doing."

"He did it to protect you," I said.

"I wish that were the case," Rebecca replied. "At least there would be some sense to that. No, he did it for that whore."

"Agnes Greenbury," I said. "He thought that if George were dead, she might turn her attention to him."

"Perhaps that is why," Rebecca replied, shaking her head in despair. "Or perhaps she convinced him to do it so she could be rid of that old goat. Whatever the case, the matter is near its end."

"How did Joseph find out that James killed Mr. Breary?" I asked. "That is why you decided to betray him, isn't it?"

When Rebecca smiled, her teeth gleamed in the moonlight. "My fool of a son went to Mr. Hodgson and announced that he'd done it. He hoped that Joseph would offer him a reward for ridding him of so troublesome a man."

"And you couldn't let that stand," Martha said.

"I might as well have tied a noose around my own neck and handed the loose end to Joseph," she replied. "I cannot allow anyone to have such an advantage over me. No, once James confessed his crime I had no choice but to act against Joseph."

"Joseph can still accuse him of the murder," I pointed out. "Even through broken teeth."

"And who will listen to an accused witch?" Rebecca paused for a moment. "But you make a good point. Perhaps I'll speak to the Lord Mayor and add Mr. Breary's murder to the charges against Joseph. Just to be sure." Rebecca nodded in satisfaction, leaving no doubt that she intended to do exactly that.

"I will see you at Joseph's trial," she said with a cold smile. "It should be a first-rate spectacle."

The week that followed Joseph's arrest passed with the pace and pain of a difficult birth. I did my best to think of other matters, but I could never draw my mind away from Will, Tree, and Elizabeth. Soon we received word from Samuel Short that Will and Tree, along with Stephen Daniels, had been sent to the Castle. Thanks to their escape from Ouse Bridge gaol, the Warden decreed that they would have no visitors, but Samuel had seen them when they arrived, and he said that all seemed in good health. I offered a prayer of thanks and sent enough blankets and food to keep them and their jailors more than comfortable. Of Elizabeth, we knew less, and it was this that kept me awake until the early morning hours. We knew that Joseph had sent her to live with a poor widow but, in an act of pure malice, he refused to say who it was, or if she even lived in the city.

Thankfully, the Lord Mayor sent word of Elizabeth's disappearance throughout York, and by God's grace she was discovered in Micklegate. It tore at my heart to know that she had been so frightened, and the joy I felt when she rushed into my arms was matched only by the enduring sorrow at Tree and Will's absence. I tried as best I could to live as if all would be well, but even Elizabeth could sense my worry. She wondered where the guards had taken Will and Tree, and if they had gone to live with poor widows as well.

"They are back in gaol," I explained. "But the man who put them there is soon to be punished, and then they will come home." That was what I prayed for, at least.

And there were signs that the storm had indeed passed. Rebecca Hooke recanted her testimony against the women still in gaol, and she claimed that Joseph had bewitched her into finding the Devil's Mark upon them. When Rebecca swore to this, the trials of other witches stopped. All told, Rebecca's scheme to overthrow Joseph seemed to be proceeding apace. But Grace Thompson's death had shown me—as if I needed reminding—that an easy travail did not mean an easy birth.

The week after Elizabeth came home, a boy appeared at my door with two notes from the Castle. One came from the Court of Special Assizes, announcing that Joseph would be tried the next day and ordering my presence as a witness.

The other was from Joseph. He wanted to see me.

Chapter 24

Martha paled when I showed her Joseph's note. "What could he want?"

"I don't know," I replied. "I asked the boy who brought it from the Castle, but he knew nothing either."

"Will you go?" She sounded as uncertain as I felt.

I did not know why Joseph would want to see me, or what I could gain by going. But neither could I see any danger in speaking to him.

"There is little he can do to hurt us so long as he is in the Castle," I said. "If Mark Preston were still alive I might worry, but without him, Joseph has been truly disarmed." I paused for a moment, wondering if this were true. Joseph had not come so far both in war and in government without being prepared for all eventualities. In the end, it was this uncertainty that drove me to the Castle. For the sake of my family I had to discover whether he had one last arrow in his quiver, and the only way to find out was to see him myself.

The next morning Martha and I walked to the Castle. As

we passed into the Castle yard we found the chapman Peter Newcome. He smiled and waved when he saw us, and we crossed the yard to speak with him.

"This is a remarkable turn of Fortune's Wheel, is it not?" he cried out as we approached. "The witch-hunter Joseph Hodgson is now turned into a witch, and accused of murder to boot! The printer is having a devil of a time keeping up with the news."

I could not help smiling at his enthusiasm. "I am grateful for your help in this affair. The book may not have found any readers, but you tried to help, which was very brave."

"Oh, I helped you." Newcome's smile reminded me of a well-fed fox.

"How so?" Martha asked.

"You are not the only one to come to me for news of the town. Your nephew burned the books. But you can't burn gossip, not when it concerns murder."

I stared at Newcome for a moment. "You spread the rumor that Joseph killed George Breary?"

Newcome shrugged. "I only told my customers what I'd heard. And it turned out to be true, didn't it? Else he'd not have been arrested."

"Then I am in your debt," I said. "You did not have to do that."

"I wanted to help your nephew," he replied. "That seemed the best way to go about it."

"I am grateful as well," Martha said. "Has there been any news about the women Mr. Hodgson imprisoned before his arrest?"

"Ah, there the Warden is in a bind," Newcome replied. "He can't try the women when one witness has recanted and another is accused of the same crime, can he? But if a prisoner owes him money for her keep, he can't send her home."

Martha stared at him in astonishment. "They are keeping women in gaol even if they have no plans to try them?"

"What choice does he have?" Newcome asked with a shrug. "Someone has to pay for their upkeep."

Martha started to argue, but stopped when she realized that fault lay with the Warden, not the chapman. I wondered how many women would die of gaol-fever for the crime of being poor. I told Newcome why we had come to the Castle and asked if he knew which tower held Joseph.

"The easternmost," Newcome replied, pointing across the yard. "Why would he ask to see you?"

"I wish I knew," I replied. "And there's only one way to find out."

"Well, if you would care to tell me after, I'm always on watch for a good story," Newcome called after us as we crossed the Castle yard.

We entered the tower, and after the customary haggling for fees, the jailor led us down the spiral stairs. After unlocking the door, he handed Martha a lantern and turned to go.

"You will not stay?" I called after him. "They say he is a dangerous man."

"Not any more he ain't," the jailor replied. "I got him in irons." He disappeared up the stairs without a backward look.

Martha and I glanced at each other and pushed open the door. Our breath turned to mist before us, and I could feel the cold seeping into my bones even before we crossed the threshold. The walls, which in summer glistened with water and slime, were now covered by a layer of ice and shimmered celestial silver in the flickering lamplight.

As in most of the lower cells, there was only one piece of furniture, a heavy wood bed with a rough mattress on it. Joseph sat on the bed, staring at us. He had drawn his knees to his chest, and I could see that, like the women jailed for witchcraft, he'd been shackled hand and foot. Unlike the women, however, Joseph seemed in perfect health. Indeed, so perfect was his visage that for a moment I wondered if it might not be entirely natural. Could Rebecca's accusations of witchcraft, however false in intent, have been true?

When we entered his cell, Joseph smiled at us. It was a terrible thing to behold, for his broken teeth now seemed more like fangs.

"You never could resist a summons," Joseph said. Even his voice bespoke his strength. If Joseph were going to die, it would not be of gaol-fever. "Have they released Will yet?"

"No," I replied. "The Lord Mayor said that he would wait until after your trial."

"Yes, I imagine that so cautious a man would want to do that." Joseph smiled mirthlessly.

"What do you want with us?" Martha asked.

"I don't really know," Joseph sighed. "Perhaps I wanted you to see what they'd done to me. I was awake for days as they beat me. *Who were your familiars?* they asked, and *What did the devil look like when he came to you?* I suppose I should have just given them answers and been done with it. Then, at least, they would have eased my torture."

"You never confessed?" I asked.

Joseph barked with laughter. "Everyone confesses, Aunt

Bridget. Everyone. I know not what I said, but they would not have let me alone if I'd stood mute."

"And you want me to feel pity for you?" I asked. I could not believe his audacity.

"No, of course not," Joseph said. "You are not so tender as that. But tell me, will you have a hand in sending me to the gallows? Or will you let Rebecca Hooke do that?"

"The court has called me to testify, and I will do so," I said. "But Rebecca Hooke will do her part as well."

"I oughtn't have put my trust in such a harpy," Joseph said.

"No," I replied. "That was a mistake."

"And you'll join her in sending an innocent man to his death?" Joseph asked. "You know I'm no witch. You know James Hooke is the one who killed George Breary."

"You might not be guilty of those crimes, but you are far from innocent." I wondered if he would remember speaking those very words about Will.

"I did say that, didn't I?" Joseph said with a slight and terrible smile. "But if you do this, Aunt Bridget, it will change who you are. You will be an outlaw in all but name."

My mind turned to the guards who had died during Will's escape from Ouse Bridge gaol. I glanced at my hands, still surprised that they were not stained crimson. "That will be no new thing," I murmured.

"If you testify, you will become Rebecca Hooke's maidservant," Joseph said. "And you can see from my poor example where such a joining will get you." His manacles clinked softly when he held up his hands.

He was right, of course. For months, York had talked of nothing at all except the women who had fallen into the devil's snare when they traded their souls for power over their neighbors. Yet here I was, doing the very same thing, only my devil would be named Rebecca Hooke. Once Joseph was hanged, Rebecca and I would be comrades of a sort, partners in his murder. The problem for me, of course, was that her ruthlessness would give her the upper hand in all our future dealings. I could no more escape her than a witch could escape Satan.

"Join me," Joseph said.

I looked at him in shock. "What do you mean?"

"I'll tell them I have more to say. If I accuse her, and you testify with me, we can see *her* hanged in my place. You can tell the jury that she bewitched you and demand to search her for the Witch's Mark. I'm sure you could find it if you looked. We both know that there is no more dangerous a woman in York."

"In England," I corrected him. And for a moment I considered his proposal. But I knew such a scheme was unlikely to work, and even if we were successful Joseph would be no less deadly a foe than Rebecca. One of them had to die, and I chose Joseph. Without another word I turned to the door.

"I'll find a way through this," Joseph called after us as Martha pulled the door shut. "And when I do, I'll hunt you and I'll kill you." His voice, with its terrifying mix of panic and fury, echoed up the stairs.

"He means it," Martha said as we hurried across the Castle yard.

"I know." My mind raced as we passed through the Castle gate toward the city.

"Do you think it's possible? With Mark Preston dead, Joseph seems as good as hanged, but if he somehow escapes the noose . . ." she trailed off.

"If he doesn't hang, we'll pay with our lives," I said.

"Then what can we do?" Martha asked.

I did not answer. What *could* we do?

In a coincidence that struck all who were present, Joseph's trial for witchcraft was to take place in the same hall that Hester Jackson's had. Fortune's Wheel turned round indeed, and we'd come back to where we started. The location, however, was where the similarities stopped, for the trial of a poor old woman could hardly compare to one in which the accused was among the city's most powerful men. The hall was packed with scores of men and women, and others braved the cold outside, just to be near the spectacle. The Lord Mayor had dispensed with the aged fool who had tried Mother Lee, and the new judge, whom I knew not, took his duties seriously.

Joseph stood to one side of the bench, his eyes searching the courtroom. His hands were shackled, but they'd removed the fetters from his feet. He had also convinced (or paid) the guard to bring him clean clothes, and he'd washed himself well. He looked far better than he had any right to, and except for his broken teeth he seemed little different than he had before his arrest. I asked the bailiff how things would proceed, and he told me that there were just two witnesses against Joseph: Rebecca Hooke and me. I felt a pang of dismay at this, for I'd hoped to spread the burden of convicting Joseph a bit more widely, but there was little to be done now.

The judge demanded quiet, and the crowd complied. The charges against Joseph were announced, and the bailiff summoned Rebecca and asked her name. I should have known that something was amiss as soon as she began to speak, for she'd abandoned the stentorian voice she'd used to address the Aldermen and now sounded meek and compliant. I pushed my worries aside, but they returned in force as soon the prosecutor asked her about the book containing the names of all York's witches.

"I thought I saw it, and that's what I told the Council," she said softly. "But I may have been wrong. It may have just been a bead-roll of the Town Watch or the garrison."

I heard Martha gasp, and I am quite sure that the surprise on my face was a match for the prosecutor's. The crowd began to murmur as well—this was not what they expected.

The prosecutor did his best to recover himself before returning to his questions. "You told the Lord Mayor himself that you'd seen a list of witches' names, a list written in the devil's own hand," he insisted. "You told the entire Council that Mr. Hodgson had bewitched you!"

"That is what I believed," Rebecca sighed. "But I am no longer so sure. The book might have been something else. And it might not have been Mr. Hodgson who bewitched me, for he is known to love the Lord above all else. Someone else may have bewitched me. I cannot say if I was bewitched at all. I am but a poor widow, and easily misled."

With those words it seemed as if a riot had broken out in the hall. Some dashed from the room to tell those outside what had happened, and everyone present seemed compelled to discuss the matter with his neighbor.

I grasped Martha's hand as I tried to control the panic that welled up within me. What in God's name was Rebecca doing? I looked at Joseph and found him staring at me. When our eyes met, an infernal smile crossed his face. His mouth seemed to form the words *I told you so,* but with all the noise I could not hope to hear him.

With a wave of his hand, the prosecutor dismissed Rebecca from her testimony.

"What the Christ has happened?" Martha hissed in my ear. "Has he joined with Rebecca? What are we going to do? If he goes free, all is lost."

She did not have to elaborate. If Joseph escaped the noose and returned to power, my family would be destroyed. I would lose Elizabeth, both Will and Tree would hang, and the trials of witches would begin once again. And with Rebecca's hint that someone other than Joseph had bewitched her, I could not be sure that Martha and I were safe. Within weeks, we could all be dead.

The prosecutor came to me, panic clear in his face. "What has happened here?" he demanded. "The two of you are making a fool of me!"

Rebecca had disappeared into the crowd, and Joseph stood tall, his shoulders thrown back, every inch the cavalry officer he'd been a few years before. A handful of Alderman had crossed the room to speak with him, a sure sign that they thought he might go free. I considered the choice of paths that lay before me, and the toll that each would demand. But in the end the decision was not a hard one.

"Call me as a witness, and I will see this through," I replied, and told him what I needed him to do. After I explained my plan, I glanced at Martha, who nodded in approval.

"Your scheme had better work," the prosecutor said. "Or we'll both suffer."

"I know that far better than you," I breathed.

As the Judge and bailiffs tried to return the hall to some semblance of order, I closed my eyes and said a prayer. I did not know if God would aid perjurers in their work, but if He did not I would lose all that I held dear.

"Lady Hodgson," the prosecutor began. "You have known Joseph Hodgson for many years, have you not?"

"Yes I have," I replied. "I came to York when he was a youth, and I was married to his uncle." All the jurymen knew this, of course, but the customs of law must be obeyed. I found it curious that for the first time in my life the truth felt strange on my tongue. No doubt it was because I knew the lies that would soon follow.

"When did you begin to suspect he was a witch?"

"In truth, it was soon after he began to hunt for witches within the city. He had never done such a thing before—what could he know of witches?—yet he discovered them wherever he looked. I wondered how that could be." As I spoke, I looked from the prosecutor, to the judge, to the jurymen. I had no desire to see Joseph's reaction to my lies.

"My work as a midwife brought me to the Castle," I continued. "Here I talked to women who would soon hang for their witchery. When they heard his name, they quailed in fear, and I wanted to know why."

"Did they tell you?"

"Aye. It took some doing, but I convinced a few of them to tell me the truth. They did not deny their crimes, but they claimed that my nephew, Joseph Hodgson, had tricked and enticed them into witchcraft with false promises and feigned affection. I then realized that *he* was their imp, sent by Satan himself to lure them into damnation." The jurymen glanced nervously from my face to Joseph's. I knew they would be torn: They would not want to hear that a man such as Joseph had fallen into the Devil's hands, but they would believe my words because I was a gentlewoman and a midwife.

"And more than one woman told you this?"

"Half a dozen," I replied. I sounded so sure of myself, I could almost believe my own lies. "They came from different cells in the Castle, but they told similar tales, so I believed it to be true."

"Are these women still living?"

"No," I said. "Joseph saw to it that they were hanged before they could expose him for his crimes."

"If you believed that Joseph was a witch, why did you not accuse him?"

I laughed at this in the same way I imagined Rebecca would. "Because I saw what happened to those who opposed him."

"What do you mean?"

I turned to address the jurymen directly. "When George Breary tried to stop the witch-hunts, Joseph murdered him."

As I'd hoped and expected, the jurymen stared at me in amazement. A great hubbub broke out within the hall, and I heard a strangled cry from my left. I took this to be Joseph's objection, but I kept my eyes on the jury. The prosecutor waited until the judge had quieted the room before he continued.

"Joseph Hodgson murdered George Breary?" he asked in amazement. His surprise was feigned, of course, but nobody who heard him would have known. "How do you know?"

"Because George told me this before he died."

Once again the crowd began to murmur, and Joseph tried to object, but the judge demanded silence.

"Tell me what happened."

I told the jury the story of George's death. I omitted his awkward marriage proposal, of course, but when I told how

Will, Martha, and I had found his body, my lies began in earnest.

"When we discovered him, he had been beaten most terribly," I said. "We carried him to my home and comforted him as best we could. It was then that he told us what happened. He said that he had been in his home when Joseph Hodgson came to his door and asked to speak to him outside. George thought it strange given the late hour and the cold, but never suspected Joseph might kill him.

"Once they were outside, Joseph struck him. George fled, but he could not escape. We heard his cries, but by the time we arrived, Joseph was gone and George could not be saved. He lived for an hour after we returned to my house. When he first told me who had done this, I refused to accept it. What woman wants to believe her beloved nephew is a murderer? But he swore on his soul that it was the truth."

"So you believed him?"

"No dying man would imperil his soul by telling such a lie. The danger is too great and the profit too small."

"Was there anything else that convinced you of Mr. Hodgson's guilt?" The prosecutor was playing his part admirably. The only shame was that he was aiding perjury.

"Aye. When Joseph and the other Aldermen came to my house to view the body, a strange and wonderful thing happened. It could only be a sign from the Lord." I paused for a moment, knowing that I held the jury in my hand. "Mr. Breary had been dead for some hours, and his wounds had long stopped bleeding. But as soon as Joseph entered the room, his wounds began to bleed afresh, as if he'd only suffered them moments before."

The jurymen nodded to themselves. There could be no surer mark of Joseph's guilt.

After I'd finished, the prosecutor summoned Martha, who echoed my story, adding a few details to secure Joseph's guilt and execution. Joseph protested as the bailiffs dragged him from the room, but none paid him any mind.

Martha and I waited while the jury considered the case.

They found Joseph guilty both of witchcraft and of George Breary's murder. He was, of course, sentenced to be hanged.

Tears froze on my cheeks as Martha and I walked home.

Chapter 25

By the time we got home my tears had stopped, but Martha and I had not yet spoken. She broke the silence when the door shut behind us.

"It was the right thing to do," she said.

"My nephew is going to hang for a murder he did not commit," I replied. "How can that be the right thing to do?"

"If an innocent man is going to hang, better Joseph than Will. Better that icy-hearted beast than someone we both love. And do not forget that he threatened to hang us, or that your lies saved Tree's life and kept Elizabeth in your home. Those may have been lies, but they were among the finest words ever spoken and the world is better for them. This was a war, and you cannot lament the enemy dead. Not until they are safely buried."

"What of the guards who died when Will and Tree escaped?" I asked. "What wrong had they done? Why should they die while Will and Tree live?"

"Because death was their lot. Because Will and Tree are

yours, and the guards were not. Mourn them, comfort their families, pay school fees for their children, do what you must. But do not think you took the wrong course."

"School fees will not bring back their fathers or replace the love their widows have lost," I replied. Without warning I was overcome by weakness and tumbled into a chair. I felt as if every drop of blood had been drawn from my body. "School fees will not salve my conscience."

"Your conscience needs no salve." Martha knelt next to me and took my hand. "You did nothing wrong. The preachers tell us we live in a fallen world. So much of what they say is mere baggage, but in this they are right. This week we all drew lots. The guards drew Death, as did Mark Preston, Joseph, and all the women he hanged. You were lucky. You drew Life. Do not forget that it could have been otherwise."

I felt a sad smile cross my face. "When did you start listening to ministers?"

"It is the one sensible thing they've said," she replied. "And I don't need a sermon to tell me the world is a cold and heartless place that has no regard for the weak."

I sat for a time, considering her words. Although I knew it was too late to change course, I tried to imagine a way to save Will, Tree, and Elizabeth that did not require Joseph's death.

I could not find one.

The next day—the day Joseph was to be hanged for witchcraft and murder—I stayed in my house. I prayed that the Lord would wash my hands of the guilt that I still felt, but that prayer only put me in mind of Pontius Pilate, and I felt all the worse. That afternoon a boy from the Castle came to us and told us that Joseph was dead.

In the days that followed, York's gaols slowly emptied of the women accused of witchcraft. Without Joseph or Rebecca to push them, the courts had lost their thirst for blood. The women who could not repay the city for the cost of their imprisonment languished in their cells until their relatives could gather money enough to satisfy the Warden. I later learned that half a dozen women died of gaol-fever because they were too poor to buy their freedom.

I sent nearly twenty shillings to the Castle in hope of speeding Will and Tree's release, and the day after Joseph's death Samuel Short wrote with the joyful news that Tree had been restored to him. As soon as the note arrived, Martha, Elizabeth, and I dashed to the Castle. We brought with us a new suit of clothes for Tree and as much food as we could carry.

"Do you think Will is there as well?" Martha asked as we wove through the crowded streets. The fact that we'd heard nothing of or from Will worried us both, and we did not know what it could mean. Perhaps he'd fallen ill—or worse.

"He could be with Samuel and Tree, waiting to surprise us," Elizabeth suggested. I prayed that was the case.

When we entered the Castle, the sight of a three-legged mare greeted us, nooses still dangling from the crossbeams.

"They must have hanged Joseph here," Martha ventured. "More private than the market at least."

I looked away from the gallows. I had no interest in dwelling on my role in his death.

As soon as we arrived at Samuel's tower, Tree dashed into our arms. When I was able to free myself from his embrace, I looked him over. Samuel had shaved his head to free him from lice, but aside from that he seemed as fit as could be. There could be no doubt that the Lord had watched over him with especial care. While Tree and Elizabeth devoured the cakes I'd brought and talked of their separate adventures—Elizabeth's visits to the market seemed no less remarkable than Tree's time in gaol—Martha and I turned to Samuel.

"Have you heard any news of Will?" Martha demanded. "Why wasn't he released with Tree?"

Samuel's brows knit in confusion. "All three of them—Stephen Daniels, Will, and Tree—walked out of the gaol together, nearly three hours ago," he replied. "Will told me he'd go straight to your house. You haven't seen him?"

Martha and I looked at each other. The relief I'd felt upon seeing Tree turned to concern for Will.

"How did he seem?" I asked Samuel. I could not imagine where he could be.

"He was distant, to be sure," Samuel replied. "He wandered as if in a daze, following close behind Daniels. He didn't even bid Tree farewell."

"We must find him," Martha said. She nearly managed to keep the worry from her voice. "There aren't many places he could go."

"Wait," I said. Something else seemed strange. "They released Stephen Daniels as well? He killed the guards."

"I didn't ask why." Samuel shrugged. "The gates opened wide, and every prisoner who could walk fled as quick as he could. I saw him and Will leave the Castle together."

Tree and Elizabeth refused to be separated, so we took them both to my home and put them in Hannah's care. We then turned to the question of where Will could have gone. A penniless man newly freed from gaol had few options before him.

"Perhaps he went to Helen Wright's," Martha suggested.

"After spending so many nights in gaol, he may have wanted the chance to bathe and change his clothes before coming home."

Martha's was the best explanation we found, so we kissed the children farewell and walked south toward Micklegate Bar.

Helen's maidservant answered our knock and ushered us into the parlor. Helen hurried in a few moments later. Gone were the days when she would make us wait simply because she could. She smiled broadly when she saw us (another first), embraced Martha, and grasped my hands. More remarkable than this was that I welcomed the gesture and *I* embraced *her*. If the Lord could let a fallen woman wash His feet, perhaps a bawd and I could become fast friends. Helen called for a warming drink, and I explained why we had come.

"Will didn't come home?" Helen asked. The surprise on her face only increased my own worry.

"We thought he might have come here," Martha said. I could hear the fear in her voice. "You haven't seen him at all?"

"Stephen is sleeping, but for this I'll wake him," Helen said.

Helen returned a few minutes later with Stephen Daniels at her side. He had shaved his head, but even so there could be no mistaking that his time in gaol had taken its toll. His cheeks were hollowed, and his eyes had dark circles beneath them. He smiled wanly when he saw our reaction, and he ran a hand over his scalp.

"Samuel Short said you left the Castle with Will," Martha said. She had no time for idle talk. "Do you know where he went?"

"We entered the city together, and parted ways when we reached the Ouse Bridge. I came south, and he turned on Coney Street. I assumed he was going straight to you," he said. "Where else could he go?"

"That's what we are trying to find out," I replied.

"Samuel Short said that he seemed strange when he left," Martha said. "Was he not pleased to be free?"

"He was pleased at the prospect," Daniels replied. "But after the hanging he seemed overcome by melancholy."

"Hanging?" I asked.

"We could see his brother's execution from the window of our cell," Daniels replied.

"Oh, Christ," Martha said. "And he watched?"

"I tried to talk him out of it," Daniels said. "What good could come of seeing such a thing? Afterward a guard told us how it had come to pass."

"And what did he say?" I asked. A knot of fear began to grow in my guts.

"That you testified against Mr. Hodgson and accused him of witchcraft and of murdering Mr. Breary," Stephen replied. "It was all the talk in the Castle. It's not often that a man like Mr. Hodgson finds himself on the loop-end of the hangman's rope."

"What did the guard say?" I demanded. "Did he tell you what I said to the jury?"

"Aye, every word. He said he was in the hall when you spoke. After that Will sat in the corner of the cell until we were released."

"And he said nothing?" I asked.

"He prayed some," Daniels replied. "And he told me he was going home. That was all."

I thanked Helen and Stephen for their help, and then Martha and I began the journey home. The cold seemed to bite more fiercely than it had earlier in the day, and though the sun shone brightly it provided little warmth.

"He knows I lied about Joseph," I said. "He blames me for his brother's death."

"*We* lied," Martha said. "And he knows we had no choice. He cannot blame you for it."

"Then where is he?" I asked. "He only had to walk a few more steps, and he would have been home."

Martha did not reply. What could she have said? We arrived home to the joyful noise of children full of cakes, but Will had not returned.

That night I knelt and prayed that the Lord would deliver Will from whatever melancholy afflicted him and bring him safely into my home and into Martha's arms.

When I heard a knock at the door the next morning my heart began to pound in my chest. I did not think that it would be Will—why would he start to knock now?—but I feared that it might be a messenger with ill news. I opened the door to find a young man standing outside.

"My lady," he murmured with a low and practiced bow. "The Right Worshipful Lord Mayor Matthew Greenbury requests your presence immediately. And your deputy's as well."

"Can you tell me what this concerns?" I asked.

"No, my lady," he said. "He simply asked me to deliver the summons."

"Of course," I replied. "I shall have to dress. Tell the Lord Mayor I will call on him within an hour." The lad bowed once again and set off.

I called for Martha and told her what had happened. I could see the worry on her face.

"I don't think it is related to Will," I assured her. "If something had happened he would not be so formal."

Martha went to change into her best dress, and I summoned

Hannah to help me do the same. Within the hour we were on our way.

"Could he know that we discovered his wife's adultery?" Martha asked as we walked. "Perhaps he simply wants to warn us to keep his secrets." We had crossed the Ouse Bridge and entered Micklegate Ward.

"Perhaps," I replied. I had no idea what he could want.

We knocked on the Lord Mayor's door and the footman ushered us in. He sent Martha to the kitchen to wait with the rest of the servants and led me to the Lord Mayor. As we passed the parlor I could not help remembering our conversation with young Agnes. Had it only been a few weeks earlier? Her infidelities seemed so small compared to the carnage that had followed.

The Lord Mayor was sitting at his desk when I entered. He did not rise, nor did he bid me sit. This, it seemed, would be a formal visit.

"You have caused a great deal of trouble in recent weeks, my lady."

"We live in troubled times, my Lord Mayor."

The Lord Mayor smiled at this, but I found little warmth in his eyes. "True enough. But I am unused to it coming from a gentlewoman."

"No, my Lord Mayor." I lowered my eyes, hoping that my deference might purge him of his ill humor.

"Your scheme to destroy your nephew would put Machiavelli himself to shame," he said after a moment. This was why he'd summoned me.

I could think of no response that would satisfy him, so I lowered my eyes once again and remained silent.

"I should thank you, I suppose," he continued. "It was clear to all that Joseph intended to make himself lord of the city. I did not know how I would stop him until you and Rebecca Hooke laid him at my feet, as neatly as a spaniel with a fowl. You and she make a fine brace of dogs."

I found the comparison to be irksome, and my pairing with Rebecca hateful, but I held my tongue. I did not know where our conversation would end, and I did not wish to anger him.

"If you have any similar scheme to rid me of James Hooke, I should be equally grateful," he said. "I would rather not have a murderer walking the city's streets, gloring over my wife."

I gasped and looked up. "You know James murdered George Breary?"

"Of course," the Lord Mayor replied with a laugh. "The fool told Agnes what he'd done, and she came straight to me. I know few would recognize it, but she is a good girl in her own fashion. So long as she was discreet and kept me warm on these cold winter nights, I could tolerate her youthful dalliances." His mirthless smile returned, and I could not help thinking that he believed he had the better part of their agreement.

"I saw the bruises on her wrist," I said. "They are not the sign of someone so liberal."

"Oh, that wasn't for her jumbling," the Lord Mayor corrected me. "It was because I had to clean up the mess she made. The city might forgive adultery, especially in one so young and trifling, but if she became enmeshed in Mr. Breary's murder? That would be a far more serious matter. And I will tell you, hiding her relationship to George Breary was neither easy nor cheap."

With this admission I realized I could answer one more question about George's murder.

"You are the one who burned George's papers."

"Well *I* didn't, of course," he replied. "I paid one of his servants to do it. Who knew what that besotted fool might have written down? It is better to be safe."

"What do you intend to do about James Hooke?" I asked.

"What *can* I do?" He shrugged. "You saw to it that your nephew hanged for George's murder. I can't hang another man for the same crime even if he is guilty. The people are often senseless, but they are not so forgetful as that."

He paused for a moment and stared into my eyes.

"I should warn you," he said, "James Hooke's guilt in the matter is a private affair. You will tell nobody. Do you understand?"

"Yes, my Lord Mayor." What else could I have said?

I stood in silence for a moment, reflecting on what had just happened. Once again, the law had failed to provide justice, only this time I'd had a hand in its failure. I wondered if perhaps the preachers were right when they said that the summer's heat and the winter's brutal cold were the Lord's punishment of an unjust nation. But I was a part of the nation, wasn't I?

"One more thing," the Lord Mayor said. "Will Hodgson is here. You should probably see him before you leave the city."

Chapter 26

My head spun as I tried to grasp all that the Lord Mayor had said. At first my heart leaped at the prospect of finding Will, safe and sound, but what did he mean by *before you leave the city*?

Greenbury rang a bell on his desk, and a servant entered. "Bring Mr. Hodgson," Greenbury said. "And Lady Hodgson's deputy as well." The servant bowed and slipped soundlessly from the room.

"I will leave you alone," the Lord Mayor said. "But we will talk again before you go."

Before I could answer, or ask him to explain his words, he strode from the room.

Martha came in first, her eyes wide with excitement. "He is here?" she asked. "He has been here all along? How so?"

I started to reply, but the door opened again and Will came in. I was shocked by his incongruous appearance, for his clothes, which the Lord Mayor must have gifted him, bespoke a man at the prime of life: rich wool was matched with fine silk, and the style could not have been more in fashion, nor could the suit have been better cut to Will's figure. But the clothes seemed to have been made for a dead man, for Will's shaven head, sunken cheeks, and hollowed eyes gave him the look of a corpse. As soon as he saw us, his face crumpled, and he began to cry uncontrollably. He stumbled across the room and in to Martha's arms.

Half carrying Will, and now crying herself, Martha found her way to a padded bench that sat against the wall. She leaned back and cradled his head in her lap while he sobbed. My heart bled for him, for the two of them, but all I could do was stand to the side, a useless spectator.

After a time, an eternity it seemed, Will pushed himself upright and looked at me.

"You killed him, Aunt Bridget," he said. His words accused me, but his broken tone begged me to deny the charge.

"Will, I had no choice," I replied. "I saved your life, and Tree's life as well. He took Elizabeth!" I could hear my voice rising as I spoke. I crossed the room and knelt at his side, desperate to make him understand my actions.

"He would never have done any of that," Will insisted. "He would never have let me hang. He was simply seeking an advantage against you. At worst, he would have driven you from the city. We could have left together, all of us."

"Will, that's not true," Martha said. "He sent Mark Preston to kill us both."

"No." Will shook his head, unwilling or unable to hear our words. "Joseph would never do such a thing. Preston must have come on his own, without Joseph's knowledge. *He* might have murdered Mr. Breary, but my brother would not."

"Will, your brother was not simply playing at this," I insisted. "He killed in the war, he hanged the witches, and he would have hanged you and Tree as well."

"So you joined with Rebecca Hooke to see him hanged. How could you not have consulted me in this? He was my *brother*. Can you not see that you were in the wrong?"

"All of that is unimportant right now," a voice announced from behind us. The Lord Mayor had returned. "Joseph Hodgson is dead, and while my powers are wide, I cannot unhang a man." He smiled to himself, clearly enjoying his little jest. "What concerns me now is not his past but *your* future.

"Lady Hodgson, I have seen your nephew's worth," the Lord Mayor continued. "And I have determined to keep him with me. He is a capable young man, and in our present times such men are invaluable."

"He does not need you," I snapped. "With Joseph dead, Will has come into his father's estate."

The Lord Mayor shook his head sadly, but the sorrow did not reach his eyes. "It is a terrible thing. The war took its toll, and Joseph did not have half the head for trade that his father did. It took only a few months, but he borrowed far beyond his ability to pay. There is nothing left, not even the house."

"And I presume the debts are owed to you?" I asked.

"Among many others on the Council," the Lord Mayor said. "But I am not such a fool as to turn Will onto the street. I have offered him a place in my house, and he has accepted. I am certain that he will serve me well."

"And what of George Breary's estate? You burned his will, but surely some provision can be made for Will out of his fortune."

Greenbury offered a pained smile. "The only surviving will is from last year. According to its terms Will and Mr. Breary's other godchildren will receive five pounds each. The rest of his estate will go to a cousin."

"A cousin?" I asked.

"In Durham of all places." Greenbury turned to Will. "By burning Mr. Breary's papers, I have done you a grave disservice. I am genuinely sorry for that, but there is nothing I can do."

Will did not reply.

"Will may stay in York but the two of you are less welcome in the city." Greenbury turned back to Martha and me. "Indeed, I have come to mislike your presence above all others."

"We have done nothing," Martha started to object.

"Nothing?" Greenbury gasped. "You were entirely wrapped up in the business of witches. You killed Mark Preston, and you sent Joseph Hodgson to the gallows. If that is *nothing*, I cannot stand idly by and wait for you to do *something*. The city might not survive it."

I wanted desperately to point out that my hand had been forced in each of these cases, but I knew my words would have no effect. "You cannot drive me from the city," I said softly.

The expression on the Lord Mayor's face made it clear that I'd overstepped my bounds.

"*Cannot*, my lady? Do you presume to tell me what I *cannot* do?" His words had the sound of newly forged steel, and I knew that there would be no appealing his decision. "Your brother Edward is dead," Greenbury continued. "George Breary is dead. Your nephew is a pauper in my service. Who will defend you? You have no friends beyond the city's gossips, nothing to protect you except your name and your wealth. At other times your name alone might have been enough to save you, but we do not live in other times. You remain in York at my pleasure, and my pleasure has run its course."

"What do you mean for us to do?" I asked.

"You and yours will leave the city before the month is out," he replied. "Where you go is none of my concern, but go you must."

"When can we return?" I asked. "You cannot banish us forever. This is our home."

"Return?" he asked as if the thought had not occurred to him. "Any time after I breathe my last. Then you can come back to York and trouble some other man."

"Then you'll forgive me if I do not wish you well." I heard my voice speaking the words as if on its own volition.

To my relief (and for the first time in my memory), the Lord Mayor laughed aloud. "No, Lady Bridget, given the circumstances, I cannot fault your lack of charity." He suddenly became serious, and once again his eyes found mine. "But you will leave. There will be no reprieve of this sentence."

His voice, his expression, everything about him made clear that he had no intention of changing his mind. I bowed my head and accepted his judgment.

"Good," he said. "Your nephew will see you home. You can say your farewells then."

As soon as we stepped outside, Martha turned to Will and grasped his hands. "Come with us," she implored him. "There is no reason you cannot. We all can go to Hereford, and we'll marry there."

I felt my heart being rent in two as Will pulled his hands from Martha's and turned away. "I cannot," he said.

"Will—," I started to say.

He turned to me, his eyes wet with tears. "No, Aunt Bridget. No. Do you think that I can simply forget what has happened? What you did?"

"Will, we had no choice," Martha protested.

"You I can forgive more easily," he replied. I recognized the bitter tone in Will's voice, and knew what he was about to say.

"Will, don't——," I said. But he was not going to listen to me or any woman.

"You were misled. You did not know what you were doing. It was my aunt."

Martha's expression of surprise and pain turned to anger in mere moments.

"I did not know what I was doing, William Hodgson?" she cried. "I did not know? I'll tell you what I know. I know that your brother was a cruel and ambitious man, who would destroy anyone who stood in his way. And I know that your aunt was the only soul in York courageous enough to resist him. Out of her love for you, she hazarded her life and estate to rescue you from gaol, and then she perjured herself to ensure that you were not hanged for George Breary's murder. I am proud to have played a part in her plans. But make no mistake: I knew *exactly* what I was doing, and I would have done it myself if your aunt had not. If you are too blind to see what is before your eyes, I cannot show it to you."

For a moment I hoped that Will might see the wisdom in Martha's words, but the pain at his brother's death was too fresh. Without bothering to respond, he turned away from us and gazed toward the Minster. I resolved to try another approach.

"Will, I am the only family you have," I said. "And you can take Martha as your wife. Come to Hereford. I will make you steward of one of my estates. It will be a good life."

"Is killing my brother not enough?" Will asked, his voice tight with grief. He mourned the death of his brother, of course, but I think he had resigned himself to losing Martha and me as well. "You wish to take me from the city my family has ruled for generations? My father and his father were Lord Mayors of York! You would have me content myself with life as a country shepherd?"

"Will, please," I persisted. "Come with us."

He turned to look at both of us, sorrow deeply etched on his face. He seemed to have aged a decade in mere weeks.

"Someday, perhaps," he said. His words sang with sorrow. "I have lost so much this year. My father, my godfather, and now my brother. Someday I will forgive you for your place in all this, but I cannot do that yet. It is too soon." He turned to Martha and took her hands. "I love you Martha Hawkins. And someday I will marry you. But not now."

Without another word or backward glance, Will turned and walked away.

The weeks that followed consisted of frantic preparations for our flight from the city. I wrote to friends and family who lived between York and my estate in Pontrilas, begging their hospitality during the journey. Each day I visited a few of my city friends and, as delicately as I could, called in my debts. With that money, I purchased a carriage and horses, for I knew that once in Hereford I would need one of my own. All the while, Hannah and Martha packed our goods and arranged to have them sent to Hereford. And all the while, we hoped and prayed that Will would change his mind and rejoin our family.

For her part, Elizabeth wondered why Will no longer lived with us, but soon she was overcome by the prospect of moving. I told her about my own youth in the country, and all she could expect. It seemed a grand adventure to her, and for that I gave thanks.

The end of the month loomed before us, and while I did not know what the Lord Mayor would do if we ignored his order, I did not want to find out. The day before we were to leave, a knock at the door echoed through the halls of my now-empty house. As with every other knock, I said a prayer that it was Will, come home at last. And, as on every other occasion, the Lord denied my petition. This time it was Stephen Daniels and Helen Wright.

"I'd ask you to join me in the parlor, but the only furniture left are the beds and the dining hall chairs," I said.

Helen looked around my home and shook her head in amazement. "When I heard the news, I could hardly credit it. But you really are leaving."

"With all that has happened, it seemed best not to test the Lord Mayor's patience," I replied.

"I suppose not," she said. "So you will leave York to enjoy the country life? It hardly seems to suit you."

"I will be rejoining family and friends from my youth, so it will be like a homecoming," I said. My words sounded hollow, and I knew that the emptiness of the room was not entirely to blame. Each night I prayed that the Lord Mayor would offer a reprieve—or, in my less charitable moments, that God would call the Lord Mayor to His bosom—but I did not think I would be so fortunate.

"When will you return?" she asked.

"Upon the Lord Mayor's death," I replied. "And how long could that be?"

"He is an ancient man with a young and lusty wife," Helen replied. "Perhaps she will jumble him into his grave."

"There are worse ways to die," Stephen commented with a wry smile.

Sam Thomas

"I wonder if I could ask a favor of you," Helen said. "It could serve us both."

I nodded.

"Take Stephen with you," she said. "He will help keep you safe during your journey."

I looked at Helen in confusion. If I was right that he meant more to her than an ordinary servant, why was she doing this? Before I could pose the question, Helen answered.

"He cannot stay in York, either. The deaths at Ouse Bridge gaol turned more than a few men against him, and many are bitter at his release from the Castle. The law is a fickle thing, and who is to say that it won't turn against him? I should very much hate to see him hanged."

"You will send him away from you?" Martha asked. I had not heard her enter the room.

Tears appeared at the corners of Helen's eyes. "My business, my home, everything I have is here. And I do not have estates to which we can flee." She smiled to show that she did not begrudge me my wealth.

"And it is not forever," she continued. "Just until memories have faded. The men who died were young and without families. Thousands like them have died in the wars, and we pay them no mind. The city will forget soon enough."

I considered Helen's offer. I had hired a soldier to drive the carriage south, but I would rather have Stephen. I did not know what he would do once we reached Hereford—he seemed ill suited for a country life—but that was a question for another day.

"We would welcome his company," I replied, and with that our party was complete.

*   *   *

When the time came for us to depart, Samuel and Tree came into town to see us off. I had suggested—and Elizabeth had begged—that Tree accompany us, but neither he nor Samuel would consider it.

"I'm well enough here," Tree had said. "And without me, Samuel would have nobody at all."

I could not argue with that.

And so, with an aching heart, I climbed into the carriage. Elizabeth, who had insisted on riding outside with Stephen Daniels, shouted to the horses, and we began the long journey from York to Hereford. I did not bother to fight the tears that ran down my cheeks as we left the city behind. I cried for the mothers who would suffer without my aid. I cried for Martha and for Will. And I cried because I loved the city, and I did not know if I would ever return.

Author's Note

As with all the Midwife Mysteries, there is a good bit of fiction sprinkled in with the history. I modeled the witch hunt seen here on those led by Matthew Hopkins, England's notorious "Witch-finder General." Between 1644 and 1646, Hopkins and his fellow witch hunter John Stearne were responsible—at least in part—for the execution of approximately three hundred witches, a total that constitutes over half of all the witches executed in England between 1500 and 1800. The authoritative account of these witch hunts is Malcolm Gaskill's *Witchfinders: A Seventeenth-Century English Tragedy.* I also made great use of James Sharpe's *Instruments of Darkness: Witchcraft in Early Modern England.* One of the more controversial aspects of this book—the idea that some accused witches might have believed in their own guilt—is drawn from Lyndal Roper's *Oedipus and the Devil: Witchcraft, Religion and Sexuality in Early Modern Europe.* Finally, the difficult labor of Grace Thompson is based on a case described by German midwife Justine Siegemund in her book *The Court Midwife,* which has been translated by Lynn Tatlock.